WANDERLUST

Stories on the Move

WANDERLUST

Stories on the Move

Selected and with an Introduction
by Byrna Barclay

thistledown press

Thistledown Press Ltd.
410 2nd Avenue North
Saskatoon, Saskatchewan, S7K 2C3
www.thistledownpress.com

Library and Archives Canada Cataloguing in Publication
Wanderlust (2017)
Wanderlust : stories on the move / Byrna Barclay, editor.
Issued in print and electronic formats.
ISBN 978-1-77187-135-8 (softcover).--ISBN 978-1-77187-136-5 (HTML).–
ISBN 978-1-77187-137-2 (PDF)

1. Travel--Fiction. 2. Short stories, Canadian (English). 3. Canadian fiction (English)--21st century. I. Barclay, Byrna, editor II. Title.

PS8323.T7W36 2017 C813'.010832 C2017-901111-1
C2017-901112-X

Cover: Joe Fafard, *Horse Diamond*, powder-coated, laser-cut steel, 2015.
Photography by Gary Robins
Cover and book design by Jackie Forrie
Printed and bound in Canada

Canadä

Thistledown Press gratefully acknowledges the financial assistance of the Canada Council for the Arts, the Saskatchewan Arts Board, and the Government of Canada for its publishing program.

WANDERLUST

Stories on the Move

CONTENTS

The Wanderlust *Road Map*

THE IDEA FOR WANDERLUST began at a barbeque at the home of Linda Biasotto when Shelley Banks suggested the prose writers attending go on a tour together, reading from their work at designated stops. To do that, they would need an anthology. I agreed to compile and edit the manuscript for submission to a publisher. Everyone would submit stories or excerpts from novels, but only one may have been previously published.

As the first reader of this collection, I was surprised and delighted to realize that in every story a person embarks on a journey of discovery. Although a theme had not been discussed each writer had submitted a travel story. At once I felt the wanderlust in the characters, that need to roam, the longing for surprise, sometimes the thrill of just recognizing the threat of danger, and finally the nomadic roaming simply for the sake of moving, or that restless and endless quest for a new beginning — even if it means the end of one life and the start of a new one as witnessed in Annette Bower's stories about aging.

How fitting, then, to begin with an excerpt from Brenda Niskala's novel-in-progress, *Pirates of the Heart,* for the Vikings may well have been the first Europeans to yield to the wanderlust. In this story, two hundred people on three Norse ships row east on a trading voyage in 1065.

Linda Biasotto takes us to Italy where the "Virgin in the Grotto" comes alive in the form of a bitter and desperate spinster taking care of her invalid mother. At the heart of this story is the revelation of a life-changing car trip when Christine's father took her and her brother to a family wedding.

From Italy, we fly with a Canadian scholar named Vivan on a quest to find the Cro-Magnon Man in the south of France, but discover "Women from Snow" and a new interpretation of the cave drawings at Lascaux. This is my first story in the collection.

On the slopes of Mombacho, the sleeping volcano in Nicaragua, an aging Canadian woman, Nash, is driven by a *need for numbness, for oblivion.* Longing for something stronger than water, Nash experiences the heat at the height of the mountain, but also the temperature of her emotions, for like the volcano Nash is ready to explode. What has brought Nash to this point of being *well beyond tears, well beyond sadness, or any feeling other than anger, impatience, the practical ones?* "Mombachu" is Brenda Niskala's second story.

In James Trettwer's "Godsend", Rex is a classic alcoholic who loses his wife, his job, and so much of his ability to remember he forgets his daughter's birthday. We witness his trips to rehab, how he encounters the alter ego of his youth, Kingsley, who tries to halt his descent into oblivion, with its shakes and blurred vision. Can his daughter be his godsend?

Trettwer's companion story, "Leaving with Lena", takes place in a potash company where a disgruntled and jaded office worker is tempted in different ways by his co-workers to leave it all behind and take off to an exotic dwelling place that may or may not be an interior flight of the imagination.

Next, the collection of stories takes us on a romantic ride on a jigger — called a railway handcar today — and a train ride with trekkers at the time of the 1935 Regina Riot when thousands of out-of-work transients were interned in the Exhibition Grounds. This excerpt from my novel-in-progress is about three sisters in love with the same itinerant handyman, who wanders for the thrill of finding a new persona in every farm or town or city along the way.

This brings us to "Redwing", Saskatchewan, by Shelley Banks. While attending a cousin's wedding, Anna drives her mother to the cemetery and the valley farm. In this story about memory, about differences in perception, Banks reveals the irony of the mother's secret when, on the way home, a flock of red-winged blackbirds *rise, wheel, and turn above the marsh and shimmer like black rainbows.*

"Bus Ride", a chapter from Kelly-Anne Riess' novel, at first blush appears to be a girl-meets-boy story. Tara, a shy, self-deprecating girl, failed as a student of engineering at university and, fed up with waitressing for three years, has accepted a job in a gift shop. The journey to Jasper represents her need for a fresh start, her longing for adventure, and desperation in seeking such a dramatic change.

Now we arrive at the heart of the theme of *Wanderlust,* with Shelley Banks' story, "As the Crow Flies", about a woman named Maggie travelling across the prairie with her husband Rob and baby Jenna. Heeding the call of the road itself, that adventure and the danger, Maggie mourns the loss of her freedom, which is far greater and far deeper than the normal frustration of a cooped-up new mother. *Even Rob likes the travelling itself, the intrinsic value of the challenge, destination irrelevant, sights on the way, mere distractions, motion the only thing that matters.* Will wanderlust lead her to thumb a ride with a passing truck or an old blue Thunderbird? What is the game called Roadside Roulette?

Annette Bower's characters find themselves at the closing of their journeys. In "Beating the Devil", Adrianne plays cards while talking to her dead husband. She tells him that *Birds fly into blades on wind farms. She wants answers to euthanasia, war, overspending, and the thong.* This leads her to the Seeing Soul Congregation and their Vault of Self-Discovery. Adrianne goes through a three-week journey. She finds answers that surprise and amuse.

In Bower's next story, "Hello In There", Muriel drives her friends, Nora and Inga, out of their hometown of Destiny in the Qu'Appelle Valley to the capital city of Regina, each seeking a different ending to her long journey on earth.

"Flying", the last in this collection by Linda Biasotto, may be a flight of fancy, a dream with a sexual awakening, or an out-of-body experience. No matter what we call it, it is the ultimate inward journey.

The urge or longing to wander is true to so many of us, sometimes hidden, often breaking out, as in the characters in this anthology. The writers of these stories wish their readers an invigorating, thought-provoking, and challenging journey.

— Byrna Barclay, November 28, 2016

Pirates of the Heart

Brenda Niskala

The year is 1065, the beginning of the sunset years of the Viking Age. Almost two hundred people on three Norse ships sail east on a trading voyage. Vaino, Leena, and their twelve-year-old daughter Ritva have been taken hostage by Sundvold, an ambitious Norseman. Leena was left for dead in Gotland, but Sundvold picked up Tuomi from the slave pits of the harbour there. Another Norse trader has already taken Tuomi's family as slaves. Sundvold has promised freedom for his slaves once they reach the trading camps in the desert and complete their trading.

TASYA STRUGGLED WITH REPAIRING THE simple hide rope, the one the Khanty had captured her with, and her only possession. She curled her legs beneath her, as close as possible to Vaino's feet, resting her head against his knee. Like a child, but not at all child-like. She sang a sorrowful-sounding song in her strange, harsh language. That is what slaves do. They ingratiate themselves. Or they become bitter. Or silent and cunning. No, Vaino thought. They must always be silent and cunning. To stay alive. And here was Tasya, with her big teeth, with her lips so plump, her yellow hair and green eyes, and her almost cruel way of teasing him.

Owning another person did not sit well with Vaino. He could still see Leena, shivering with fever on the hide blanket. Leena dying in that place. For she must be dead now. Despite his guard, and new friend, Tuomi's gift of sight. Best to face the truth. Poor Leena, her spirit so far from the trees of the ancestors that it would never settle down. Her spirit would wander in that place, the slave pit in the harbour of Gotland, homeless, until he came to find her bones. Leena would not want him to be alone on this long journey. Leena would want him to be with someone. Maybe not a wife. No one could replace her, his partner, his home mate, mother of their children. But she would not want him to mourn. She would want him to live.

He tilted his chin up and to the right a bit, to that place where he could sometimes feel the presence of the spirits as they passed. But Leena was not there. How could she be? Still, he tilted his head and asked the grandparents to intercede on his behalf, to forgive him his weakness in not being there to help her, leaving her to die. As he had since the ship set off for the east, he thought through every moment of his captivity since leaving Gotland. Could he have turned back, jumped ship, returned to put her to rest?

Maybe when they were trading for the Slavs. The camp was a temporary trading place, shaped like a triangle, with a tent forming the narrow peak opening to the water side. Vaino should have escaped then, instead of going into that smoky chum, that tent that rose on crossed poles like the homes of his little cousins, the Sami, only much larger. But run where? The river meandered between low banks, and beyond, miles of flatland, tall grasses and nothing more as far as the eye could see. That was the problem. The Norse, and the Khanty, and everyone else on those plains would see him for hours, could simply ride out after a leisurely visit, pick him up, put him in the slave tent.

But Sundvold the Pretender and his crew were not looking for grizzled old slaves like him for the eastern markets. No, when Sundvold's men pushed Vaino and Tuomi into the reindeer-hide tent, their eyes adjusted to meet the eyes of the girls, children really, and a few boys too, all bound by harsh hide, hands and necks. Many had dried blood and angry swollen bruises on their faces and torsos, and their clothes were in rags. Their eyes were dull, for the most part, as if they were beyond caring, beyond fear. They had been left to sit and lie in their own excrement. Vaino's stomach clenched, and he glanced at Tuomi, who must also have been thinking of his own women, tied up and abused, somewhere on this trail.

Vaino and Tuomi could understand the speech of the traders, nomads who attacked and herded the farming peoples. The Khanty carried on a perpetual state of warfare against the Slavs and did not consider them equals because they stayed in one place. The people of the Volga did not worship the tortured man. The Slavs did. The horsemen did not consider the Slavs human, because they had abandoned the bear. The bear makes sense as an all-powerful totem for people who strike out and move on. The Khanty were little cousins to the Finns, but wilder even than the Sami, who herded reindeer, and stayed close to their home forests.

Seeing the slaves they were expected to load for the first time, Vaino knew he could not be a part of this. He would not. These children were not so very different — not different at all from his own child, Ritva, who would soon be travelling on the same ship with them. Speaking with them. Realizing how the Norseman's trade would change their lives.

Vaino touched Tuomi's arm, his mouth pursed in a show of the stubbornness the Finns call *sisu*. He reached for his woodsman's carving knife. Tuomi nodded. There was no escape for the Finns, none for these children. The Finns pulled out their blades.

The two sleepy slave guards, caught by surprise, did not have time to pull out their curved and polished scimitars. Vaino sliced the tent stays and Tuomi opened the wall by slashing the hides. The guards escaped as the tent fell on the bound children, and on the berserker Finns.

The captive Slavs were not comforted by their possible rescuers. They did not run from the Khanty camp. They pulled each other from the wreckage of the tepee, screaming in an odd, mournful way, as if they had no energy, had already accepted their fate. Their cries brought in the Norse, who circled the captives. As the young Slavs came close to the Norse, they became silent, in awe of the massive axes, the heavy broadswords, the cruel blue eyes.

As Vaino and Tuomi pulled the last of the lamenting youth from the tent, the Norse stepped back as they always did, to assess what would happen. The Khanty guards, no longer sleepy and joined now by a fierce and fiery array of male and female warriors, seized Vaino and Tuomi, and thrust them to the camp's packed earth, kicking their backs, their faces, their ribs with hard-hide riding boots. They were chanting a word neither Vaino nor Tuomi knew. "*Bogatyr! Bogatyr!*"

Their cheering and jeering became deafening as the warriors stepped back and a massive Khanty appeared before Vaino and Tuomi. He was almost six feet tall even with his bowed legs, and he appeared even larger from the ground. He wore the slashed tunic of a horseman, and moved like one. "It's your fight," Sundvold said, half smiling at the Khanty but loud enough for everyone to hear. "This will be our entertainment today." He turned his back on Vaino and Tuomi as they scrambled to stand.

Bogatyr swaggered like a warrior who was used to being called on for just such moments. Like someone who had never lost a battle. The Norse had already formed a spectators' wall around Vaino and Tuomi, the newly released slaves. Like Sundvold, their body language made it clear they wanted no part of the madness that could ruin their trade with the Khanty.

Vaino had only his knife, which had never drawn human blood. Tuomi carried a sword, but its edges were well worn. Between the two of them, there was not a lot of hope, and they faced a fully armed Khanty warrior. Bogatyr carried a broadsword on his back, a shorter Khanty sword in his belt, an axe in his right hand, a shield in his left. He wore leather and metal mail that would have held back the sharpest sword. He faced both Finns without hesitation.

"Crouch down. Move like a hunter," Tuomi said. He moved away from Vaino, so Bogatyr would have to choose which one to face.

He chose Vaino. Bogatyr's face was scarred on one side. He had no lip to cover his teeth and no eyelid to protect his eye. The healer in Vaino was amazed at the damage this man had already sustained, apparently as his people's champion. Did he have a choice? Yes, he was large, the largest of his people, but did he like to fight?

The blade of the axe suddenly before his forehead resolved any doubts Vaino had about fighting spirit. Saved by his shortness, he dodged the thrown axe, fell to the ground, and rolled to a crouch. The broadsword swung back over Bogatyr's head and swooped down towards Vaino's neck. He lunged to the left, feeling the rush of cold air as the blade rent his sleeve and skinned his right shoulder.

Tuomi prodded Bogatyr's mail with his old sword, but Bogatyr chose to not even grace him with a swipe. His focus on Vaino was terrible. Bogatyr pulled the huge blade back and swung it in a half circle before him, as easily as a scythe. But Vaino, recovering from his rage at the manner in which the slaves were abused, was full of the quick hunter's energy. Bogatyr roared and swung. Vaino dodged and ducked, leapt and leaned. The massive man's blade glanced off Vaino's leather wristband and dug into his forearm, which he'd extended for balance a moment too long. Vaino did not give him the satisfaction of a groan, nor did he glance at the wound, which burned like fire before his arm became numb.

Bogatyr dropped his broadsword, which was not serving him well in such close quarters and with such a swift-moving match, and pulled his short sword, his killing weapon. It was a beautiful thing, its curved blade gleaming in the late afternoon light, the red of the sun through the dusty air giving the illusion of blood. Vaino held his own *pukka* knife in his good hand, his injured arm curled in front of his chest like a shield. The *pukka* knife was not a weapon, only a tool to ward off the worst of the sting. Bogatyr had dropped his shield after the first swing of the broadsword, and now held the scimitar with both hands. Vaino backed towards the river, although the watching crowd did not let him move too far. He could not run from this.

Bogatyr's curved blade swished the air in a zigzag. Vaino watched the blade tip, like the claws of the great bear coming down on him. He kept his eyes open, prepared to remember every second of his last moment. With this new weapon, and Bogatyr's awful mastery of the wavering blade, Vaino could not decide which way to move, how to block. He straightened himself, quiet and dignified.

The blade faltered, slashed slowly across the space where Vaino had crouched, and dropped to the ground. Vaino heard Tuomi yell. Tuomi stood behind Bogatyr, the champion's broadsword in both hands. Blood spurted rhythmically where the sleeve of leather ended, just above the coils of silver on the giant's thick upper arm. Bogatyr's grimacing face became even more horrible as he groaned. His right arm was a useless thing, hanging by a few threads of skin to his shoulder. Vaino backed out of reach, and watched the falling Khanty bat at the wound with his left hand.

Firmly, almost respectfully, Tuomi pushed Bogatyr to his back and held the sword at his neck, as if to behead him. He looked at Vaino, who nodded, held out his arm in a gesture of peace, and smiled. "You're bleeding, Vaino."

"Brother, bring us some tar," Tuomi shouted to Sundvold the Pretender. Sundvold tilted his head to one side for a moment in amazement, then ordered one of the Norse to go to the ship.

Tuomi held the blade of the sword over the fire pit. Vaino had gently pulled the giant's weapons out of harm's way, and had torn a length of linen from his shirt. He pushed the cloth directly into Bogatyr's arm socket. The warrior winced, his strange eyes wide in pain, but not terror.

A woman from the Khanty camp rushed forward with a basket of herbs, and pulled the glowing broadsword from Tuomi. She ripped the cloth from the bleeding amputation, and applied the wide edge of the hot sword on the wound herself. The stench of burning flesh, of hot blood, was overwhelming.

Ritva ran from the ship with a wooden cup full of tar. She gave it to the woman leaning over Bogatyr. The woman sniffed the tar, smiled tightly, and smeared it over the seared skin. When she stood, five men cradled Bogatyr's legs, shoulders, and head, and carried his shuddering body to their camp. A sixth supported the barely connected bleeding arm. The Khanty turned their backs to the Finns, and the riverbank was silent.

Vaino wanted to follow, wanted to meet this healer, to learn about the herbs in her basket, which had obviously kept their champion alive for many seasons. She had nursed him through the horrible cut to his face, through a cut to his thigh, which was likely the source of the man's swagger as much as the riding muscles of a man of the steppes. But Sundvold had already loaded the slaves, prepared to leave with or without Tuomi and Vaino.

Sundvold had smiled like an old friend as he clapped Tuomi's back, and gripped Vaino's arm. Vaino finally moaned. "Blood," Sundvold said, and they smiled quietly at him, and at each other. Ritva was storming towards Vaino. This was a look he recognized. Men and their foolishness, she would say. That could wait until they were on their way. It was definitely time for the Norse, and the Finns, to leave.

RITVA WAS TAKING A DIPPER of water to the child slaves. Vaino approached her. Now was as good a time as any.

"Ritva, I need to tell you. Sundvold — "

"Lied. I know. He would have left you, Father. He took the slaves from those people without trading."

Vaino was startled. He had not thought that through, Of course, of course. At what point would Sundvold have completed the trade? Vaino and Tuomi had won for them. No, win or lose, Sundvold had just taken the Slavs. "Sundvold was deciding the best for many people," Vaino said.

"And so were you, "Ritva said. "He would not have stayed around for you except his men wanted to watch the fight. You had no weapons. Any one of them could have given you his sword. It was an execution. He had decided to let you die. So he could get richer, Father. I see him. I see him now."

Vaino was surprised at Ritva's clear analysis. It was true. He and Tuomi were meant to die. "But we never expected any help from Sundvold at all. Nor from any of the Norse. It was our fight."

"And Sundvold took advantage of your foolish outrage," Ritva said, and smiled fondly at her father. "Let me see your arm."

Vaino lifted his bloody forearm, grimacing. The wound was ragged but not hot to the touch. "You'll live." Ritva dabbed the cut with birch tar. "You sure can move fast."

"When I need to. It's like dancing. I was a good dancer. That's how I won your mother."

"And Tuomi is a good hunter."

"Yes, he is." Vaino had complimented his friend on the clean cut to the giant's vulnerable spot. Tuomi had shaken his head in disgust.

"Pure luck. I was aiming for his head." The men laughed much harder than necessary at that. Bogatyr's head would not have been a good place to land with the edge of a blade. It would only have made him angry.

Tuomi kept the broadsword. "It's too big for you," Vaino told him.

Tuomi had pulled it out from behind his back in a slow steady arc, a huge grin on his face. "We Finns have longer swords, and we know how to use them," he said, and Vaino joined him in a battle cry, their voices travelling over the water, so both ships on either side also heard them and saw Vaino duck, and Tuomi lift his new sword high. The men around them, and then all the people in the three ships of Sundvold, had joined in a triumphant chant for Vaino and Tuomi, the slayers of the giant.

"If only your mother could have heard the cheering," Vaino said.

Ritva bowed her head. "Sundvold lied about Mother, didn't he?"

"He did not leave her with silver to find us a new home in Gotland. No, my daughter, he left her on a hide blanket in the slave pit, shivering with fever."

"So she is dead," Ritva said.

"Tuomi says she lives. He has the sight."

Ritva's eyes were glassy with unshed tears. "Tuomi is right. I can't see her in the spirit world. But maybe that is because she died too far away."

Vaino nodded. His assessment exactly.

Ritva's jaw was clenched as if she had one too many hardships. "So now you want me to know this. You could have told me before. Months ago. I am not a child, Father." Ritva pulled her blouse tight to her body. Beneath her new breasts, Vaino could see the unmistakable mound of belly.

"Sundvold's?"

"Of course."

Vaino closed his eyes tightly. "That lying, cheating, child-stealing pretender. That pillaging pig. I promise you, my child, I will kill him."

Ritva frowned. "Not until this heals, Father!" She pokes his forearm hard. He winces. "There was nothing you could have done. It was my choice, *Isa,* and even if he is a terrible man, he is still the father of my child."

Vaino leaned his head forward, deep in thought. "All right, I'll kill him later. I am too tired today anyway." It was true. The famous Finnish rage that had helped him through his combat, that had prepared him for death, was just not there. Instead, another emotion was rising from his chest. He couldn't help himself. He hugged his daughter. "A baby! I will be a grandfather!"

And Ritva cried now, finally, in relief. Then stopped herself. "And now you choose to tell me about Mother, because you don't want me to hate you. Because you want me to understand that you haven't forgotten about Mother. But that you also want Tasya?"

Vaino's daughter really was no longer a child. He was speechless before her ruthless honesty.

"Tasya will be my helper." Ritva patted Vaino's forearm firmly. "She will be our family thrall. I have seen how she snakes around you, Father." Vaino pulled his arm away and hung his head. Ritva was not done. "She has a good heart, *Isa,* and I think she is smart. I will not ask you to push her away." Ritva smiled at her father, her tired eyes so like her mother's.

And that was that.

The Virgin in the Grotto

Linda Biasotto

IN THE TOWN OF MANNA, the bells of San Martino toll as though in warning for the woman who fights death in an upstairs bedroom. For Cristina, who climbs with a supper tray, the bells announce a new life.

Perhaps tonight. And she imagines how it could be the next day: She, entering her mother's room, unhooks the shutters, casts them open to the autumn morning. When she turns, she sees the face slack, the blue eyes vacant.

Cristina's left knee drags and she takes the stairs one at a time. Soup slides to the bowl's brim, slides down again, leaving behind a glistening film. The recipe for the broth came from Dr. Rossi: boiled beef bones from shank, carrots, onions, celery, and oregano. Next to a glass half-filled with red table wine is a soft bread roll.

A small landing separates two parallel flights of stairs. After the earthquake of '76 opened wide cracks along the walls of the stone house, Cristina's stepfather had the bathroom re-plastered, then tiled in blue and white. Here, she sets the tray onto a bureau, dampens a facecloth, and continues her climb.

Upstairs, white sheers at the double balcony doors filter the waning light; the rest of the hallway is dim. Peripheries of a cushioned chair, edges of a commode crowned by a plant, and framed sepia photos of the family dead merge soft and nebulous against the pale plaster. Cristina turns toward the sound of muted voices. Inside a large bedroom, the full-length mirror on a massive *guardaroba* reflects her entrance. She doesn't look. She has avoided mirrors most of her life, has believed in the image created by her mother's taunting: *You are too tall. You are too thin. You must wear your skirts long to hide the scars on your knee. Your breasts are no larger than walnuts; you could pass for a boy, especially with that oversized chin.*

A lifetime ago, a young man once admired her brown, almond-shaped eyes and kissed her. She no longer remembers the boy's face or his name, but she can remember the kiss itself, the warmth of it on her mouth in spite of her mother's voice afterward: *There must be something wrong with that boy if he wants to date a cripple.*

At two windows, white curtains foam onto the dark tiles, and on one curtain clings a humped green beetle. The grey-painted shutters, half-closed, reveal narrow bars of sky. The room smells of sweat and something sour.

Cristina passes a long dresser covered by white crocheting, a still fan, and a porcelain doll, which stares across the room with round, dark eyes. The voices murmur from a television set, which squats at the end of a king-sized bed. Cristina mutes the sound with a remote.

Tray on lap, she sits next to the bed. Not until she taps the spoon against the bowl does Bruna Bozza turn her head.

Her face, made flaccid by a stroke, sags like soft putty. From her forehead to the back of her black hair runs a skunk-like strip of white. Her limp arms rest on the bed as though she is a marionette waiting to be pulled to life.

The spoon clicks at the bowl; the invalid sucks at the spoon. When her mother finishes the broth, Cristina breaks a piece from the roll. "You'll be happy to know, Mamma, that I walked to the church this morning to light a candle for *Papà*."

Her mother's mouth tightens then opens to receive the bread.

"If you could speak, I'm sure you would approve. And yesterday I ordered a new granite monument for his grave from DeCecco's and told him the new inscription will read: *Forever Remembered By Your Loving Daughter.* I haven't yet decided on your stone. Something small. Like the one you chose for *Papà*."

Bruna Bozza sips wine with her eyes closed. After Cristina wipes the pale mouth, she picks up the remote and once again releases the voices into the tepid air. The channel airs continuous news programs, the type her mother hates.

On her way from the room, Cristina stops before a black-and-white photo hanging near the door. A pretty woman sits before a painted backdrop of round Tuscan hills and holds a plump baby on her lap. Next to them is a girl of three or four with a huge bow tying back her long hair. She ducks her head as though afraid of the camera. On the girl's left shoulder rests a hand, disembodied because the fourth figure has been ripped away.

To Cristina, life before her *papà* died appears in postcard images. The three-story stone farmhouse looms grey against an orchard backdrop where sunlight sifts the leaves of apple and pear and plum trees, transmutes greens from lime to dark olive. In the yard, poultry peck where the mule stands harnessed to the wagon, flipping its rope tail at flies. Against the byre, a golden haystack, the byre itself dark with the heaving shadows of two milk cows.

She can see herself on her *papà's* knee being tickled by his large moustache whenever he kisses her. And there is Alessio. Adored and pampered Alessio. Trailing after her, calling to her with his baby lisp, blond curls a halo about his chubby cheeks.

BEFORE SUNRISE AND FIRST COCKCROW, when heavy fog hung motionless to the ground, Cristina's *papà* carried Alessio to the tiny Topolino and laid him, still sleeping, on its front seat. Mamma tucked a blanket around him as Cristina climbed into the back, clasping her only doll against the buttons of her brown wool coat. Taking up the rest of the seat was a basket, its food aromas mingling with the bitter smells of gas and tobacco smoke. She'd never ridden in a car before and, not knowing what she was allowed to touch, sat rigid.

Three of them were travelling to a wedding in Udine, because her *papà*'s sister had finally managed to snag a husband. In the first trimester of what was proving to be a difficult third pregnancy, Cristina's mother was forced to stay behind. She had argued to keep Alessio home with her, but her husband was adamant about showing off his first son and heir. And to spare the children a long train ride on the wooden seats of third class, he'd managed to borrow a car.

Cristina's mamma leaned through the driver's window, kissed her husband, and then blew a kiss toward Alessio. To Cristina she said, "Be careful with your dress. And behave yourself."

The gears crunched as her *papà* pulled back on the shift. When he set a tentative foot on the gas, the engine choked and died. Chagrined because his wife laughed, he restarted the engine and stomped hard, pebbles bouncing against the undercarriage as the car surged forward. In the darkness and mist, he circled the yard, beeped the horn, waved his arm through the window and hollered: "*Ciao! Ciao!*" like a happy lunatic. Nervous and thrilled, Cristina clung to the door handle with one hand and, with the other, clutched the doll to her thumping heart.

SHE PAUSES IN THE FRONT HALL. A curtain of black and white chenille cords, hung across the doorway to discourage the entrance of insects, sways in the barest of breezes, rich with the scents of ivy geraniums and roses, ripening grapes and pears. There's the sound of a car stopping outside the front door. She hurries to the kitchen, scoops two dark berries from the counter, and drops them into a drawer, managing to reach the front hall just as Dr. Rossi calls, "*Permisso!*" He steps inside with his medical bag in one hand and a handkerchief in the other. Beneath his suit jacket, the open collar of his dress shirt reveals the round neck of a white undershirt. "Good evening," he says while swiping at his broad forehead and thinning white hair. "Your house is pleasantly cool."

Cristina places herself between the doctor and the kitchen. "Good evening, doctor. I wasn't expecting you until tomorrow."

"I had business in town, so I thought, why should I make two trips when I can make one? And how is our patient today?"

Cristina looks at the floor and manages a quiver to her voice. "No better. Perhaps worse."

Dr. Rossi sighs and shakes his head. "Ah, these are sad times for you, truly sad times." When they climb the stairs together, he slows his pace to match hers.

Inside the bedroom, Cristina opens the shutters wider. Her mother turns her head as Dr. Rossi drops his bag onto the chair and takes her hand. "*Signora,* I see some colour in your cheeks today. Do not worry; we will have you out of this bed in no time."

Cristina knows this is a professional lie meant to comfort a hopeless case. He doesn't bother looking into her mother's eyes while he speaks, but when he takes a tiny flashlight from his bag, he peers into her like a man making a cursory inspection for a soul.

From below the window comes the sound of voices. The neighbour, Rita, speaks to her son. Cristina strains to make out the words, and then flinches when the young man starts his motorcycle, revs the engine, and roars off.

Dr. Rossi snaps his bag shut. "Her appetite is the same?"

"All she wants is the broth, but I coax her to eat bread, too."

"*Signora*, you must try eating vegetables. And a bit of boiled chicken. I will see you again in a few days. *Ciao*." On his way from the room, he wags his finger at the fan. "Cristina, you must remove it. In your mother's condition, any draft could be fatal."

"I had no idea. Of course, I'll be careful."

Downstairs, Dr. Rossi sets his bag on the floor and wipes his glasses with his handkerchief. "You must have courage, Cristina. You two have been together all your lives and now this. But." He tucks his glasses into the breast pocket of his jacket. "I must say I still do not understand your mother's inability to speak. Stroke victims usually regain some speech. Does she try talking?"

Cristina claps her hands together as if to pray. "How many times I have tried to get Mamma to speak." She drops her arms. "But you know how stubborn she is. Sometimes . . . sometimes I believe she has given up."

"Ah, it happens." Dr. Rossi shakes his head. And to think, only a short time ago, she had the vigour of a young woman. She could have passed for your sister." Oblivious to any offence his words might cause, he continues, "But your mother has a wonderful nurse, and you are a good daughter. No one could give your mother better care."

"Any daughter would do the same."

"Oh, no. The stories I could tell you."

And because Cristina knows Dr. Rossi lingers in the hope of her offering him a glass of wine, and time to sit and gossip, she says, "I admit I am always busy. Even now I have laundry waiting." She glances toward the back of the house, but is careful to keep her voice regretful, because she needs this man, depends on his lack of imagination and his complacency. A younger physician would inquire more closely into her mother's illness.

Dr. Rossi rocks back and forth on the soles of his shiny shoes. "And you? How do you get on these days?"

Cristina forces brightness into her voice. "Much better, thank you."

"Those pills are helping, then. Good. Well, I won't keep you from your work."

From the doorway, she watches the doctor's Mercedes disappear around a bend in the street then returns to the kitchen, aromatic with the smells of boiled beef and oregano.

She takes a box tied with ribbon from a cupboard. It's a narrow, white box with a name lettered in blue along its top. Folded within sheets of tissue paper is the black silk slip the saleswoman talked Cristina into trying on. How sexy she looked in it, the woman enthused. Wasn't the fabric soft and smooth? When Cristina stood at the till to pay, she felt both abashed and exhilarated.

How foolish. Still. She passes a hand over the blue ribbon. She will take the slip upstairs and try it on, again, later. She leaves the box on the corner of the table.

Because the September sun still radiates enough heat to burn the potted cyclamens on the two window ledges, she keeps the kitchen shutters partly closed during the day. Now, she flattens them against the outside wall.

A corner shelf to her left bears a candle, a bud vase with a single white rose and a statuette: an exact replica of the Virgin, which stands within a trellised grotto at a nearby convent. Under her blue wimple, the Madonna's serene pink and white face inclines benevolently; a serpent writhes beneath her sandaled feet.

Cristina removes a pan of creamy *pasticcio* from the oven, ladles out a portion of noodles and white sauce, and sets the plate onto the tablecloth. She pours herself a glass of Merlot. She likes to watch her favourite program, *Quiz Show,* while eating. Whenever the camera gives a close-up of the host, a handsome man of forty, she smiles. He banters with the contestant, a plump, middle-aged woman with a circle of beads around her throat, who receives yelled encouragement from her daughter in the audience.

The host asks the plump woman: "Dom Pérignon invented champagne. What was his occupation?" As usual, the answer is multiple choice. Cristina decides on the correct answer by elimination. Blacksmith doesn't seem right. Pérignon might have been a soldier, but she settles on abbot because monks usually grow their own food and grapes.

While the contestant ponders, the camera zooms in on a voluptuous young woman, alone on a pedestal and wearing a glittering, bikini-type costume. Every time she breathes, her exposed skin glitters from scattered sparkles. A poised distraction, an erotic showpiece, she keeps the audience's attention every time a contestant takes a long time answering. Unsmiling and silent, the luminous woman stares at the camera with calm eyes.

Like someone seeking the revelation of a mystery, Cristina watches the shiny bow mouth, high round breasts, and cupola-curved thighs. Of what does a beautiful woman think? How much happiness does her beauty bring her?

When the camera goes back to the contestant with the excited chins, Cristina turns off the television. She pours the leftover broth down the sink, then scrubs and rinses the cooking pot several times. The berries in the drawer are for the next batch, but she needs to gather a few more.

One step separates the front door from the narrow street, and here she stands to shake out the tablecloth. Rita's daughter calls, "*Ciao*," and waves as she climbs into her car, speeding off into the twilight to whatever it is the young do while away from their parents. Maybe she will meet her boyfriend, a slim-hipped fellow who greets Cristina with the type of nods he likely reserves for unattractive and aged women.

She ties back the chenille cords for the night, shuts and locks the door. On her way to the back of the house, she passes the storage room stocked with bottles of water and wine, jars of pickles and brandied cherries she has canned over the years. Draining in a colander in the back sink are white mushrooms, a gift from Rita, who picked them during her usual morning hike into the hills.

Whenever the neighbours see Cristina, they inquire about her mother's health, give advice, and recount their own experiences with illness. Sometimes Rita will sit with her mother while Cristina runs errands, but she uses her mother's worsening condition to discourage visitors. This is not difficult. Her mother's sharp tongue and affectations during her second marriage put people off, and now she doesn't have many friends. Except for nieces and nephews in other countries, there is no family left.

Years ago, it was Giorgio Bozza who saved Cristina and her mother from the reluctant charity of relatives. Her mother arranged to be introduced to him, a newly retired broker who had moved to Manna to spend his retirement years in rural tranquility. The man was flattered by the attention of a pretty widow. Until the day he died of cancer, he believed the whirlwind courtship and marriage had been his own idea.

From the beginning of that marriage, Cristina's mother fell into frequent bouts of melancholy, spent days in bed, crying and sleeping. The doctor explained to Giorgio how one could expect such behaviour from a woman who had suffered much. This was a young Dr. Rossi. "*Signor* Bozza, you must have patience and understanding."

Giorgio Bozza had too much pride to tell the doctor how his wife shrieked commands from her bed until she got up from it before rushing about in a manic fury, screaming, "Why isn't this done, why isn't that?" He soon learned to grab his hat and desert to one of the neighbourhood bars, leaving Cristina to bear her mother's tantrums.

Now Cristina steps onto the back patio of red stones. Clay pots, like chubby soldiers, stand in a straight line with red or pink ivy geraniums cascading over their brims. Other plant pots contain oregano and basil and laurel. A square yard with a garden separates the patio from the rear wall of the neighbour's house, which looms against the darkening sky.

She crouches on the patio to break off dead leaves and pinch faded blossoms she then tosses into a pail. In a corner grows her mother's belladonna with the bell-shaped flowers, and from it Cristina takes a few black berries and drops them into her apron pocket. Lastly, she waters the pots with a hose, returns inside, and locks the heavy oak door.

It takes longer to climb the stairs this time of day when she is tired and her leg aches. She stops at the bathroom and runs warm water into an enamel basin.

Her mother, dozing in the shivering light of the television, doesn't acknowledge the sound of a drawer opening and closing. Cristina tugs off the invalid's nightgown and unfastens her diaper. A quick dab with both sponge and towel across the shrivelled skin before pinning on another diaper. Lastly, her mother's favourite nightdress embellished with rose-coloured ribbons and white lace. A pretty gown for a healthy woman, it now resembles finery on a corpse.

Cristina takes a wasted hand into her own. "Mamma."

The closed eyelids twitch.

"You must believe this is for the best. Soon you will be in heaven with Alessio."

The imprisoned hand quivers. "Yes. I know you still miss him.

"Do you remember my first Mass after the accident? After you finally brought me home from the hospital? Because of my knee, I couldn't stand or kneel. I stayed sitting and watched how the stained glass windows held the light, saw how the apostles sparkled in a circle around the high dome. I felt a draft against my face and when I looked at the statue of Jesus near me, I wondered if it was His breath I felt.

"And the pink-and-gold cherubs. Flying about the high, arched ceiling, carrying banners among the fluffy clouds. Someone told me that Alessio became an angel in heaven and watched over us. When I saw the boy angels with their round cheeks and blond hair, I asked if one of them was Alessio. For an answer, you pinched my arm. It felt like a snake's bite.

"After Mass, when you stood with the priest, a lady took my hand. Led me to the table with the votive candles inside the red glass cups. She gave me a burning taper and said, 'Light a candle in memory of your poor little brother.' She held a candle close enough for me to reach. 'Good girl. Now light one for your father.'

"Before I could light that candle, you took it from me. You pressed your hand against your waist where the baby had been, the one you lost after the accident. And you said, 'We will light candles for Alessio, but never for the man who killed him.'"

Cristina traces a cord-like vein, blue beneath her mother's transparent skin. "When the priest gives you the last rites, all your sins will be forgiven. Your anger against *Papà*, your cruelty to me. You will have Alessio and I will have my life."

With unexpected energy, *Signora* Bozza grabs Cristina's wrist. The grip is loose and lasts but a heartbeat, yet Cristina leaps from the chair. She looks down to see her mother's eyes alive with hatred.

The look stops Cristina for a moment. Then she yanks a pillow from the bed, letting her mother's head drop onto another. There are strict orders from Dr. Rossi to keep the patient covered during the night, yet Cristina folds the blanket to the bottom of the bed and plunks her mother's feet on top.

Television off, Cristina pulls in the shutters and fastens them.

The fan. She takes it from the bureau, sets it on the bedside table, aims it at her mother and turns it on. The light fabric of the nightgown ripples.

And all the while her mother watches in silence.

In the bathroom, Cristina begins her own ablutions by hanging her clothes on the door and covering her hair with a plastic cap. Her breasts are tender as she soaps herself. Dr. Rossi had explained she had the symptoms of early menopause. She wanted to tell him he was an idiot and that she was far too young. But she stood in his yard a long time afterward and watched the leaves of the acacia tree drip moisture from the morning's fog.

Now she fastens the buttons of her nightgown and again climbs the one flight of stairs to the second floor.

The only sound from her mother's room is the fan dragging the air in one sustained breath.

In her own room, light from the street lamp drifts through the window and strikes bits upon bits of gold on the floor tiles. She leans her arms on the marble window ledge. The night air feels soft and warm as an animal's pelt. Bats launch themselves in and out of the lamp's gleam across the street, and beyond, the dark shadows of grapevines stretch like silent ranks of soldiers waiting the call to march. She can almost see the shimmering richness of the autumn air and its ripe possibilities.

She yawns and closes the shutters.

In bed she stares across the room where the dresser hunkers its long shadow against the wall and she thinks of the box she left there, the box with the slip. She reaches for the bedside light, and then pads to the dresser. The mauve tissue paper whispers when she lifts out the black silk.

The only full-length mirror in the house is in her mother's room. Cristina opens the bedroom door and flips on the overhead light. When she approaches the *guardaroba*, she sees beneath the slip's hem how her scar glows white. She sucks in her stomach and turns sideways, holds her breath for as long as she can.

Sexy.

Perhaps if she dyed her hair, got rid of the grey. She could lose weight, take a bus to the city and buy new clothes.

And then?

Who will see the silk slip? Dr. Rossi in his examination room? No doubt he would laugh the moment she left. She places the palm of her hand onto the glass and covers her reflected chin. There. That's better. Yet when she takes her hand away, she's surprised. Her chin doesn't make her look much different from the other women she knows. How is it she did not notice this before? For the first time in a long, long while she can look at herself without the old fury clawing for a way out.

She's calm when she turns to the bed, touches a button on the fan and watches the whirring subside. With a fingertip, she touches the white stripe across her mother's hair. Then she rolls the blanket upward, covering arms and shoulders. *Signora* Bozza sleeps on, unaware, her breath faint but steady.

Her mother will regain her voice and tell the doctor everything. Will he believe her story and admit he has been incompetent this whole time? Cristina can forestall her mother's revelations, convince the doctor her mother's mind has been damaged by the stroke. Cristina knows the symptoms. Besides, Dr. Rossi has witnessed her mother's irrational tirades many times.

There is one other thing. Her mother knows now what Cristina is capable of.

In her own room again, the fabric hisses when Cristina hauls the slip over her arms. She drops the thing onto the floor, pulls on her nightgown, and climbs into bed. She keeps her eyes open until they adjust to the dark and to the indistinct shapes within it.

Women from Snow

Byrna Barclay

SHE WAS CAUGHT UP WITH a stranger and borne away to Le Périgord Noir, the land of a thousand caves.

When she deplaned in Paris, her head buzzed and eyes blurred with fatigue, her inflamed left eardrum still popping from too many descents over a period of twelve hours. Her luggage was last on *Le Belt*, but the book bag containing texts about the famous Abbé Breuil, the Pope of Prehistory, was not counted among the hundreds of valises. Miming the size and shape of the bag to a ponytailed Portuguese porter, who immediately told her he wasn't French and his name was Luis Geronimo, she then waited while he disappeared behind metal doors as mysterious as the entrance to the cave at Lascaux she so desperately wanted to see so she could believe in it. He reappeared with the rescued duffle bag.

Blame it on a lazy security guard or a rough luggage handler who, instead of throwing it on the conveyor belt, ripped open the cheap plastic bag containing her books.

After the mid-air explosion of TWA bound for Paris on July 17, just before the Olympic Games, security had been tightened at airports, and maybe the dogs sniffed out grains of pot still embedded in the seams from her high-school ski trips, or the x-ray machine picked up her foil-wrapped Nicorette tablets unidentifiable to a security guard who had never wanted to quit smoking. All this was conjecture on her part. The only thing she was sure of was that the bag had to have been slashed open — the vertical cut was so clean — but why not just unzip it? The bag wasn't locked. Had someone thoroughly examined the contents? All her books were cover face-down, with her footboard on top instead of on the bottom the way she had packed them. She had no time to complain to airport officials or claim damages for a bag that needed replacing anyway, not if she wanted to make the fast, direct train to Bordeaux.

At customs, a puffy-cheeked official eyed her passport photograph taken two years ago when her hair was cropped as short as the bristly mane of a prehistoric horse and rinsed with vegetable dyes in three colours: carrot on the crown, beet on the sides, and spinach at the back. He took too long to recognize her, with contacts now instead of glasses, her naturally curly, blonde hair ironed straight, cut blunt, and falling to her shoulders. Blame the new look on Chester, who said a graduate student, especially a mature one of thirty returning to university after a failed marriage and a bankrupted career as the owner of an antique shop, should stop trying to look like a first-year student just because her banker husband had run off with his barber whose greatest ambition was reflected in his fingernails, each one painted a different primary colour.

Then she saw the stranger. In the arrival gallery outside customs, he held up a placard bearing her name: VIVAN. She didn't know anyone in France, and anyway she had only five minutes left to catch the train to Bordeaux, not enough time to inquire if he really was meeting her, a jet-lagged Canadian off on a scholarly quest that was also a flight from Chester. Then he seemed to duck into the crowd and, dashing away, disappeared, so she felt light-headed and confused. Perhaps she misread the name, a French one like Vivienne, the way she often looked at strangers when away from home and thought they looked like people she longed to see once again in a more familiar place.

She hobbled after Geronimo, impaired by an old fracture of her left ankle when she fell on snow-covered ice outside Chester's house. He'd been too afraid to go outside and clear the sidewalk. Her ankle was still puffy with fluid, stiff and unbending, so she had to lug along her exercise board that looked like a square skateboard on one roller instead of wheels, on which she balanced three times each day, tilting backward and forward, forcing the shortened tendon to stretch, the weak foot to bend.

On the long march through the airport's cavernous tunnels and galleries to the train station, she felt compelled to look up, as if hypnotized by the girders and glass that mirrored new visions of ancient rock-bound structures she could only imagine, not name. She felt drawn forward, as if lured into a cavern, yet driven to roam as if she were part of a herd.

Geronimo said the trains stopped for only two minutes and waited for no man or beast, not even a beloved French *chien*. He also told her he had been to Montreal and the French were the same there as here: they looked down their Gallic noses at strangers who refused to even try to speak French. At least that's what she thought he said, recognizing Montreal of course and *personnes* and *étranger* and *le nez*. Unless he was saying she was a person with a strange nose, because, well, it was upturned, with a dent left where the diamond had once pierced her nostril.

With no affinity for languages, a new word was not hers until she had read or seen it written at least three times, and then often she couldn't pronounce it properly. This impeded her ability to think in French, though she was swift at translating familiar words. She was born too soon, that's all, before French immersion was introduced to her western province. When she tried to speak, her tongue and lips, overly trained to flat English vowels and harsh consonants, refused the more lyrical French.

Luis the porter took her down *l'ascenseur*. Her left ear popped again, but she felt wonky, as if she were descending slowly, like Alice, down a rabbit hole. He left her in the waiting area in La Gare while he paid a visit to a friend, and returned only heart-stopping seconds before boarding time.

Le numero six. The right track, but from which tunnel would the train emerge, and her coach, *le numero deux*, where would it stop? The porter wasn't sure, he squinted at the overhead timetable that looked like a TV screen blurred with snow or a computer with a virus. Then, out of the tunnel the train zoomed, like a bellowing beast, each coach roaring by, then slowing, it halted far, so far ahead she'd never catch it, the porter ahead now, throwing her luggage onto the last coach.

Everything she needed for her survival here was now on that train: her traveller's cheques, return airline tickets, and information on how to find the house she had rented at Bézenac.

Now short of breath and the train sliding slowly away, but there, just beyond her reach, a hand ready to pull her up, and a voice pitched with urgency, calling: "*Vite! Vite! Vite!*"

The taste of blood, pain zinging in her Achilles heel and shooting like electricity up to her knee, she grabbed hands reaching down for her, leaped onto the step with her good foot, and she was up, yanked into the corridor of the last coach.

Leaving the Portuguese porter screaming about his tariff of fifty francs. She had slapped his palm with thirty, more than the rate for two bags.

There: her suitcase and book bag safely stacked on the luggage rack. The man with the sign now guided her by the elbow to a seat: 6A. First Class! He drew the curtains so the tunnel lights flashing by wouldn't hurt her eyes. These new trains travelled at 180 miles per hour and if you didn't keep your eyes trained to the far distance it could blind you. That's what she believed he said, leaning across her, so close she smelled aftershave tangy as lemon and the smell of new leather too, his jacket sleeve so soft she wanted to stroke it.

Thanking him for his help, still breathless, the blood drumming in her left ear, she groped but couldn't find buttons or levers on the armrests to lower the chair. Damn the travel agent who promised her a chair that would recline for sleeping, just as fine as those on Air Canada Executive Class, sleeping compartments gone the way of slow trains and dinosaurs. If she had known there would be four more hours to Bordeaux, then at least another two by car to Bézenac, she would have splurged on an overnight hotel in Toronto or Paris.

She wasn't as purse-proud as Chester, who fussed over his pension. Sticking too close to a budget was dangerous, couldn't he realize that? Look what government cutbacks were doing to the university, his own tenured position gone like so many others with his early retirement. And, what prospects of a teaching position would she have once she finished her degree? A job as a tourist guide at Lascaux II sounded more promising, and maybe much more fun.

Her name, the fellow repeated her name. How could he know who she was? Unless he thought she had to be the woman he was supposed to meet since no one else heeded his sign, and she was the last person to leave customs. Yes, he was the man with the placard: not very tall, Gallic features, flirty brown eyes set close beneath a Slavic forehead, hair the colour and texture of sunflowers and cut in the longish mushroom style. His darker eyebrows met in a tuft over his nose.

When Chester smiled, even now it curled her toes, his moods changing as wonderfully as the coat of an ancient cave lion she admired in her textbooks, his exposed teeth causing her to clamp her hand on the back of her neck, a primitive reflex. But this younger man's smile was solicitous, radiant, full of unspoken promises, a benediction. She thought of her pastor who arranged for the Churchman's scholarship so she could return to university. His face had glowed when he told her she had won it.

It was so difficult to interpret a language delivered as fast as this Eurotrain.

She didn't understand. Please speak slowly. *Je suis Canadienne,* you've mistaken me for someone else. As if her runners and jeans didn't give her away as a North American tourist. Only the name on the sign may have been the same.

She was named for the nurse who delivered her after a long labour in the river-stone hospital, never mind her obscure, Nordic ancestry. *Je suis Canadienne* should have said it all to a person who likely could trace his family for generations and would never understand how, in the new world, status was determined less by lineage and more by the ability to acquire houses with two-car garages.

But forgive me, he said, my name is Biron de Bézerac. Bézerac was the name of a town, where she would find a certain Madame Cordelier, a local employee of the agency, to take her to her lodging. Or was it Beynac or Bergerac as in Cyrano? Truly, her head was stuffed with clouds. When she arrived in Bordeaux, after a long sleep in a hotel, she could sort it all out, then rent a car to take her beyond the vineyards to the heart of Le Périgord, to Lascaux, called a School of Thought in the textbooks.

Permit him to explain. The agency, it made a mistake in renting his family's summer place for September. Tone-deaf to the lyrics of his language, she thought he was from the agency, not one of the owners of the house she had rented for the off-season. Then he said he was behind on his novel, something about the Hundred Years War that ended in Europe but continued on in Canada, exemplified through constitutional debate and referendum, especially now, with Quebec again threatening to separate, cede, but not yield its land and all its resources and rights. Never mind all that, he had a great need to finish it, and the only way to do that was to get out of Paris, away from its distractions, to the quiet of a house set deep on a wooded hillside. That's what she gleaned from his long, tapering fingers drawing pictures in the air of many pages of good heft, something she was only too familiar with as she was unable to finish her thesis. *J'ai un grand besoin de,* indeed.

Chester had confused the issue with his caveman tactics: a blunt verbal blow to the head, as if she were too stupid to understand the difference between typology and paleoecology or between geomorphology and stratigraphy and sedimentology.

Je ne comprend pas.

Biron offered her francs, the full amount of the rent, plus extra for the inconvenience. Like a gypsy throwing a blanket in the air — the French idiom for pulling the wool over your eyes — but she couldn't remember how to say it in French, much less put it into a question: *What kind of a trick are you trying to pull?*

Did he have to draw her a picture?

Wait. She had paid the rent in full to the agency. What he suggested was a breach of contract. She was not sorry. What else could she do?

Perhaps the agency could find her another house, probably without difficulty since the off-season was well advanced. He gestured at the empty seats. No other tourists on this coach, only four men with notebook computers and briefcases and an elderly couple in the seats in front of them, gumming ham sandwiches and peeling oranges.

She was too exhausted to change her plans. She would need to elevate her ankle for days, trouble enough locating a masseuse. No, let the agency find temporary accommodation for him, since it was all their error. *Je suis fatigué. J'ai mal à pied.* She lifted her foot to show him the tensor bandage around her ankle, but booted it against the back of the seat in front of her. The old woman with the crocheted hairdo turned around to glare at her. *Pas possible. Il fait que vous* — forgetting her declensions, *trouver* — other, yes — *une autre maison.* Was house feminine?

Not possible, he said, because then his father would find out from the agency that he'd skipped Paris and his job interviews. The father didn't know about the magnum opus. Did he really say that?

Votre père, il est un petit fou?

This Biron, the son of a count or baron, a man who owned a house in Paris and one in the country, a place that bore his name, was clearly not in as big a predicament as he was placing her. Just a grape-picking minute. The house rented for less than a hotel, so it couldn't be as grand as she was beginning to imagine, and why would the family rent it at all? Something smelled higher than a winery. He didn't actually say he was the son of a baron, she just assumed that, and even so, in Europe titles didn't go hand in glove with money; it usually meant the opposite: renting the castle or opening it to tourists to pay for upkeep, or, if newly purchased, the rent would go toward the mortgage.

Did she really care if Baron or Byron or Biron from Bézenac was more or less than what he appeared to be? She just wanted a bed and a pillow and a long sleep. She separated the curtains, looked out the window, and was almost blinded by another tunnel's lights flashing like yellow cats' eyes. She yawned, and her ear popped again.

He rubbed his hands in the air as if clearing a slate or erasing words from a blackboard. Nothing humble or apologetic in his manner, and the word *hauteur* leapt to her mind.

Share the house with him?

He said it slept eight, but she thought he said *Sleep with me,* though *huit* and *moi* weren't even close.

Sleep, oh sleep. Here in the birthplace of *Homo sapiens sapiens,* the man-who-reasons, the man-who-knows.

When did she ever encounter a reasonable man? Look at Chester. Afraid to even leave his cavernous house and drive on icy roads to the university tower of medieval study, he refused to accompany her on her search for something beyond historic reasoning. Chester, Chester. She could just see him: unlighted pipe clenched in the corner of his mouth, now settled in his tapestry chair before the wall-to-wall windows closed against the evening fear of being alone, gazing up at the open-beam ceiling, his plate of cold beef forgotten in his lap. Soon, he would be afraid to leave the house even in warm weather to fetch his favourite tobacco and the books he ordered from Paris. And then where would she be? Toting cups of hot chocolate, turning down his bed, then fighting for sleep on the chesterfield. That's what she deserved, he said, for falling in with her widower advisor on the eve of his retirement, even if it was merely a partnership of convenience, of small comforts to two people all too familiar with grief, with loss. He wanted someone to cook for him, and she needed solace, but she was stifled in the airless house, even when she threw open the windows.

In the doorway, she'd set his breakfast tray on the threshold, and announced: "I have to get out of here!" She didn't just mean to an English-titled French movie at the library or a beer at the faculty club. "I need to see where it all began. It won't make any sense until I do." She didn't trust the texts. If she couldn't see the past unearthed, it was all dead, dead, just as her earliest studies of Canadian history meant nothing to her until she went to Batoche and saw the Métis_trenches and bullet holes and Louis Riel's chair with its wicker webbing indented and sagging from his weight. And before that, in high school, Wolfe and Montcalm and separatism and the distinct society were only names and ideas that couldn't give her an identity of place or time, until she rode in a horse-drawn carriage driven by a red-headed francophone named Pierre O'Leary down the cobbled streets of Quebec City to the great Plains of Abraham where she found her breath in her own living history. Though she belonged to neither founding nation, she was Canadian, and without Quebec she'd be halved and never whole again, like a salmon split open and its backbone torn from its flesh.

And then she read about the Huguenots, religious dissidents, cliff dwellers who were torn from their homes built into five rock-walled terraces by an order of the Catholic king, Henry III, in 1588. The Roque Saint-Christophe, a natural fortress once inhabited by the Neanderthals, was beyond her imagination, even further removed from what pre-historians articulated in the textbooks. How could they do anything else but impose their own religious and social constructs upon people who left no record of their existence apart from magnificent drawings in caves? She had to see Lascaux.

She said to Chester, "How can a person raised on land flat as a table ever imagine a cave as anything more than a hole in the ground dug by a gopher?"

"Prehistorians refuse to let their imaginations run riot," Chester said, lighting his pipe and pacing before the windows. "They don't know why so many spearheads were found — broken — at Lascaux. Nor do they know why they were engraved."

"If I see the rock paintings in this so-called Sistine Chapel of Prehistory at Lascaux," she said, "then I'll sense the meaning of those six-rayed stars, the elongated saltire cross, even the plain horizontal line; all the emblematic punctuations." Were they signatures, pre-language signs, or symbols for the four directions?

"You can't develop a thesis on your senses," he said.

And she left the room, slamming the door to the kitchen, muttering so he couldn't hear her: "And you can't live if you're so afraid of dying you can't even drive the car in winter anymore, let alone take an airplane."

She stopped trying to coax him into the trip of a lifetime, visiting the castles and dungeons and places whose histories he had studied all his life, without ever seeing them.

She called a travel agent.

So no, she didn't need another alliance of convenience, not even for a few weeks.

She tried to sleep, leaning against the window, with her jacket bunched for a pillow that slipped, and she banged her head, jerking awake, then her head dropped onto her chest.

And so she awakened four hours later in Bordeaux, unable to hear with her left ear, her neck so stiff it hurt to lift her head, and her left foot so numb she couldn't put her weight on it.

Biron tossed her luggage down onto the platform, turned abruptly, sensing her fall even before her ankle twisted on the second step down, the pain so piercing she saw stars in flashing colours of red and yellow. She fell. Like a snowbird toppled from its perch by a stone.

He caught her.

The last thing she saw was a grey sky lowering over a cavernous, domed building.

And rain.

Blame it all on the eternal mist rising in early morning above the Dordogne and Vézère rivers.

The Lookout

THE SUN BURNS AWAY THE haze by the time it reaches its height above the Black River.

Perched in the natural lookout chipped and cut and carved by wind and water into the rock face — only room enough for one man in the small square vault — he sees in the wind-driven clouds: a bison chased by a man with feathers in his hair astride a horse larger than any he's ever seen, with a long mane, a bannered tail. The light of the sun behind the clouds illuminates the horse and rider, providing a backdrop for the massive bison head. He feels as if the hunter — or no, the animal itself — is calling him.

Above the opposite, darkly greening embankment, he sees a grey-blue river carrying a strange floating oak tree bearing pyramid-shaped, striped sails, the prow a tree-woman carved and painted in the same colours he finds in the sediment on the cave floor: red and yellow ochre, charcoal black from his dead fires. She rides low in the water. These men with horned hats bring the end of the Cold, but also the end of peace. He can see that in the torches they bear, the spears for fighting, not hunting, made of something as shiny and hard as wet rock and they catch the light of the sun. They push on, downriver, from the place of the everlasting Cold.

When the wind drives too hard, the clouds dissolve and the lower, closer ones shape themselves into Now, the time of warming when the herds move north, with fewer and fewer seen on the trails, at the fords, at the Melt where the cold mountain waters spill from the cliffs into the Black River. He is afraid it's the end of the Warm. All he knows is that the reindeer, bison, and mammoth continually move, slowly northwards, even the red-deer and roe-deer becoming scarce, so few now too often he brings home only frogs, fish, and snails. And it's harder now for his mother, her eyes weakening and joints cracking when she scrabbles down to the valley to pick berries, roots, and nuts. He feels pulled towards the plains, his need to roam as great as the reindeers', yet driven as if by a lone stalker. If it weren't for his ailing mother he'd go in search of the reindeer.

Ah, there: so low, so close to the river's edge, where mists rise like smoke from large fires, he sees a strange woman thrust forward onto her knees, a female with hair falling over her face, hair as long and tangled and as thick as a woolly mammoth's coat. She's kneeling, mounted from behind by a male. On his haunches, Peta leans forward, the better to see, his belly quaking with laughter.

The mist clears, and now he can see the black berries hanging in great clumps from a bush that shakes as if disturbed by bison rubbing back-to-back, itchy where the fur is thin and skin bitten by insects. Wait. There's no need for the male's bone javelin, not while rutting. That's what's making the bushes shake. He's bashing the weapon against them, and beating the female's neck and back. Clenching the neck with one hand or biting it doesn't hold this female still enough to mount, or long enough to make him spurt like crystal water sluicing from a crevice in a rock shelter.

And then, all is stilled, even the wind. And he can see the male better now, crashing through the bush like a stag startled by a wolf. It's a harpoon raised above his head, not a bone javelin as he had thought. The male's head-hair is cropped short as if he's in mourning, spiked like the mane of a horse. His skins are turned white-side-out, or no, it's the hide of a mountain animal he wears, that of an ibex.

Clearly, they are not People who follow the reindeer.

Reindeer. So easy to track, their tendons crack with each step, their feet wide as if webbed. If only he could just call them home.

All he can see of the female now are her blood-streaked legs protruding from the thick brush. Her feet are bare, not wrapped in hide bound with sinew. Foolish one, not to protect herself from sharp flint and hard pebbles thrown up by the Black River. She is stilled, not sightless in death, surely, though it wasn't a rutting like any he'd seen before — from behind, yes, but not that kind of beating, and never done so quickly, not even by the impatient blue fox.

If there are two people, surely there will be others not far behind — one family or a group of three or more. Perhaps they know why the hunt is so poor, where it runs better. He needs to know what brings these strange People of the Ibex so far to the place of the reindeer.

He must track them.

And see to the strange woman from Snow, who must be forced down and beaten for the rutting.

Using the rope his mother wove from tough bison tendons, he leaps backwards in a flying arc, out of the Lookout, falls a short distance, winging towards the rock wall, his hide-bound feet giving him leverage; he lets the rope out, jumping out and down, in a wider arc this time; and he's descending, like a giant spider, swiftly, till he touches bottom.

Leaving the rope dangling free for his return, he hastens through the scree, taking the slope to the river in great sideways bounds, like a sure-footed horse, until he's racing through river-grasses to the black currant bushes. Parting. A figure appearing, and yes, it's the woman from Snow, stunning in a white ibex hide, her wild hair flowing around her like the blood-rays of the sun. Pale, her skin is so light it makes her black eyes burn like embers in the deep sockets of her eyes. She has three fingers in her mouth, the juice of the black currant trickling down her wrist, and her cheeks are smudged with the flesh of the berry.

Surprised that he wants her, by his own rising, feeling of desire, he skirts the tracks left by the man, assured they only circle away from the river and don't double back.

Why didn't she follow her man? Will he come back for her?

Turning back, he finds her unmoving, save for the crossing of one leg around the other knee, blood oozing down to her bare feet and pooling around the roots of the currant bush. He lifts the ends of her curly hair, separating them from the drying blood and swellings on her neck where the man had beaten her with his harpoon. He finds old scars there too. Sniffing her hair, he detects only a faint smell of burnt wood; it's a long while since she lay by a fire, and judging by how rapidly she stuffs her mouth with berries, too long since she turned a reindeer rump over a spit. She has travelled far and long without stopping, such great haste to get away from the man. He must have tracked her far, punishment his only motive, otherwise surely he would have driven her back.

Around her neck hang bone pendants, stag's teeth, a butterfly fossil, and a large pebble with strange markings. This last piece he takes between his pointing-finger and thumb, turning it over and over, finally realizing that the image is of a headless woman with swollen belly, overly long straight legs not properly bowed for hauling long distances. She smacks it from his hand, then draws back, but not afraid, she plucks more berries from the heavy root-stems, and offers them to him.

Mee-nah, she moans, not a word so much as a sound erupting from deep in her throat. The woman from Snow cannot talk, her tongue cut to a stump the size of a small truffle. Spittle dribbles down her lips and she's unable to lick it away. She opens her mouth for another morsel, and he sees the black hole gaping like an opening to a burial mound. He turns his back to her so she won't see the water leaking from his eyes.

She spins him around, and moans again. He grunts, not knowing what she means, but deciding that must be her name: Mina.

— Peta, he says, hand over his chest, as if that will still his heart beating so fast it seems to be trying to burst from his ribcage. His mouth is dry now too, but not from fear.

He doesn't know what to do with her so he leaves, scrambling back to the safety of his rock shelter within the pockmarked and tiered cliff, so massive it once housed so many families of Slant-heads Peta cannot count the now empty openings on fingers of both hands.

Only once does he look back.

The woman from Snow follows him.

La Palétie

HOBBLING AND WITH THE AID of a crutch Vivan followed Biron from his car to what appeared to be a back entrance to a fieldstone house. A sign on a limestone fence read: La Palétie. She hopped to the door, her left foot and ankle now encased in a light, plastic cast.

After she fell from the train, driving all her weight onto her twisted ankle, Biron examined her foot, so purple-yellow it looked like a fig burst from its casing. He took her, against her protestations, to a hospital at Bordeaux. An English-speaking doctor x-rayed her ankle and declared it the worst mangled mess he'd ever seen, the original star fracture not set properly, the tendon freshly torn, and a new hairline break parallel to the old. He said it might have to be re-broken and reset when she returned home, but for now he gave her a packet of painkillers, told her to keep the foot elevated and packed in ice, then tighten the cast when the swelling went down.

How could she ever pull on her hiking boot, drive a car, scale a cliff, or make her way into the tunnels of Lascaux II? How would she ever face Chester again, if she returned home, having seen nothing of the Sistine Chapel of Prehistory at Lascaux II or the Great Roc at Les Eyzies?

Now, after a blurry drive from Bordeaux of which she remembers nothing apart from feeling woozy but pain-free while listening to Biron's tape of the Beatles' singing *I believe in yesterday*, and dimly aware of vineyards heavy with grapes for the harvest finally yielding to farmsteads and fairy-tale castles defying gravity on the top of treacherously steep cliffs. And then she hobbled after Biron into a fieldstone house from three centuries.

The centre of the house was a small medieval tower called Le Pigeonnier, its spiral staircase leading to a loft. To the right, she found the oldest part of the house, once a barn and now an enormous farm kitchen that opened into an equally large living room furnished with antique sideboards, dining table, and newer stone fireplace.

The floor-to-ceiling shuttered windows opened onto a small terraced garden of fig trees and pampas grasses, their upswept plumes like giant ostrich feathers; and beyond them, sun-dried cornstalks, frost-blackened sunflowers on a hillside that sloped towards the river. From open-beamed ceilings, antique gas lamps with glass shades hung, shrouded with cobwebs.

Biron left the bags of groceries he bought at L'Alimenation in St. Cyprien down the road on the oak table in the kitchen. Vivan noticed a gas stovetop, a dishwasher, an old fridge that couldn't hold much more than foodstuffs for one day. She was suddenly hungry. Biron switched on the electric radiator. The house, closed and unheated for too long, smelled of mildew. He trudged ahead with their luggage, down three treacherous flagstone steps, where she found a closet containing one toilet at the foot, then around a corner and down an Italian-tiled corridor that opened into a bedroom with two single beds and an armoire. He left her panting at the bottom of another spiral staircase while he toted their luggage to the second floor.

If I make it up those stairs I'm never coming down. But he was back, pointing at his rump and slapping it so she understood he would take her up piggyback; and both laughing so hard she didn't care if he dropped her, he clumped upwards and around and around, she hanging onto his shoulders for dear life, he gripping her thighs and jouncing her back up every time she slipped down; until he carefully deposited her before a bathroom with a sink and shower stall, no toilet. Time to resurrect his great-grandmother's chamber pot, no doubt, and sure enough there it was on an oak washstand.

This was the newer part of the house. Two enormous bedrooms at the ends of a short hallway, with doors opening towards each other; Biron's room was just opposite hers.

In her room, the green velvet draperies were tied back, and he opened the shuttered windows. The furniture was old but not from antiquity, the armoire and headboard similar to those found in Quebec country houses: scrolled posts and diamond point engravings. No shelf for her books. Tables draped with flowered chintz and reading lamps on each side of the double bed. Framed mirrors on the walls. No art or family portraits anywhere. It was an old farmstead, now a summer place, often rented to tourists.

And then she managed a shower with a plastic garbage bag wrapped around her cast, unpacked her toiletries and a night shirt with long sleeves. She crawled under a French duvet, elevating her foot on two French pillows, the square kind, with envelope cases.

Far below, Biron clattered about in the kitchen. Then his footsteps rang on the stone stairs, and she welcomed the cup of hot chocolate, an omelette with truffles, a croissant and apricot jam on a tray. "You're far too kind," she said in English, not sure how that translated, so much irony contained in the phrase at the best of times, now not being one of them.

He left her leaning against three feather pillows, watching the clouds though open windows. She imagined overly large hips, bulbous breasts, a wild-flying woman with legs wrapped around the torso of a man with massive biceps and hairy chest. The last image she saw, before falling into a sleep deeper than the black river, was the head of a man with a slanted forehead, curling hair shading from grey to black, an enigmatic curve to his mouth, neither a grimace nor a smile, but both of these.

Grotte du Grand Roc

IF YOU KNOW HOW TO look you can find *L'homme de Cro-Magnon* everywhere in Le Périgord Noir.

That's what Biron told her the next day over a heavy, six course lunch at L'Abbey Hotel in St Cyprien, the first of many versions of the same meal he would order every day: *escargot, potage du jour, fois gras, canard d'orange,* ending with *crème caramel.* Before he finished his soup, he poured red wine into it, then slurped it up, lifting the entire bowl to his mouth. "*Chabrol!*" he said.

On her notepad she drew a picture of a force-fed goose to show Biron how she felt after the meal.

Armed with a French-English dictionary, a notepad, and a ballpoint pen, she was ill-prepared for her fortnight in the south of France, though she scribbled on the pad every French word she mispronounced that he couldn't understand, and even sketched maps showing landmarks, with her own hieroglyphics: arrows or dots or a series of exclamation marks pointing to rivers and routes and caves she wanted to see.

It seemed that Biron, rather than write, preferred to talk about his novel, most of which she understood only when words of Latin derivative cropped up in his *l'histoire,* and then she couldn't imagine how he could write any of it without visiting Les Bastides, the villages built by the English and the French during the Hundred Years War. He talked on, it seemed, just to hear his own voice, which made her think of trees felled in a forest, that crashing.

He promised to help her with her search in the Birthplace of Mankind. It turned out that most were closed on Sunday like everything else except the ancient *églises.* Monday was a holiday, and those under national jurisdiction were shut up tight on Tuesday.

During the first week, they visited the medieval chateaux and ancient churches. She took photographs and made notes for Chester. Her letters and the stories she would tell him when she returned could never equal the experience. She hoped he would understand her brief attraction to Biron, the magnetism of his language and culture. In her notepad she wrote: *With Biron, nothing will ever finish, nothing ever last.*

He wanted to know about Canada, how she could bear the cold winters. He was always chilled, he said, even now in September when the rains were warm and the golden cattle dozed like sun-worshippers in the valley pastures. He had a motorcycle but wouldn't ride it when it rained. He was afraid of the sharp turns in the winding roads, so slippery when wet.

By noon each day, Vivan was so warm she shed her sweater and either opened the window on her side of his red Renault or turned on the air conditioner. Biron wore layers of T-shirts under a flannel shirt and reindeer-patterned sweater. She discovered that one night before the fireplace when they disrobed, but slept under three blankets piled on top of a cowhide rug. Before light, she awoke in a sweat, and crept back to her own bed.

By Wednesday of the second week, the swelling in her foot was so reduced she tightened the plastic cast, and could walk without aid of the crutch. She was clear-headed after sleeping deeply for ten hours each night, and no longer needed painkillers.

Today, they would visit Grotte du Grand Roc at Les Ezyies.

The Magdalenians were so close now she could almost feel their presence in every cliff face or rock shelter under an overhanging ledge, or lookout. Here, in 1868, when the Périgueux-Agen railway was carved through the rock, five skeletons of the first human, Cro-Magnon, were found, establishing the lost link between prehistoric and modern man.

She now imagined him in the Valley of Vézère, squatting in lookouts in the sheer cliffs, in grass huts and wooden forts hewn into the rock face, in shallow caves pitted and hollowed out by the river. And finally, there, in La Capitale de la Prehistoire, she found him, not in Paul Darde's monolithic statue of a golden man with massive forehead raised to the sun, not even in the museum containing evidence of the whole evolution of the human race.

She saw the Cro-Magnon Man in the Great Rock cave.

THEIR CAVE IS A GOOD one, too high for wolves and brown bears but not too high to lug the meat from the hunt. Close to water and wood, deep enough to shelter them from wind and rain, with scree masking the opening of the rock shelter, the mouth of the cave is not too close to the firepit.

Mina helped Peta's mother, Sheeya, build a thatched hut where they store berries and roots, his spears, and their tools for chopping and scraping. Here, they busy themselves inside with women's work, much laughter filtering out for him to hear, and it's strange how his mother always understands what Mina gestures and signs but must always draw for him.

When they first entered the cave, they stumbled over then shrank back from a skeleton near the firepit as if the Slant-head died while sleeping and had no one to bury his body, with gifts for his journey, in a dolmen protected by rock-slab from wolves. Mina pointed to the rock wall and a fresh scar, and then touched a boulder near the head of the skeleton, so he understood that no bear had felled the man. Peta's mother hid her face behind the tangled moss of her hair.

Though he can't remember him, Peta's father, too old for hunting, had fallen down a pit while chased by a cave lion.

Peta's mother and Mina busy themselves with women's work while Peta hunts, then when the catch is good, help him drag the reindeer home where they scrape the hide and sew coverings for their bodies and for sleeping robes.

Together at night, the dark time he looks forward to more and more, before the firepit, he works on his arrowheads, the chipping always so fine — a finely honed point can pierce the eye of a mammoth. Mina sighs deeply and shows him her teeth. They glint like crystal rock pebbles on the bottom of the shallow part of the Black River. His mother says that the flat edge of flint is good for scraping, not admiring, but that's what raises pleasure-bumps on his arms and legs: Mina's sighs over his work.

With her bird-beak point, Mina scratches on the rock floor a picture of a large stone hut, and he laughs, pretending he doesn't understand what she wants now. Isn't this cave and her hut big enough for the three of them? He stretches out on the bear hide, watching flames casting shadows on the ceiling and illuminating the natural shapes of the spirits embedded there: the snout of a running stag, the long jaw of a reindeer, the rump of a horse; all waiting for his colour-rocks. Black for the outline, berry-red, cloud-white, sky-blue, and yellow ochre blown from his bone-pipe fill in the bodies.

Since the woman from Snow arrived he hasn't had time or the inclination for drawing. She keeps him busy in the currant bushes. The colours are few and not strong in this cave. He needs to sharpen more nodules into colour-points, though Mina has shown him a new way to *grind* and mix colours to get different tints, pale-to-strong.

After first light and the mists have disappeared, she ducks out of the three-sided hut, leaving his mother to sewing a rabbit skin with sinew laces. She will gather nuts and berries while he thinks of her lifting her ibex-hide to show him her swelling breasts and lead him out, wanting him again, or will give him the woman-stone she wears around her neck on a thong, telling him by drawing on bark that she feels the presence of the reindeer — perhaps a large herd — and he's to take the stone for good luck on the hunt. But no, she's been carving and drawing on a stone again, in the hut instead of making him new wraps for his feet, something his mother says would have brought punishment on her backside from his father. He's too soft with the woman from Snow.

He leans close to her, admiring the woman-stone carved with bulging belly.

His mother shrieks from inside the hut as if startled by a bear, and they rush to her.

On the cliff-side wall facing the river, just under the stone shelf, he finds a narrow crevice, into which his mother has dropped something; it fell from her hands while reaching up to leave it in its place on the shelf.

Mina loses the new colour that brightens her cheeks now, and she drops to her knees, keening, as if she's lost something of more value than she can bear. And she has: her skin-bag, the one that holds her secrets from the Snow that he's never allowed to see.

On all fours, Peta reaches into the crevice with one arm, patting here and there as far back as he can reach, a small draft of air raising the hair on his arm, but he cannot find the bag.

Together, they lift and cast away the loose rock, widening the opening until it's large enough to accept his head, then his body lying flat. He peers in, but it's black as the river, darker than night. Mina lights a tallow-lamp and cups it in the hollow of his palm, then urges him forward by patting his rump.

The floor slopes gradually down, and he can see the skin-bag fallen to the right. The ceiling slants upward, and he's able to stand with head bent. Just as his free hand lifts the bag, he sees strange lumps scattered like walnuts and figs.

Mina's bag slung around his neck, he moves forward enough to see what looks like sticks rising from the rock as if someone had started to build a hut, except the stumps are made of rock.

Then: what he sees is more terrifying than facing charging bison without a spear.

They're growing up from the rock, down from the cave roof, some as small as figs, some as long as spears, some joining together. At first, he believes they're icicles, but they're not cold to his tentative touch. The colours are dazzling: sun-yellow and fire-orange, the flesh-coloured ones almost pulsing. The grey ones with white spots look like the back of his mother's hands, but are so much wider than her fingers; they look like old roots.

He darts around a pillar, then has to drop to his knees and crawl around them. More. More, so many more above him than even the stars above the Black River.

Who could have done this? Severed the members from so many beasts — or no — they could have — many did — belong to men! Some great power beyond his knowing and almost beyond his believing has done this, and that's why the reindeer are deserting this place.

It isn't the fire that keeps bear and wolf away from his cave. It's the dark spirit, the One who has severed life from man and beast.

The hair on his body rises and stiffens, he's so frightened of the clear liquid dripping on his head and shoulders. It might poison him, or dissolve his body, leaving only his erect manhood sealed forever there.

Clutching his shrinking pouch, he crawls backwards, his heavy breath snuffing the tallow, the lamp scraping against something hard and wet and lumpy as knuckles. It's a mammoth foot turned to stone, only one, the rest of the massive body dissolved by the poison dripping dripping dripping, not even a bone or jaw or enormous tusk left. Yet it's almost as if the spirit of the beast is calling him, not only to take his family to a safer place, but to do — something more. He calls out, a long howl, the way a sentinel wolf will alert the pack.

Maybe the Power is female, a giant without a male, who pleasures herself by sitting on one and then another but never able to draw seed to produce young. If he weren't so terrified he would laugh. What a story-picture to draw for Mina and spook her so she will creep into the comfort of his arms.

Peta ducks back into the hut, still protecting his poker, sweat streaming down his broad forehead, high cheeks, jowls. Crouching, he hops about, waving his left arm, yelling at the women to pack up, now. Move and move some more, roam with the herd, until he finds more than just a safe place. But the herds are disappearing, and he needs to call them back — but how can they hear him until he finds them? He feels as if he's nothing more than a leaf whirling before a wind, that harbinger of snow.

His mother laughs at him, rocking and crooning over a small, squawking bundle. Mina rests on a sleeping ledge, her face red and wet as if she too has crawled through the tunnelled rock and seen for herself the severed staffs of men and beasts growing from the ceilings and floor. She claps her hands, and he realizes she's not as happy for the return of her lost skin-bag as she is with the small, hairy head tucked into the rabbit-skin hide.

Too frightened to be angry at the females for sending him off on a false search so they could take care of birthing, he begins to stack rocks like a wall of the hut Mina wanted him to build and so seal the opening to the cave.

We follow the reindeer, he tells his women. It's time to leave.

He has a place in mind, not far from the massive rock-shelter of the Slant-heads who long ago left mounds of reindeer bones for the taking, many antler racks, mammoth tusks. There, he will make an offering to the reindeer and create a safe place for Reindeer People and the good animal that gives them food, antlers for weapons, sinew for ropes and thread, its hide for warmth.

He will find a way to do more than remember the good spirits, to bring them back.

He will make a sign too, a warning to those to come here after him not to enter the cave.

Lascaux

THE DORDOGNE FLOWS THROUGH A wide valley of Dark Périgord. Downstream, it gouges out a grand passage through cliffs, carving out caves and rock-shelters and slicing into uplands, hills, and mounds for easy burial of the dead.

On the left bank, the yellow and iron-rich rock reddens under the sun.

This is what the First Man searched for that day of his leaving, the site radiant in colours for his new visions of reindeer, horses, and even ibex so his woman would never forget her own land.

Driving with Biron towards Lascaux, the story begins its shaping for Vivan. How they brought with them all they could carry, following the river's passage. They would have avoided that place of a thousand Neanderthals she could only imagine now, the Slant-heads who were so stupid (Peta's mother said) a person couldn't reason with them, so thick-headed they left the safest place in their known world — and disappeared. Others arriving long after the People of the Reindeer left would build a great fortress against the Horn-heads from the north who would bring in their floating-trees, clay bowls and metal pots for cooking, but also spears so heavy and sharp they could behead a man. And later, the river would bear men with still fiercer weapons: giant balls that explode and destroy a rock-shelter; and the fighting would never stop, not for more than a thousand winters.

These first Magdalenians would have laughed at being called such a name; they were the wandering People of the Reindeer. Peta meant to go deeper, so safe and so far into the rock no other man or beast or Spirit could penetrate its secret. Peta wouldn't have stopped until he found these underground passages opening into galleries containing the shape of running hoof, massive head, elongated jaw, the horns of the ibex too. He simply brought back to life what he saw: the spirits of the departed. Just as he called to them and they answered with their stories that leapt and raced and even fell into place on the walls and overhanging rock ledges and ceilings of caverns, the sight of running hoof and charging head lifts Vivan's spirit and moves Biron. Wild and free. Not just under the covers at night, but while wandering through woods, along the banks of the dark river, scaling the cliffs.

He would have seen it just as Vivan saw it now: its porch and rock-awning wide open at the foot of the sheer cliff but hidden from predators by stunted oak, pines, hazelnut bushes, and juniper. The arid plateau above looked sun-drenched.

Vivan was so deep into her discovery now, she was only dimly aware of the few tourists lined up for the tour, of the guide's passionate story of the four boys in search of a legendary treasure lost in the Middle Ages, who discovered Lascaux on September 12, 1940 when one of them fell down a hole, just like Alice after the rabbit. With Biron's arm around her waist, she picked her way along the wide excavated entrance, where Abbé Breuil found thousands of bones and flints, so much evidence of the Cro-Magnon Man.

Using a flashlight to illuminate her story, the guide shone it on a black-and-white negative on the opposite wall, pointing out a total of four hundred emblematic signs they were to discover once they entered the cavern: Single or multiple sticks drawn in parallel lines. Branch-shaped signs. Fan-shaped or hut-shaped signs. Interlocked signs. Quadrangles. Clubs and bows. Punctuation marks. Dotted lines. And the wondrous stars with six and sometimes eight rays.

"No one knows what they mean," Biron said, whispering in her good ear, his breath feathering her neck.

Art began here, thirty-five thousand years ago, with engraving, sculpture, painting in geometric, symbolic and abstract forms in bas-relief, high relief, stumping, wash-drawing, and even stencilling. But Vivan couldn't picture it.

Show me. Now.

With a flick of a switch, the guide lighted the way, the electric lamps as low as the tallow-lamps found here that once gave light for the artists' labour.

And there: The Great Hall of Bulls.

Vivan lost her breath, all sense of now, the deepest part of her circling with the ring of primitive horses, dominated by four large bulls that sprang into motion around her. *Follow us. Come with us.*

The paintings were arranged along a plateau halfway up the sides of the chamber. Every irregularity of the rock face was used: a calcite chimney bringing life to a stag's expression of urgency, a bump becoming its belly, a larger imbedded boulder its chest.

The first thing he must have painted was the two-horned animal that now resembled a unicorn, though its hide was spotted like that of a leopard, its tail short like a stag's, its hump as large as a bison's. Its snout was muzzled as if preventing it from speaking, and Vivan wondered: *to whom and why?* Was it an imaginary creature drawn here, likely for the girl-child, a story to help her fall asleep? Perhaps the woman drew it, the first bedtime story? The unicorn's belly was overly round, ready for birthing, but its sex organs were phallic beneath human legs. Its realistic style didn't differ from the others, proof to Vivan that the prehistorians were wrong: these were done by one artist, not many. Why did they assume the paintings were done by men? Or that they didn't live here because it reminded Abbé Breuil of a church? He discounted the animal bones he found in the chamber he called the Apse. So much for objectivity. It had never served Vivan. She trusted her senses, her instincts.

Opposite the entrance, they moved into a narrow passage called the *axial diverticulum* in the textbooks that opened into Father Breuil's famous Sistine Chapel of Prehistory. And suddenly Vivan smelled the tallow of a hundred lamps burning, and her eyes stung, an aching lump in her arched throat, her chest tightening and ribcage closing, her mind refusing the predetermined religious theories imposed by the pope on a sanctuary. Yes, it was a safe place. The spirit of the artist — man or woman — was light-years before and beyond the recorded histories of mankind's religious wars. The sight removed her from all reason and all motivation apart from what always prompted the creation of great art itself.

Peta or Mina or both had simply brought to life what they saw in the rock face walls and domed ceiling by employing a cunning double perspective (his and hers?) with the animals in profile but head and horns turned in a three-quarters view, a technique not rediscovered until the time of the Renaissance. Horses leapt and bounded, red cows circled, a black bull charged, the bison rubbed back-to-back, and another cow leapt high on the wall. And there, at the end of the passage a horse, its belly swollen, its legs detached from its body to give a sense of depth. Why it was drawn is less important than its creation.

And there: another horse, red mane bristling, while yet another fell, legs in the air.

Returning to the Great Hall, through a second corridor, Vivan found herself in another vast chamber depicting a massive black cow and two bison, savage in expression. Opposite them, five reindeer stags swam a black river — leaving or returning?

Through a smaller and difficult passage to hobble through, even with Biron's cautious arm, she entered a small cave-room alive with drawings of yellow cave lions with no manes, tufted long tails. A depression opened onto The Well, and here Vivan found at last the Woman from Snow.

THOUGH SHE CAN MAKE SOUNDS the child understands now, a high-pitched gargle of warning and call to stay by her mother's side and a rumble in her throat when she's displeased or wants the child to stop her play to learn how to scrape and stitch and carve, Mina is tired of the close, tallow-scented air, the unnatural light of oil lamps.

Sheeyah lies by the firepit, directing with withering hands and bird-claw fingers the shapes she sees on the ceiling for Peta to bring out with his tuft-of-hair brushes, his blow-pipes, and flint. He outlines the shapes of returning spirits. She says the reindeer soon will come and claim her, her last shallow breath saved for the sight of them when she can finally release her own spirit and let it go with them.

And so, confined to the cave to help Peta and care for his mother, Mina creates for the child a kind of language: males and females scratched on pebbles to wear around her neck, the man always misshapen, clumsy, half human and half animal. They ward off the return of the Slant-heads. The females with exaggerated breasts and hips will make it easy for her daughter when her time comes for rutting and birthing.

Mina's larger wall-drawings are always on the edge of a chasm or pit or in places difficult and dangerous to reach, indicating BEWARE OF FALLING ROCK or SLIPPERY WHEN WET.

Never mind what frightened Peta or what makes him paint endlessly, rarely sleeping, eating only enough to sustain him, her paintings show far more than a story. Perhaps Peta wants to preserve his own memory of the reindeer, of all the hunts. By honouring the animals, their strength and stories, he offers a prayer for their return — for his own child, yes, but also for Tomorrow People.

By the light of a tallow-lamp, she mixes minerals with sand and clay, crushing them in a hollowed rock and binding them with water and her own spit. Then, drawing pictures on bark for Peta, she shows him how to build a false floor from stunted oak, how to cut deep holes into the rock face to hold beams or wedge logs into ledges of slotted rock. And later, in the Bull's Chamber, they use roughly lopped trunks to build the scaffold so he can reach beyond the natural footholds and handholds in the rock-wall. She cuts the saplings herself for the climbing poles, and at night she weaves ropes from vegetable fibre, saving one for her own descent into The Pit.

When finally his eyes glaze with frenzy and he can't rest, won't even come down for roasted hare, she leaves him there, and tends to her own work. Here in the deepest corner of the cave, at the sharp, downward turn, she warns the child to be careful by drawing a falling horse, on its back, with legs up, head rounding the ledge and toppling into the hole. Then, with a braided vine-rope she lowers herself into the pit, only lighting the tallow-lamp when she reaches bottom.

She begins her own double-barbed sign, a spear-thrower topped by a white bird from the land of Snow.

WHEN VIVAN SAW THE HEAD and arc of uplifted wings, she told Biron to lower her into the well; she had to see the rest of the painting and that she was going down, deeper, with or without his help. Her own left foot dangling like that of a wounded sparrow, her right scrabbling against the rock wall, she inched her way down, groping as if blind, until Biron said he had to pull her up or let go of her; and she hollered, "I'm down!" Then he released her into the painting in the well. Lighted only by a single electric lamp that might have been a magic lantern, it glowed as if by its own internal sun.

She knew it was for a child, not just a warning or a story-painting, but a memory of what happened before the great porch collapsed and the falling rocks and boulders closed the sanctuary — Mina must have believed — forever.

Before she left, Mina broke all his spears, more fierce in her grief than ever she was in rutting, and she saved one, his finest, to bury with him.

She left Peta's body inside, hidden in a dolmen sepulchre, his belly ripped and torn open by horns, the stone pendant of the woman with child carefully placed in his right hand, his spear in the other, and she put his colour-points and a tallow-lamp beside him to see him on his journey.

Before she departed with their child, Mina painted on the wall sixteen feet deep in The Well what happened to Peta.

HE STALKED THE BISON, too weak after the reindeer left and never returned, his eyes nearly sightless from squinting in weak tallow-light at the reindeer spirits on the ceiling, his legs bowed and back bent from crouching on the scaffold for too many winters. A good hunter, he was careful tracking spoor, massive droppings, hoofprints in the soft river earth, the scattering of pebbles when the great beast, closer now, plunged ahead, yet he was surprised when the bison charged out of the thicket. Swift to hurl his spear, he ripped open its belly, blood spurting and darkening the earth. But the bison did not fall. With the spear and its entrails hanging out, it charged again, head lowered and swinging in a great arc so its right horn pierced and caught Peta up and, tossing his head, flung the hunter to the ground.

And suddenly his hair turned to feathers, his nose into a beak. He became a spirit-bird ready for flight, the last one, and seeing the reindeer scudding across the sky, he felt the woman-stone cold against his chest, and with the final raising of his manhood, he was thankful for the hunt.

He scratched in the sediment a double series of punctuation marks only Mina would understand and explain to their child.

LEAVING THE VILLAGE OF MONIGNAC, they see smoke spiralling, from the lookout. Traffic blocked ahead, they are forced to wait behind four trucks until a gendarme waves them into the left lane that will take them through the tunnelled underpass.

This is no place for a serious argument that begins at breakfast every morning now her visa has expired and new tourists arrive at La Palétie tomorrow. She has begun a last letter to Chester. *I didn't plan it, some things just happen when we least expect it. I hope you'll understand why I have to move on.*

He wants her to stay in France. He'll show her Paris, its Eiffel Tower, L'Arc de Triomphe.

"Uffington!" He shouts, his garlic breath steaming the front windshield. "No one knows how to cook *canard* there. *Les Anglais,* they eat something called suet pudding that looks and tastes like boiled rubber gloves."

"I have to see it to know who created it." A turf artist, surely. As old as the caves at Lascaux, the White Horse of Uffington is best seen from above, stylized and running right out of Prehistory, carved into the flat hilltop, with deep trenches filled with white chalk. It says so in the book she found in a wondrous shop in the village of St. Cyprien. She clutches the book to her chest, her breath now caught by the sight of a Renault, overturned on the midline, like a humpbacked beast, its seatbelts and buckles dangling like entrails. From the opened doors, articles have spilled out onto the road: a plastic, ribbed backrest, baguette wrappers, Coke cans, blue Lucite-framed sunglasses, a green writing pad with gold lettering, torn pieces of notepaper that flutter and swirl when caught by a new wind. One, lifted and taking flight like a fledgling out of its nest and testing new wings, smacks against the windshield, its leafy edges curling as if its trying to hide drawings of six-rayed stars too smudged to understand their meaning.

No sign of the occupants or even an ambulance. The gendarmes seem to be waiting for a tow truck.

They check the buckles on their seatbelts. He tells her not to look, to cover her eyes, the sight might frighten the child stirring within her.

Turning about, they drive on, in a new and opposite direction, away from the darkly brooding river, the cliffs pocked with caves, away from the Valley of the Dordogne.

Mombachu

Brenda Niskala

THE TROPICAL SUN BEATS ON Nash's uncovered head, perhaps even more merciless in the thin mountain air. Rico, the tour guide, drones on ahead of the staggered and staggering line of hikers. "There are thirty-five different kinds of orchids on the volcano," he says. "I will show you many."

Okay, Nash thinks, *This tour guide's got me pegged as some sort of green orchid-loving old lady. When all I really want right now is a drink.* Bottled water just doesn't cut it. Nash pulls out the crinkled plastic anyway, and slugs back a third before pausing to breathe, to gulp in the sulfur-laced air.

"And this is the — I think you say in English — green frog? *Muy venenosa.* Very poisonous." The guide pries open the concave bromeliad nesting the amphibian and each of the *touristas* on the volcano tour dip and peek at the frog, then back away.

"This my favourite spot. Wait, wait. Luck is possible here." He leaps to another thatch of undergrowth, *like a leprechaun,* Nash thinks. A Nica leprechaun. She'll have to ask the cigarette girl if they have little people in their folklore. Rico is some sort of magic, though. She's never actually seen his legs move. Just as she glances up, he appears to settle from a vertical leap by a clump of waving flowers. "Begonias," he says, his thick dark fingers cupping the blossoms like a butterfly. "There are thirty-five different kinds."

Nash nods in polite appreciation. She grimaces as a septuagenarian Nicaraguan woman strides past her, on some everyday business up the trail. *Maybe I'll be that wiry in twenty years,* she thinks, but then remembers her own mother leaning into the walker she used until her death. Bad genes.

How the hell had she let Helen talk her into this? God, she does not do tours. She could have been absorbing the Nicaraguan culture from the veranda of the Colonial Hotel with a perfectly good guava and rum. There she could appreciate as much as she needed to of the flora and fauna from her perch over the central *marketa.* Rather she would have done with Mike, if he'd stayed around long enough. They would have made up stories about the country, about the people. They would not have done guidebooks, would have found their own small miracles, their own poisonous frogs.

But Helen insisted, waving the guidebook, and claiming it would be good to stretch her legs, to see something other than the bottom of a glass. That's how she put it, the bitch.

Nash agreed to go, though, and wouldn't you know it, Helen had already purchased a hiking ensemble for the event. For Nash, though, the appeal of checking out the volcano arose from a vague memory of a book, required reading in her first and only English literature class, part of her unfinished degree. Decades ago. She didn't finish the book either, but remembers the growing discomfort with the story while the main character searched in vain for something in his garden, in his home. What was he looking for? She remembered feeling disgust and alarm, almost panic, at his restlessness.

She could be letting the world come to her — the boys and girls laced with strings of pottery, drooping with handmade hammocks — those would look great in her condo — and later, the women with trays of gum and cigarettes at twenty-five cents a smoke, the men with boards of pirated CDs and DVDs, five bucks each for American releases. So there was culture. She had even cultivated a relationship with her own cigarette girl, who sometimes also came by with small bags of cashews and succulent sliced mango.

"No smoking in the nature reserve, *Señora*." How had he known she was even thinking about cigarettes? Perhaps he's more of a gnome, she decides.

And Helen, the witch, connived and cajoled until Nash agreed to keep her company, but her friend disappeared the moment she spotted the empty seat beside *Señor* Egret, the guy with the camera and binoculars slung around his skinny neck, practically crushing his scrawny chest. The only single male on the tour. There's a friend for you.

Well, it's been a few years since Nash has had an adventure that did not involve Mike holding her elbow, a *maître d'* at the door, and a glass of cooling bubbly set on white linen, but if she keeps her eye on the prize — ah yes, there would certainly be drinks after! — she'll be just fine.

"In the third ecosystem on this mountainside," the gnome says, then pauses to make sure everyone can hear him. Nash has missed the explanation of the first two. No, wait, one was where the coffee grew. She even had a cup on the plantation veranda, while she watched the armed guards watch her, unsmiling, their hard eyes jumping from tourist to tourist. Maybe the second one was the rainforest? "In the third ecosystem you will feel the radiating warmth of the lava. Next we will view some vents."

Okay, will there be a test after? She thinks back to the air conditioned bus — ah yes, now that was ecosystem *numero uno*.

And then there was the second ecosystem of the tour — according to Nash, the dusty paddock where the tourists milled inside fences, awaiting the arrival of the green army personnel carriers, while the locals seemed to float by on the steep road, driving humpbacked cattle. Just kids, these Nicas, really. Why weren't they in school? Every one carried a baseball bat instead of a cattle prod. Three boys had stopped to stare back at her when she lit a smoke and tapped her toes in the dirt of the tourist kennel: clear brown eyes, menacing in their lack of expression. She tried one of her toothy smiles, the one that won over pedlars from the *marketa*. Hadn't these boys ever seen a middle-aged blonde before? Should she have given them some *cordobas,* these country children, so different from the city beggars? The children who come to the veranda of the Colonial hug her, their fingers searching for anything they can pry loose. She is less than fresh prey on this mountain, however. She could feel the impersonal harshness in the way she was being studied: a specimen of only passing interest, deemed unusable while they continued up the rocky roadside path carved into the mountain wall. Their tour would pass these boys, would leave them in the dust, squeezed against the sheared rock.

Nash found herself pressed against the mesh of the fence, following the boys with what could be called a gaze of longing, of recognition, maybe, until they rounded the first switchback, out of sight.

To not need. It's been a long time, but Nash remembers when she was that complete child, watching with detached curiosity the flinching and coiling of the restless adults around her. How had she arrived at this pitiful place, where she hates the alone part? Fears it. How could Mike betray her like that? She'd given him her life, dedicated herself to his successes and his failures, to his friends, to his appearance and to his happiness. God, she could use something stronger than water right now!

The gnome is waving them all towards a steaming slash near the stony path. As if she needs a sulfur facial?

"In this lava lives Chalchihuehe, the evil lady." Rico's eyes twinkle as he lowers his voice. "Carefully. She eats innocents."

So then Helen's not the only witch on the mountainside. But not to worry about any innocents in this troupe. Nash ducks dutifully over the heated hole and exclaims like every other gringa. So we're on a volcano. She admires the heat vents, the heated floors, the field of wild begonias clotted with orchids apparently unique to these slopes.

"Also, do not pick flowers, ladies and gentlemen. Those who have done so never come back down this path." Rico's eyes narrow, as if he would ensure such an abandonment.

Nash pauses to tighten her laces. What she could really use is a proper bath, bubbles and soft music, her feet resting above her heart in this heat. The Nicaraguans do not get the concept of baths. Their precious water, even in the hotel, is only available in one temperature, whatever comes out of the pipe, in a shower that must be driven by gravity, it is so lethargic.

Cold showers, once Nash gets used to the shock, feel good in the heat, and are her main defense, her friend in the nights that only cool to ninety-four degrees Fahrenheit, her lifesaver when the fans stop, as they often do in yet another power outage, when she spreads herself naked on her bed, then falls into a stupor. Not passing out, exactly. It's damned hard to pass out in the tropics. She will have to be more dedicated, she decides. Dedicated to numbness. To oblivion.

"It's not so much farther now, *Señora.*" Rico jumps in front of her face, his ingratiating smile making her teeth grate. "We have a little climb, then a — how it is? — tunnel, and then a little bigger climb, and then we rest." There are twenty or so following him, but his eyes are on her for the moment, not smiling.

Nash nods, nonchalantly. Okay, so they'd leapt from stone to stone through the jungle undergrowth, across the heated plains, and into the rocky chasms, but mostly she realized, they'd been going steeply downhill. Surely someone would come around with the personnel carrier and pick them up now. Nash had come perilously close to ending the tour before it began when she realized she would have to climb a ladder, then swing into one of the metal seats bolted to the floor of the back of the Nicaraguan army's version of a four-wheel drive. Oh no, she hadn't signed up for an open-air tour, jungle vines and branches swooping into her face while the truck bounced and ground its way up the steep incline.

"This path will take us from zero to three thousand feet above sea level," the gnome exclaims.

Big deal. Where Nash comes from, the Cypress Hills are almost five thousand feet. The Rockies are fourteen thousand feet up. They call this a summit? Nash can see Helen and *Señor* Egret far ahead and climbing.

Don't look up. Trudge. Remember to breathe.

A drip of perspiration, not the moisture from the *palapa* of exotics, all of which have been named by the gnome. What was this? A drop too salty to be dew or the morning's rain. Into her eyes. Blink clear. Stinging like tears.

No! Definitely not tears.

Nash is well beyond tears, well beyond sadness, or any feeling other than anger, impatience, the practical ones. This must be a side effect of the heavy breathing. God, will her legs hold out? The steady climbing, stone to slippery stone, the gnome dancing in front of her. "Just a few more steps, *Señora.*"

The heat, will she ever cool down? So hot.

"And here is a little surprise." The gnome leaps far to her right and opens his arms to direct the small group — all puffing, but are they gulping the air like her? Are their diaphragms close to bursting? Their faces are not the deep flush, dark as she knows hers is, as if she's just swigged some cheap red wine.

Oh, any wine will do right now. She moves to the railing, to appreciate the view, gather the breeze. Let there be a damn breeze; even a hot wind will be cooling. She shakes her blouse, pulls it away from her back and breasts, creating a miniature plough wind inside the polyester knit. No place to sit — well, except where Helen now perches, completely focused on something the birder has spotted towards the horizon.

Nash has been abandoned by her travel companion, has been left to fend for herself. Again. Oh, self pity, please stop. Nash knows where this leads. He's gone. Pass the bottle. He's gone and she imagines how much better it would have been if he'd simply drifted to another relationship. At least he'd still be here to hate, to berate.

The gnome has not stopped talking, is not breathing heavily. He skips from one side of the panorama to the other, pointing out details of the city and the countryside far below. The vast fields of sugar cane, rice and, on the mountainside, coffee, fed by the volcanic soil and the moisture preserved by the jungle in this otherwise desolate land. The white graveyard is significant only because there are blue and yellow graveyards in this country too. And because it's so old. Much older than Nash. It dates from 1540 or so. Old. Another volcano in the distance, slate-black and steaming. Some touristas actually sign up to climb that ugly slag heap in order to catch a glimpse of the churning lava. Not for her. Not for her.

If only Mike had kept their damn pact, and made sure she went with him. That was supposed to be their final solution. Easy, elegant, leaving no survivors, no messy mourning. But no, he had to sneak out the back door. Massive heart attack. Why are these things always massive? Oh, I miss him.

"*Señora,* will you be all right?" The gnome singles her out. How embarrassing. But the rest of the tour had proceeded without her while she leaned over the railing, gulping in air, pretending to appreciate the view. She has not spoken for hours, and can't catch her breath to speak now. She nods yes, and pushes one foot in front of the next, in the general direction of the gnome's dancing heels.

The ground crumbles beneath her. She can't tell whether it's a crack in the soil opening to boiling liquid, or the bones of her feet and ankles snapping, the tendons twanging, her movement forward impossible, or whether it's simply waking up to how really alone she is.

Part of her doesn't care. Open a bottle of wine. Another part weeps and thrashes as if throwing a tantrum. A third and secret part of her, as feral as the brown eyes of the boys on the road, knows that it doesn't matter, nothing matters. She will experience this and move on. Or die. This third part is a great friend of death, of the peace that passes all understanding, of the place where nothing matters, and where everything matters equally. Where rock and lava and steam, the beginning and the end, meld. Snake and tail. Infinity.

Sweat-blinded, heaving and stumbling like some mad jungle beast, the slip feels natural, the air rushing past her body as she falls like a fan opening in slow motion. She has time to decide what not to break — don't hit my head on the rocks, don't over-compensate and wrench my back, don't over-reach and crack my arm bone. Keep light on the feet, like a leprechaun, protect my ankle. Nash even has a moment to worry about the gash in the knee of her new Bermuda shorts.

"I told her this was not a suitable tour for someone in her condition." Helen's voice. No time has passed. What condition? So thirsty. But mercifully not moving forward for the moment. Resting.

"*Señora?*" The gnome's face is right over hers. In the relentless sunlight, she cannot see his features, only the halo around his head. "Some water, *Señora?*"

"Nash, can you talk? Say something to me!" Helen is silhouetted by the light.

"Fuck off, Helen." Nash manages to say the words very clearly.

On the volcano there is supposed to be molten lava, sulphur, and searing heat. In the rainforest there is supposed to be rain.

Godsend

James Trettwer

THERE WAS SOMETHING I NEEDED to remember. It wasn't work, I was already there staring at my bloodshot, bruised-looking eyes in the washroom mirror. I'd even made it on time because I had crashed at my friend Darryl's apartment, a ten-minute walk away. My clothes were a bit wrinkled but I'd been at work in worse shape before. Darryl even let me use an extra toothbrush. So what was it I had to do?

I had already called Esther at her house. Her answering machine said *leave a message*, which I didn't. Her work voicemail said she was away. I didn't leave a message there either.

The last time we spoke she told me I whined like a mule. "That's creatively original," was my less-than-creative response. "By the way, nice mixed metaphor." Not that I know what a metaphor is, but I'd heard her say the same thing.

We had stayed married for about twenty years. The things we do for our children. Or our only daughter in this case.

A recollection just started to crawl up from the depths of my addled brain when Darryl found me.

"Miller, there you are. Lorne's looking for you and he is seriously pissed off."

"How does he know we're hungover again?"

"You shouldn't slobber down a co-worker's cleavage first thing when you come into work. Especially if she goes to the same church as the boss, you dumb shit. And not we. Just you. I'm not the one who looks like he's still wasted."

"You always drink more than me and look like you just had water all night." I blinked at his reflection in the mirror. Darryl's white, tapered shirt, crisply tucked in, revealed his broad-shouldered upper body underneath. His black hair was perfectly groomed, without any of the grey which was spreading like a fungus from my temples.

"It's all in the genes," Darryl said. "I told Lorne I'd go find you — I kind of figured you'd be here puking — so at least I could give you a heads-up."

"I'm not puking. It's the dry heaves." The near constant pain in my stomach surged and I leaned my face toward the sink. Nothing happened.

Darryl clicked his tongue. "Whatever. Just get moving."

I turned toward the door and tried to properly tuck in my wrinkled Walmart dress shirt, which stretched across my belly and ballooned across the lower back.

Darryl grabbed my arm. "And, hey. Keep me out of this. I'm not the one stupid enough to get caught. Again." He passed me his apartment keys. "Just in case," he said.

I made my way to Lorne's office. He sat behind his desk and immediately made eye contact with me. He dropped a sheet of paper he was reading on his spotless, uncluttered desktop. He did not stand up or offer me a chair. I thought he surrendered the psychological advantage because he was a large man and would have towered over me had he stood. Especially if I sat down. Instead he leaned back in his chair and folded his hands across his massive midsection, his thick arms resting on the chair's arms. Without preamble or the usual lecture on company image, he said, "You are being suspended without pay for the rest of the day. The reason: inebriation in the workplace after multiple warnings."

I briefly wondered how Darryl divined the purpose of the meeting and gave me his keys. "You can't do that." I vaguely waved my finger in Lorne's direction. "You can't even talk to me about this without a union representative present." I heard movement behind me and turned to see a uniformed contract security guard and a barrel-bellied retired cop from the internal security department hovering at the open door.

Lorne glanced at his watch. "I am intimately familiar with disciplinary procedures because of you. You can have your say to the union at a hearing on Monday morning in the Manager of Staff Relations office in Personnel. Now that's Monday — three days from now. This coming Monday morning at 8:30 AM."

"All right. Monday. I'm not stupid."

"I want to make sure you don't have one of your convenient 'misunderstandings'." He picked up the sheet again and held it toward me. "This note reiterates what we've just discussed and, in bold, indicates the time and location of the meeting. Don't forget to report via the security kiosk. Until then, please leave." He nodded to the two men at the door. The ex-cop, whose name I couldn't remember if my life depended on it, placed a gentle hand on my shoulder.

"I'm launching a grievance, you know."

"Fine." Lorne did not move.

"Come on, Rex," said the ex-cop, and squeezed my shoulder ever so lightly.

My security entourage followed me to my desk and watched me fumble for the union office phone number. I threw the telephone directory aside when I couldn't immediately find the listing. "Screw it. They're in on this conspiracy anyway."

Darryl was nowhere to be seen when I was escorted outside of the main entrance to the building. The ex-cop asked me if I intended to drive home; he could call a cab if I needed one. "I intend to walk," I replied, "to my buddy's place, where my stuff is, and have a sleep. Thanks for the send off, boys."

They both went back inside without another word. I headed to Darryl's, fondling his keys in my pocket, for a well-deserved nap before going for a well-deserved drink.

Later that day, I sat with Willie, the permanent resident who haunted the doorway of our bar, The Coffee Cavern, across the street from the building. He scratched his chin under his scraggly beard and flakes of dead skin drifted down onto the table. He drained his supper of a glass of Guinness. "Jeez Rex, that's tough. Sounds like them bastards are going out of their way to do you in."

"They're probably going to send me to rehab again."

"Ow, that bites. You should get a lawyer or something. Especially if them union guys are in on it. You could probably sue them for a couple hundred grand, eh?" He waved his empty glass at the server. "Do you mind?"

"I'm kind of short at the moment," I said. "I need money for something coming up." I still couldn't remember.

"Oh, okay." He looked around the bar. "Oh, hey, I just thought of something I got to do. I'll see you later."

In The Cavern's slightly oppressive, subdued lighting and dark woodwork, I saw Willie talking intently to some other regular drinkers standing around the black marbled bar. He disappeared after a few minutes. I ordered myself another Guinness and some cheese fries. My rehab comment made me think back to my time there the year before.

The company's "intervention team" had arranged for that visit and Esther dropped me off. Instead of letting her escort me to the door, I insisted she just watch me enter the two-story house on Victoria Avenue. The neighbourhood was too rough at night for her to walk back to the car by herself; so I told her. I pretended to buzz the outer front door and leaned down to talk into the speaker. I reached for the doorknob, turned and waved, and Esther drove away. I promptly walked to The Cavern a few blocks away. Darryl was there with a couple of our mutual buddies. I don't remember the rest of the night.

I do remember waking up in the play area of Victoria Park the next morning. I was beside a little playhouse and a young girl, with a snotty nose, was poking me with a stick. Her mother, sitting on a nearby bench and rocking a baby, kept yelling at her to leave me alone. I heaved myself up by clinging with both hands to the window opening of the playhouse. The girl ran away with a squeal of feigned fear.

"Good thing the cops didn't find you, eh?" The mother smirked when I staggered by.

"You bet. Do you know what time it is?"

"It looks like it's time for a bit of hair of the dog for you, eh?" Then she laughed.

I wandered to a coffee shop across from the park and ordered a large Dark Brazil roast. While sitting in a half-doze and stirring two tablespoons of brown sugar in my coffee, I heard a voice say, *You really look like you could use that.*

This guy sat across the table from me. Dressed like a tree-hugger in a vest with a million pockets, he was my height and his face was smooth with no crow's feet or black rings under the eyes. His dark hair, without a hint of grey, was pulled back in a ponytail much like the way my hair used to be twenty years back in those carefree days at university. Those days before the grinding tedium set in at the regional office of *Can-Co Assurance and Mutual.*

Back then, I studied while listening to alternative and garage music; once lectures and final exams were done, they were done. The beer after that stress was a relaxing, well deserved pleasure. Not like now, with finals-level stress day after day after day of actuarial stats and quotas and cover-sheet counts and that peaceful oblivion, the only hope to plough through just one more day.

The guy extended his hand and said, *Kingsley*.

With hesitation I reached forward and my fingertips tingled as if from a firm grasp.

What would your daughter say if she saw you in this condition?

"My condition is none of your business, you jerk. And I don't let her see me in 'this condition' anyway."

Are you sure?

"Daddy?"

I swung around and knocked over my coffee. "Christine? What are you doing here?"

My eighteen-year-old daughter stood over me. Her lower lip quivered. She looked so vulnerable, her entire body tense and hunched as she let out a long breath before saying, "You promised you were going to rehab."

"I was. I mean, I did. I am. I'm on my way there right now. I just wanted a quick coffee."

"Mom said she dropped you off last night."

"What? Why does she lie like that? I'm supposed to be there today. As soon as I'm finished my — " I looked around the coffee shop. Kingsley was gone.

I pushed myself up with both hands on the table. "Christine? Did you see that guy?"

She was already sopping up my spilled coffee with a handful of paper napkins. "Why do you do this? Why do you lie to me?"

I gently touched her shoulder. "I'm sorry, honey. I had stuff to do yesterday, but nobody would listen. So I pretended to go in last night just to keep the peace. I was just on my way there. Honestly."

She blinked hard, but did not tear up.

"Do you have your car here, sweetie?"

She nodded.

"Good. Could you drive me over there right now?"

"Okay."

I held her cheeks with my fingers and kissed her forehead.

She threw the napkins in a garbage can and apologized to the staff for my mess while I leaned against the storefront outside, resting my head against the cool glass.

I managed to last the two weeks in rehab because I would have been fired otherwise. Darryl made sure I didn't suffer too many ill effects during my stint by smuggling in a flask in his cowboy boots. We covertly finished the flask's contents during visiting hours when we were alone in the smoking area outside. I was a model attendee and fully cooperated and participated in all of the therapy sessions. If the rehab staff suspected anything, I'm sure they were too overwhelmed with work and constant funding cuts to bother with a hopeless case like me.

After my release, it took Esther less than an hour to discover nothing had changed. She packed up and took the dog. We've been apart since then.

Now, I poked at the coagulated glob of cheese on my cold fries.

Darryl and Willie sat down. "Close call there today, buddy." Darryl waved three fingers at the server. "I thought they were going to fire your ass."

"It's not over yet. I have a meeting with Personnel on Monday."

"Pah, you'll just get another disciplinary letter. Maybe suspended for a week or something. Big deal. But come on, pal. It's Friday night. We got all weekend to party."

"Wait a minute. I have to call Esther. There's something I'm supposed to do."

"What do you want to talk to her for? She'll just bring you down. Willie, my man, here's some coin. Fire up the jukebox. You know what I like."

"No. I have to call her." Or was it Christine I had to call?

Darryl grabbed my sleeve. "Hey! You dodged the bullet today. I'm here to help you celebrate. And it looks like I've got a lot of catching up to do. You can't leave me in the lurch. I'm your best buddy."

I hesitated.

"Look, here's our brewskies."

I don't remember much else of that weekend.

THE PHONE WAS RINGING.

It was Lorne and he told me I was an hour late for the meeting in Personnel.

"I've got the flu," I replied. "I took some heavy medication last night — from the doctor — and I don't think my alarm clock is working."

"You were able to see your doctor over the weekend?"

"He was at his 24-hour clinic. If you don't believe me, call his office."

Lorne sighed. "When can we expect you?"

"I'll be there in an hour."

I sat on the edge of the bed and tried to orient myself. The pain in my stomach was constant. I showered quickly and skipped shaving to save time. The dress pants I had been wearing for the last week had mud and grass stains on the knees and butt. I kicked them behind my toilet and snippets of the weekend came to me.

I had drunk a lot. Puked a couple of times. I'd slept at Darryl's again and spent Sunday afternoon at his place watching football and drinking beer. I'd then gone to the north shore of Wascana Lake.

I remembered weaving along the shore. With no one in sight, I'd stopped and chucked a rock at some geese on the water. My throw landed nowhere near the birds but it did spin me around and I fell to a sitting position. I felt a hand on my shoulder. The guy with the many-pocketed, pretentious vest and sporting my old ponytail loomed over me. "Kingsley?" I said.

Well, well. I am amazed you remember me.

"So am I, actually. What the hell do you want? And how in hell did you find me?"

I just happened along. Did you ever remember what you were supposed to do?

I drew a blank. "What do you know about it? Or know about me?"

I know more than you might think.

"What do you care? And I say again, what the hell do you want, anyway?"

Simple. I want what's best for you.

I staggered to my feet. "Oh, I'm totally sure of that. And what if the best thing for me is to smack you in the face?"

Go ahead. Remember, though, you missed those geese by a mile.

I tried to plant my left foot to deliver a right hook but only stumbled.

Kingsley stepped forward, grabbed my shoulders, and steadied me. *Perhaps you should direct that anger at what's causing your memory loss. You will have a revelation when you least expect it. And you will be filled with remorse.*

"Remorse? I'll only be remorseful if Christine finds me like this again. And that isn't going to happen." Just then, someone called my name.

It was Darryl. He strode toward me, swinging his arms, hands balled into fists. "You idiot. Do you want to get tossed in the drunk tank?"

"How did you find me, too?"

"Too? What are you talking about?"

I turned around, but Kingsley had disappeared again. There was a dark-haired guy with a ponytail walking away in the distance, but he was wearing a black T-shirt and shorts. "Did you see the guy I was just talking to?"

Darryl pushed me away from the water. "Come on, let's get you out of here. You look like a freaking rummy. It's a good thing I found you."

"Why did you bother to try and find me, anyway?"

"When I saw your car still parked in front of my place I knew you weren't on your way home so I came looking for you. I was the last person you were seen with. I don't need hassle from the pigs if you get into more trouble."

We didn't say anything else to each other. Darryl drove me home in my car and I went straight to bed. How he got back home, I don't know.

But now, all that mattered to me was that my car was parked in its space and I was able to drive to the appointment I was more than two hours late for. The meeting itself lasted about an hour. Lorne, the union representative, and the Manager of Staff Relations talked about me in the third person. I was addressed directly only once by the union rep when he asked me if I agreed to the terms.

I said, "Sounds good to me." Then I signed some forms, made a quick stop at the bank, and I was at The Cavern shortly thereafter.

"I tell you, Willie, it's the best thing that's ever happened to me. They terminated me with a week's pay for each year of service plus all outstanding vacation pay, plus one month's pay in lieu of notice. And they handed me a cheque for that amount right on the spot. I've got full access to my pension. I just have to call a broker from a list they gave me and get a RRIF set up. One of the forms I signed said I wouldn't sue and she was a done deal. I didn't even bother to clean out my desk."

"It's a real godsend, pal. Work was interfering way too much with our drinking anyway." Willie licked his lips when our order arrived.

After our second round, I called Darryl from the bar and told him to join us after work. And then, I went and threw up what I had just drunk. That continued for a while. I'd drink, then throw up. The stabbing pains in my temples steadily worsened and my vision blurred. I had to send Willie out for some painkillers and antacid tablets.

Then finally, finally after a few boilermakers with scotch, I achieved that euphoria that had eluded me all day. I was back to normal and ready for some action.

The bar had filled to capacity and Darryl was at another table chatting up a lanky blonde woman in a short leather skirt and white blouse with the top two buttons undone. Shortly after, a swarm of young, seemingly drunk girls came shrieking into the bar. I was trying to get a good look at them at the bar counter when Darryl sat down across from me.

"I'm going to be cutting out of here pretty soon with my new friend over there. She's got a 'BFF'," Darryl quoted with his fingers, "who she'll bring along or ditch depending on your frame of mind. Sorry Willie, she only has the one friend."

Willie nodded and disappeared into the crowd.

"That's what I like about you, Darryl. Always looking out for me."

"That's what I'm here for, buddy. What do you want to do?"

"First, I want to check out those girls who just came in."

"Whatever." Darryl stood up. "Don't take too long. When our drinks are gone, so are we."

"I'll let you know in a couple of minutes."

At that point I saw the girls through my blurry vision only from the back. I found myself particularly interested in the one sitting on the periphery of the group. She hunched over the bar and seemed detached from her friends and just a bit out of place. There was a sense of vulnerability about her that I found intriguing.

She faced the black marble-topped bar with her back to the crowd and her cohorts to her right. I approached from the back and squeezed in between her and the wall.

I said, barely audible over the din, "Hi. I don't think I've ever seen you in here before."

"Daddy?"

I staggered backward, the bar disappeared, and I was left alone in a circle of light, surrounded by blackness. Christine's eyes were wide, near tears but dry, her lower lip quivering, the same expression I had seen countless times before.

Kingsley stopped me from crashing to the floor. *Coveting your own daughter now?*

My head ached. My stomach burned. My heart hurt. I remembered when Christine was born. Esther said she was our godsend.

How much more of your antics do you think she's going to take? By the way, did you remember what you were supposed to do?

Christine's nineteenth birthday. I had promised to spend it with her.

"What have I done?"

You know what you've done.

I heard Darryl telling me to hurry. I raked my fingers over the stubble on my face. Willie was at the edge of the light staring at Christine. He licked his lips.

"Come on Miller, hustle up," Darryl said. "These wenches aren't going to wait all night."

There was a ripping hurt all across my chest. "Scuttle back to the hole you came from and die," I said to Darryl. "You too, you lecherous old bastard."

Willie faded into the blackness.

"Suit yourself," was the last thing I ever heard Darryl say to me.

Your daughter. Enduring you all these years. And now she's at the very place you've called home longer than you've been at home with her. What do you think she's likely to do next?

"Help me fix this."

Only you can fix this. Kingsley did not let me fall. His face reflected in mine, unblemished, like mine used to be. Like Christine's. He made sure I was standing upright when I returned to the bar, the noise, the stink.

Christine breathed deeply, silently counting. Silently enduring me, yet again.

I stammered, "What are you doing *here*?"

"Celebrating my birthday. Because you didn't. My friends decided to take me bar-hopping."

"But you don't drink."

"Yeah. Funny, that. Designated driver at my own legal drinking party. Coming here of all places. Irony after irony of my life with Father." She turned away from me and indicated to her friends that she was leaving.

The girls glanced repeatedly over at me, expressions of contempt obvious and unbridled while they gathered their things and prepared to leave.

That ripping had to end now. I touched Christine's shoulder. She didn't turn toward me but did say, "What?"

"Do you think your friends would mind if you drove me somewhere?"

"Where? Isn't there enough booze here?" She then did turn and looked at me the way a curious child would examine a misshapen worm caught on concrete after the rain, before deciding whether to put it out of its misery and step on it. She wasn't hunched.

"No. I need help, Christine. Can you help me? Please."

I PRESSED THE EMERGENCY BUZZER and muttered my name into the speaker. After a few moments, the door lock clicked and I opened the door. I turned to wave goodbye to Christine, watching me from her car.

Leaving with Lena

James Trettwer

DILLON POKED AT THE SCUM floating on his coffee with a stir stick. He then leaned back in his chair, an ergonomically correct, high-backed tilter. These types of chairs and the desktop computers with flat monitors were the only new items in a department full of furniture that looked like it was salvaged from an early '80's office disposal sale. His chair did not match the hideous beige of his forty-eight-inch-high cubicle panels. The two guest chairs, intended for visiting external sales people, also a vague and worn beige, sat in front of his dark brown, teak-laminate desk.

Rubbing his eyes, he signed into the Procurement Request system on his computer. His first requisition was for drills and drill-bit sets for the general maintenance department at the mine site. He sat back again and wondered if Lena was already at her battered secretarial desk across the office, out of his line of sight. Maybe he should clean the coffee maker instead of filling orders. "Or not," he said out loud. "Not in my job specs."

"What's that you're muttering there, *Dial-on*?" said Buck, a co-worker in internal supply and distribution and sometimes drinking buddy. He plopped down in one of the guest chairs. His convenience-store thermal cup, with the vendor's name worn off, was so full, coffee slopped out of the holes in the lid.

"Exactly. Just muttering, *Puck,*" replied Dillon.

"Geez, sitting around talking to yourself, pally? You really need to get laid. Anyway, have we got a story to tell you. You know Johnathon the summer student?"

"Never heard of him. The only summer student I know around here is Lena, doing some sort of religious studies master's degree. I do know a Johnathon who's a co-op admin student slotted as a junior buyer for his work term."

Buck took a noisy and exaggerated slurp of his coffee. "Dick-less, *Dial-on*. How could I forget, that rhetoric is not in your repertoire. Mr. *Litter-alley* himself."

"Well, at least I have a marginal command of the English language, unlike some Bumbling-Bucks I could name. Do you even know what rhetoric means?"

"Doesn't matter. I came to tell you that we all went for beers last night and I had to come back for my gym bag. We got kinda goofing around and got into the dare thing. So, we dared Johnathon to smell Lena's chair seat and he did it."

"That's not even a good try at a joke. You're losing what little talent you never had to begin with." Dillon took a swallow of his coffee. "Try harder."

"It's no joke. It's totally true. And totally weird. Like, I mean, he got down on his knees and really took a whiff. A normal guy would just jerk around and then pretend to sniff and come up laughing when everybody groans. But he stayed there. And when he came up, he kinda had this look on his face."

"What was he looking at?"

"No, you moron. He had a weird look — on his face. He wasn't even laughing. He just kinda smirked. The guy's on something or he's a total jerk-meister."

"And you're not all of the above? You idiots and your enfeebled attempt at a new urban legend is a total fail. How many beers did it take to come up with this stupid story? As if."

"I'm serious. Give Elmo or Billy a blast. They'll confirm."

"Oh, sure, let me *confirm* with Mr. Buck Van-Pretense's not-so-stealthy stooges. Elmo, your personal version of Chester from the *Bugs Bunny* cartoons. And Billy, King of E, who's always so wasted he'll believe anything you tell him because he can't remember a thing. I'm supposed to call them after you all talked about it so you could get your story straight? The co-conspirators lending credibility to the fables of Aesop sitting across from me here? Good luck."

"Shit, Dillon. You're such a boner since you and Tiffany hit the skids."

TIFFANY AND DILLON were together for over three years. They had first met when Tiffany was a sales representative for a stationary company selling office supplies to Liverwood Mines. After Tiffany started working for an agency selling general lines of insurance, and any perception of corporate impropriety was eliminated, Dillon asked her on a date. Six months after that, he moved into her condominium.

Dillon had initially hoped he could calm her down, steer her away from her self-destructive binges; bar-top stripteases down to her underclothes. Get her away from the Buck-like slouches who leered at, and slobbered over, her model-runway body and exotic, shoulder-length black hair. Then came her venomous and unjustified accusations when Dillon even looked at another girl. This only ended with him eventually matching her drink for drink. They both spiralled downward with booze-saturated puke on the bathroom floor or in the kitchen sink, then one or the other sleeping on the couch too many times. After a 500 milliliter container of margarine splattered on the wall inches from Dillon's head and his fist flew a centimetre past Tiffany's face, punching a hole in the gyproc wall, Dillon moved to his own place.

BUCK SWIRLED THE COFFEE in his cup. "You're better off without her, you know."

"That much I've figured out myself. Haven't you got work to do?"

Buck stood up and turned to leave. "I don't know why I bother with you these days. My advice to you still stands."

"Duly noted, *pally*. And hey." Dillon waited until Buck turned back. "Come up with a better story."

Buck shook his head and wandered off.

Draining his cup, Dillon proceeded to work through a few requisitions for hand tools, bearings for roller assemblies, and a portable 6.5 HP generator. He called different vendors and checked online for best prices and delivery to the mine site, all the while thinking about Johnathon. The guy was in his early thirties, the same age as Dillon and Buck and their office cohorts. Unlike Dillon and the others, who all went right from high school to Admin Degree graduates to some sort of office drone — which is what Dillon felt he presently was — Johnathon had spent ten years working in various fast food kitchens, nighttime security jobs and even a year long stint as a 'swabbie' on a container ship. It was only after his time at sea that Johnathon finally enrolled in university under the Administration Degree, Co-operative Work Term Program. He occasionally tagged along for after-work drinks but only when cajoled and only when Dillon was there too.

Dillon wondered why Johnathon went for drinks without him the night before.

JOHNATHON SAT BY HIMSELF, tapping on his Android tablet at one of the round, white laminate tables in the break room. A half-empty orange juice bottle sat on the table beside him. Dillon poured himself a cup of coffee and approached the table. Johnathon looked up, nodded, and gestured for him to sit by pushing one of the white plastic chairs away from the table with his foot.

"Solo today?" Johnathon said. "Where's Buck and buddies?"

"Who cares. What's this I hear about you going for brewskies with those clowns last night without me?"

"We went over to The Cavern for a few drinks and a bite to eat, yes." Johnathon hesitated. "I expected you to show up."

"I was on suicide watch last night."

"Problems with your ex still? Uh, her name is . . . "

"Tiffany. She seems to think I owe her money for unequal living expenses paid over the years. Keeps calling to nag me about it. I don't know why I bother to listen. I guess it's easier than hearing the phone ring every five minutes until I answer and let her have her little vent."

"I'm sorry to hear that."

"Not your problem. Anyway, I didn't come here to whine."

Johnathon turned off his tablet and set it down. "So, Buck told you about the chair?"

Dillon was reminded of how quick this guy was and said, "What's the scoop with that?"

"That's what I like about you," Johnathon said. "Straight to the point. Not like Buck and his clique — always up to something. I did not smell her chair. When they dared me, I said something like, 'I've already done better.' I should've kept my mouth shut."

"And?"

"And nothing. I blurted that out because I am so tired of their stupid jokes. I just wanted them to shut up about Lena and maybe finally leave her alone."

Dillon pushed any thought of Lena from his mind and studied Johnathon. He had a mass of dirty blond hair, always in disarray, and his slightly bulging eyes had an open innocence about them. Like Buck, Johnathon stood six foot two, with huge hands and broad shoulders. Unlike Buck, Johnathon had a spongy body. Dillon knew that Buck worked out and suspected his bulging muscles more than likely involved steroids. He said, "So you really expected me to show up last night?"

"Why wouldn't I? Buck said you were coming. And I hoped you would because I've been wanting to talk to you about a couple of things."

"Oh?" Dillon said.

"One, I've been meaning to thank you."

"For what?"

"For not indulging in the constant dirty tricks they play on me. It's nice you and I can talk about something other than the latest sporting event or the contours of some woman's breasts. Like now, a half-assed, decent conversation."

"Uh, huh." Dillon drank some coffee. "And two, you were going to admit you have a thing going with Lena."

Johnathon cheeks reddened and he smiled. "Not exactly," he said. He took a drink from his juice bottle. "Hmm, I thought we were keeping it low-key. How did you know?"

HOW COULD HE NOT HAVE known? Since the first moment he met Lena. On her first day of work as receptionist for the Procurement Department, she was already at her desk when Dillon arrived for the day. She gave him a friendly and welcoming good morning and warm smile when he walked in. A thin, but well-proportioned, plain-faced girl with freckles on her upper cheeks, and strawberry-blonde hair that hung in a curled mess down to her shoulders, her petite nose wrinkled slightly with that smile.

Dillon introduced himself, Lena's hand gentle and warm when they shook. He immediately retreated to the break room for a sudden, desperately needed cup of coffee. In shock and awe; Lena, he perceived, was some sort of angelic antithesis to Tiffany. They had been broken up for two months at that time.

Back at his desk, Dillon thought that Lena's friendliness was also the total opposite of the overt hostility permeating the underlying dynamic of the whole department. He wondered how long that attitude would survive. Only until that first day's afternoon coffee break, it turned out.

That afternoon, Dillon went to find Buck and the others for the break. He found the three of them around Lena's desk swarming like wasps at an open pop can.

He couldn't remember the exact words Buck and the boys used at that moment, but "go for a ride," with an extended pause "on my motorcycle," and a blatant "get naked and do stuff," plagued his mind.

"Come on *chumm . . . ps*," Dillon said, attempting to deflect attention away from Lena. "Break time. Let's go."

"Hey Dillon," replied Buck, putting his hand on Lena's shoulder, "Have you met our new acquisition?"

"This morning. It's coffee time." Dillon marched toward the office exit but the others didn't budge. Lena kept typing, her shoulders taut, expression neutral, that cute smile nowhere to be seen.

Dillon turned back and intended to grab Buck by his shirt collar but Johnathon appeared. With a near yell he said, "Hey, Lena. I understand you know stuff about spreadsheets." He elbowed his way between Lena and Buck. "Can you open file manager and go to the budget shared drive? I think I screwed up a range of cells in one of the files." He leaned over her shoulder and verbally directed her to the appropriate network drive.

Lena's shoulders visibly relaxed while Johnathon hovered near her. After a minute of an obvious work-related discussion over Lena's monitor, the wasps finally ambled off to join Dillon for coffee break.

From that moment on, Lena politely said good morning or good afternoon but Dillon never again saw that nose-wrinkling smile cast in his direction.

"IT'S OBVIOUS, ISN'T IT?" Dillon replied with an exaggerated sigh. "The way you hang around her desk all the time, like some sort of sentry. The way you almost rest your chin on her shoulder when you're looking at her computer screen over the most contrived problems I've ever heard. Your Freudian slip over the chair." He poked at the scum on his coffee with his finger.

"I just wish they'd leave her alone. They all keep hitting on her, all the time." Johnathon paused a moment. "I guess that wouldn't stop them anyway, would it?"

Dillon shook his head. "Those guys will fish off of any dock, including the company one."

"And they're all married or attached too, aren't they?"

"Just Buck. Billy's single and is always too stoned to stay with any one girl for more than a night. Elmo considers himself single now because he just split with his wife."

"He doesn't seem bothered by it."

"Not like it bothers me, you mean?"

"That's not what I meant."

"No worries." Dillon didn't want to have that conversation again. "You said you wanted to talk to me about a couple of things?"

The question remained unanswered. Buck and company stormed in for more coffee after their break and wouldn't leave until Dillon and Johnathon had.

DILLON SAT AT A TABLE in The Coffee Cavern bar and finished his chicken burger. He had a swallow from his pint just as Johnathon appeared at the entrance. He waved his glass and Johnathon spotted him. Nodding once, he made his way to the table.

"Hey, Dillon," Johnathon said and sat down. "Thanks for meeting me. And thanks," he pointed at the sweating glass of tonic water with lime that Dillon had ordered for him.

"I hope it's not too warm," Dillon replied. "Anyway, I'm here most nights so no big deal. At least I don't have to drink alone. You know what they say about that."

"I do," replied Johnathon. "Are the guys going to show up?"

"The clowns are off to an NHL pool draft. It's never too early for an NHL pool draft, yeah?"

"I guess." Johnathon took a long drink, seemingly taken aback at Dillon's sarcastic tone.

Dillon said, "Where's Lena?"

"Choir practice."

"So, tell me, how long have you two been an *item*?"

Setting his glass down, Johnathon thought a moment. "Quite a while, actually. She was the lab instructor in a Psych class I took as an elective last year. We pretty much hit it off. Must have been the age thing. We were coffee-buddies on campus and hung out together when we were there. You know, the usual stuff. She was out of the picture last semester, doing directed reading research, so we didn't see each other much. Quite the shocker when she told me she got a job at Liverwood, I'll say. We were together again within the first week. It got serious a couple of weeks after that."

Johnathon wiped his lips with his fingers. "I wanted to meet you because we never did finish our conversation from a couple of days ago."

Dillon finished his pint and caught the attention of the server. "Lena's a Christian, yeah? You must have some pretty frustrating nights."

Johnathon's entire face flushed. It took him a moment to answer. "She's not that radical. She's a caring, giving person who happens to have strong beliefs. She also acknowledges human, physical needs."

"Well, good for you two. Tell me though, isn't she going to Niger or Timbuktu or someplace when her summer job's done?"

"Ethiopia. She's going to do some mission work through her church and Campus Crusades."

Dillon smirked. At least that relationship wouldn't be in his face. He said, "Gee, that's only three weeks from now. Too bad it's Splitsville for you then. You'd better get what you can in the meantime."

"We're not splitting up."

Dillon blew a raspberry. "Good luck with that. Distance relationships don't work."

"I'm going with her."

Dillon stared at Johnathon, mouth wide open. A religious studies person taking off for mission work was one thing. But an admin student turned office drone? And that guy, still with Lena? When he could finally speak, he said, "What the hell would you do that for? You've only got two semesters left for your degree."

Johnathon shook his head. "I can get a degree any time. I want to be with Lena now. And I want to do something maybe meaningful. The guys at the office are either procuring objects or girls any way they can." Johnathon suddenly shifted, his face red again. "Present company excepted, of course."

Dillon just cocked an eyebrow and waited.

Johnathon cleared his throat. "Regardless, I don't need the kind of crap that goes on around here."

Dillon felt a heaviness. He said, "So you're just going to drop out and head for Africa? For a woman, no less? You're a ding-dong, you know that? No offence."

"None taken. Lena is the first person I've ever met who is totally selfless. And she brings out a selflessness in me I never knew I had. She makes me feel good and I feel like I owe her something."

Dillon shook his head. Here he sat across from a guy who easily managed his small part of the departmental processes, not because he was happy doing it, but because he had an escape plan. An escape with a near-angel who didn't need to drink or strip or argue.

In a boozy stupor, he had once mentioned to Tiffany that he was afraid of becoming *the scum that forms* — a vague metaphor for concerns he couldn't quite fathom, but it sounded right. Tiffany tried to focus on Dillon with her own booze-bleary eyes and told him to suck it up and stop being an infant.

And there sat Johnathon with an almost childish look of defiance. He was going to take a chance on something better.

The server arrived with Dillon's next pint. He seized the glass and drank.

Johnathon asked, "Do you believe in fate?"

"Not particularly," Dillon replied, "But don't tell me." He touched his forehead with his fingertips and closed his eyes, "Let me read your mind. You think it was fated for you to meet Lena and then set off on some African adventure."

Johnathon shook his head. "I was thinking more about the timing of our two recent conversations. And that's what I wanted to talk to you about."

"Come again?"

"I was looking for a way to talk to you privately. Without the *clowns* in tow. And here we are again, just us two at the bar."

"So?"

"So why don't you come with us?"

Dillon snorted. "Are you kidding? I thought you didn't do Buck jokes."

"This isn't a joke. The missions always need people. And they don't have to be Christian, either. I'm not."

"Why the hell would I want to go to Ethiopia?"

"Don't you always say that you're sick of the 'mindless morons' you deal with everyday? Including Tiffany and that other girl from Accounting you see on occasion, Darla, Deedee?"

"Deirdre. And what's it to you?"

"We've made some inquiries to the pastor and our mission on your behalf. If you don't mind my saying, you seem very, very unhappy. Perhaps you need an opportunity to expand your horizons. And I think your drinking will ultimately result in, well, let's just say, discomfort for you."

That crossed the line. Dillon clenched his jaw. "Well, Friar *John-oh-thon,* thanks for your concern." He stood up. "Unfortunately, I do mind you saying. And my drinking is none of your business. So keep me out of your idiot schemes." Dillon drained his beer while standing. Turning, he said, "I gotta blast."

"They're taking volunteers for two more weeks," Dillon heard Johnathon say as he stomped away.

On his way home, the night was calm and cool — incongruous with Dillon's mood. He should be furious with that pretentious cock Johnathon for making inquiries to 'our mission' — even that phrase oozed with pretension — without his permission.

And what was Lena's motive? She hated his guts. Didn't she?

DILLON DIDN'T DESPISE HIS JOB. It was something he was good at. The salary was more than acceptable, about ten percent higher than the industry average for purchasing positions. He enjoyed talking on the telephone with the workers at the mine site. He also liked dealing with outside vendors — on a professional level. No more involvement on the Tiffany side of the scale. Ever again. It's too bad he couldn't demonstrate this part of his personality to Lena.

He stared at the flashing message-waiting indicator on his telephone but couldn't find the energy to even reach for the receiver. What was disturbing was that someone would actually consider his well-being without being asked. He realized that his lifestyle and his "first world" problems were far removed from real world issues, especially in nations like Ethiopia. Yet, if he dared state this fact out loud to anyone in his current circle — miner, vendor, co-worker — he would undoubtedly be regarded as making some ridiculous, Buck-type joke, followed by serious sniggers and chugging contests to bring him back to reality.

He sighed and reached for the phone merely to shift his mindset. There was no point in wallowing. His arms didn't feel quite as heavy while he listened to a couple of price quote returns, entered prices in his Procurement software, and then deleted the messages.

A voice message from Deirdre, his occasional liaison in Accounting, was next. "Oh, *mygawd,* Dillon. I'm so sorry I haven't called you lately. I was meaning to for a while but I just couldn't find the energy. I have some news. About *him.* I'd love to go for drinks with you, get caught up and, you know, whatever. Let's cut out about a half hour early tonight and get that back table at The Cavern. I've got something else to ask you, too. I think I totally need a change."

Dillon and Deirdre had flirted on an intensifying level as his relationship with Tiffany deteriorated to the point of no return. When it was finally over with Tiffany, and afterward abundantly clear Lena would never smile at him again, the flirting turned into satisfying mutual needs. Dillon understood that there was no commitment, but Deirdre didn't seem to see it that way. Yet at the same time she was in a tumultuous, on-again, off-again relationship with someone else. When it was off again, she was with Dillon. Of late though, it was on again and they hadn't seen each other for a couple of weeks.

By the sound of her voicemail, Deirdre's relationship was definitely off. She might be a distraction. At least for a while, anyway.

Or maybe a replacement? He called her back and ended up leaving a message on her voicemail saying her plan worked for him.

Dillon smirked to himself. Now, what would Johnathon have to say about this particular twist of fate?

DEIDRE WAS LATE. The din in the bar increased while people filtered over after work. Well into his second pint, Dillon gazed around the bar. The Cavern's dark, hardwood floor was polished to a shine but the equally dark, exposed roof support beams and pillars and the brown brickwork gave the whole bar a slightly oppressive feel. The subdued lighting, probably to obfuscate the scaling of the brickwork and dry-rot of the wood, added a certain dinge factor. The black marble of the bar's counter did nothing to brighten the place.

But, the drinks were cheaper than other downtown establishments and the food was better than average. The owners had a good sense of customer service with the bar and restaurant acting as a coffee shop during the day and then both providing the service they were designed for after quitting time.

With Buck and the boys off to another hockey pool — never enough NHL drafts — and Johnathon presumably with Lena doing their church thing, Dillon anticipated being alone with Deirdre the entire night. She had the physicality of a '60's model, shorter in stature but with an ample and well-proportioned body. The really attractive thing about her was her almost waist-length, auburn hair. The annoying thing about her was her tendency to twirl her ringlets in the fingers of her left hand.

When she finally rolled in, she headed directly to the bar. She ordered her drink and then smiled and gave Dillon a finger wave. Waiting for her drink, she twirled her hair the whole time.

She slid into the seat of the booth across from Dillon and gently set down her Paralyzer. She then clunked her purse, a purple and mauve shoulder bag with long straps, in the middle of the table. Dillon recoiled and snatched his glass, saving it from a tumble.

"Sorry I'm late," she said. "Some receivables didn't balance. To the order of nine cents, no less. The boss wouldn't let us leave until he got his reconciliation. It probably cost nine hundred dollars to find the stupid inverted cents entry that caused the difference in the first place. Nine cents! Just write it off, I say, but who listens to me? I hate that place."

"Sounds like you've had it with the dump," Dillon replied. "How's life in general?"

"Oh, *mygawd.* That's exactly why I called you. I need someone to talk to. This crappy life so sucks. Does it show? I can't even begin. My *gawd,* he's taken up with a nineteen year old. Like, how sleazy can you get? Some newb little chicky he found when he was coaching community association basketball. Barely out of high school. No wonder he hasn't wanted sex with me lately. I hope he gets the clap. It happened like just last Friday or something. He took me out to a real nice dinner, then hit me with the news. 'It's nothing personal,' he says. He says he needs to live before he can be tied down with marriage and kids. As if I'm going to wait for him, while he's off on a fling with some underaged twat. I told him he had to make a choice right then or I was out. And oh, my, *gawd*, you know what he says? He says he already made a choice and that's why we were having the dinner conversation. So I spilled my drink in his lap and I said I hoped his pecker falls off from VD. I just left him sitting there. Of all the nerve. I've been so wasted ever since. But I got it together and finally called you. And you were there for me when I needed you. How sweet. You've come to my rescue." Elbows on the table, she rested her chin on her interlaced fingers.

Dillon's head spun from that barrage of information. "I take it, then, that means you're off-again?"

Deirdre's braying laugh was so loud some other patrons looked over at her. She grabbed one of Dillon's hands with her right — her left hand immediately back to her hair — and said, "Oh, you."

"Well, Deeds," Dillon said, while she smiled coyly at the familiarization of her name, "That's tough news. I'm sorry to hear it."

"Don't be sorry. All the self-help books say we have to make the best of adversity. Which is what I wanted to talk to you about. The self-help books say you should try and be selfless. And I am. I just picked a lousy bastard to be selfless with. Then you're there just when I need someone better. I think you and I should do something radical. Totally for the selfless part of ourselves before finally settling down. Something they'll talk about for years to come."

"A suicide pact?"

Deirdre brayed again. "You're hilarious. You sure know what I need and now it's a good laugh." Deirdre, letting her hair go for a moment, dabbed at her eyes with a napkin, careful not to smear her mascara. "Seriously, I think we should run away for a while to some exotic, unexpected location."

"How about Ethiopia?"

Furrowing her eyebrows, she finally let go of Dillon's hand and shook her head once. She was at a momentary loss for words. "Do they have all-inclusives there?"

"Not exactly. How long do you think this getaway should last?"

She leaned forward and whispered, not that anyone could hear her in the din of the bar. "It would be one fantastic, last fling before settling down. We'd combine this year's and next year's holidays back-to-back and take six weeks off."

"Oh." Dillon leaned back and drained his pint. He waved the glass at a server.

Deirdre shook her head. "What? Six weeks isn't long enough? How long were you thinking?"

"I'm thinking we're not thinking the same thing."

"You mean Ethiopia?" Deirdre's fingers twisted deeper into her curls. Her acrylic nails, purple and adorned with little black flowers, disappeared from view. "Isn't there like poverty and pirates there? And, *mygawd,* starving babies and grasshopper swarms? Gross. They probably don't even have beaches. And if they did, aren't they, like, one of those religious countries where women can't wear bikinis? Count me out. Why would you want to go to such a horrible place for holidays?"

Dillon didn't bother to tell her there were no ocean beaches or pirates because Ethiopia is landlocked. Instead he said, "Someone suggested I should try a new job there for a while."

"Ewww. You can't be serious." Deirdre studied Dillon's face a moment, her finger gyrations slowing as her head slowly leaned over and rested on her hand.

Dillon didn't smile. He was thinking about Johnathon's proposition. At that moment, without understanding why, the idea actually seemed a preferable alternative to another pointless conversation, another pointless night's boozing, just before another day of pointless jokes and scummy coffee. Even if Johnathon and Lena were together.

Deirdre stared vacantly at Dillon until her eyes went wide, as if she finally departed the ship at that perfect tropical, all-inclusive paradise. "Oh, my, *gawd.* I get you. You're pulling one of those silly Buck jokes, aren't you? Stop it right now. That's not even a little bit funny."

Dillon laughed without humour. "Hey, you caught me. Good job." He wondered where his drink was. He glanced at other patrons for a moment. He didn't see anyone he knew well enough to start a conversation with so he couldn't tell Deirdre he suddenly saw someone he had to go talk to immediately, just to get away from her for a couple of minutes. He was mired.

But at that moment Deirdre looked adrift and rudderless, a lost soul out of sight of the coast of the Horn of Africa, as unpleasant a prospect as that shore seemed to her.

Dillon said, "So, what places do you have in mind?"

"Well, now that you ask." Deirdre wiggled her eyebrows and pulled a stack of Internet printouts on office paper from her purse. While pints and Paralyzers flowed she presented a plethora of holiday getaways from all--inclusive Mediterranean resorts to mountain climbing in Chile to South Pacific cruises. Dillon listened patiently and drank. And drank some more.

They left at closing time and called to one of the waiting cabs. Dillon pushed Deirdre into the back seat, and said, "I need some time alone."

Deirdre tried to focus on Dillon with heavy, heavy eyelids. "I thought you were coming over?"

"Not tonight." Dillon slammed the cab's back door.

The window was half down and he heard Deirdre slur, "What's up with you?" Dillon didn't hear what else she might have said as the cab drove off.

Staggering home, his mind remained completely blank other than focusing on putting one foot in front of the other while he tried not to spin off the face of the planet.

HE FINALLY UNLOCKED THE DOOR of his downtown apartment-style condominium and stumbled inside, leaning at the entrance until the spinning slowed. He could see the message-waiting indicator flashing '2' on his answering machine. The full-sized framed poster of Dali's *Temptation of St. Anthony*, the only thing on any of the walls, loomed on the far side of the room where the answering machine patiently waited and flashed.

Dillon's walked a reasonably straight line to the machine and pressed the *play messages* button. The first was from Johnathon, which said he and Lena talked to their church pastor again and they were holding a place for him in their upcoming mission trip. Johnathon asked Dillon to call the pastor's number as soon as he got in. If it seemed too late, please leave a message. Before he could even absorb an iota of Johnathon's words the indicator for the next message chimed.

"Dillon. This is Tiffany. I want you to know that I still don't blame you for our split and I don't hold a grudge, even though it is all essentially your fault, but . . . " Dillon's bladder protested and he rushed to the bathroom. He caught only parts of Tiffany's monologue while urinating. " . . . too much smothering. Too much for me anyway. Perhaps a lesser woman . . . " He proceeded to brush his teeth, went back to the apartment door and put his shoes and jacket in their places in the front closet while Tiffany's voice droned on, slurring occasionally, " . . . we agreed each of our pensions wouldn't be touched by the other person. But over the splitting of costs over the years, I really think that I got the short end. Saskatchewan marital law states that after a year of living together, everything is a fifty-fifty split, and I know I make more money than you, but you shirked on daily living expenses and I've calculated you owe me . . . " She rambled on until the answering machine's maximum message length timed out.

Dillon thought he should finally subscribe to voicemail so he could simply delete messages without having to listen to them all the way through. But his answering machine was still reasonably new and perfectly functional. He pressed the delete button twice, eliminating both messages. The indicator showed a steady '0' when Dillon eased onto his black-leather couch.

He thought briefly of channel surfing on his forty-two-inch flat screen TV, just to unwind a bit by watching mindless commercial television, but instead he tossed the remote out of reach on one of the two matching leather armchairs. He reached for a cardigan he kept on the back of the couch, covered himself, and passed out.

OPENING HIS EYES, DILLON WAS still fully dressed. He sat up and checked his watch. He had awakened at the normal time without the benefit of an alarm. He never needed an alarm. Standing, he felt reasonably rested. He wondered how much booze it would finally take before he started to suffer from hangovers — or maybe withdrawal? Making his way to the bathroom, that rested feeling only lasted until he finished urinating. When his conscious mind finally powered up to full capacity, he thought about the night before. He wondered what was going to be said at the office about his outing. What fabrications would Buck concoct out of it? What would Lena think, even though he hadn't taken advantage of Deirdre? He felt like he was standing in the lowest level of the potash mine. A lump developed in his lower abdomen in all that heavy darkness. He hung his head and leaned with one hand against the wall above the toilet. He massaged his forehead with the other hand.

Standing up straight, he was hit with a sudden resolve, which he did not resist. He simply went with the impulse without thinking about it and made two telephone calls.

One was to his manager's voicemail to say he wasn't coming into the office. The second call was to make an emergency appointment with his doctor's twenty-four-hour clinic.

The doctor on-call there wrote a note prescribing, at Dillon's suggestion, three weeks off and some heavy-dosage antacids. He also strongly suggested that Dillon stop drinking; the advice was unsolicited but fit in with his plans.

Scanning the doctor's note on his combined scanner/printer, he attached it to an email to his manager and after another phone call to him, a three week hiatus was agreed to.

Johnathon would be able to cover for the duration of the absence. Then, his work term and Lena's summer job would both be finished by the time Dillon returned to work.

DILLON DID NOT BELIEVE HE had a drinking problem. To prove it, he spent his entire absence avoiding all alcohol. This included wine with meals. He simply made up his mind not to drink.

He whiled away the hours cleaning and re-cleaning his austere and spotless home. Twice, he reorganized the kitchenette, which opened off of the main living area, separated by two louver folding doors. Eventually, nothing sat on the countertop with all small appliances, including the coffeemaker, flour, ground coffee, and all accoutrements in plastic containers stored behind closed cupboard doors.

A warm glass of water with lemon or a cup of fresh-ground coffee — the grinding process prolonged, the smell of the beans savoured — satisfied any urge to drink, which lasted roughly a week. The only time Dillon ventured out was to buy groceries. Otherwise, he watched movies or weekly TV series online, and never turned the actual television on other than to watch the news. He checked his email daily but deleted all of his messages unread, except those few from his manager who asked for an update on his health.

Dillon tried not to think of the office, Deirdre, Johnathon, or especially Lena. Yet their upcoming trip, and Johnathon's offer, crept into his mind constantly. He rejected the idea each time it emerged from the dark mine shaft. There was simply too much to leave behind. He couldn't even entertain the possibility.

Keeping Tiffany out of mind was another matter until Dillon took direct action. He received a number of phone calls from her all of which he ignored. He played any messages with the answering machine's volume turned right down and deleted them immediately. He finally answered one call on the second ring. He said, after recognizing the number on the call display, "Look it, Tiffany, with this fifty-fifty thing I can easily go after half your pension and half your earnings. Would you like that? So why don't we just let this living expenses issue go and let's move on with our lives, shall we?" He hung up.

The next day, Dillon deleted her number from his telephone's directory and call list. He was certain her number would soon reappear but the confirmation beep was so satisfying, he proceeded to delete all the numbers from the lists.

This included the pastor's number, which Johnathon had called from a number of times before.

IT WAS DILLON'S FIRST MONDAY back at work. Johnathon and Lena would now be in preparation for their mission to Ethiopia, leaving the following Friday.

A new girl, blonde, with heavy black mascara, and a body type that reminded Dillon too much of Tiffany, sat at Lena's desk. Dillon walked past her with a cursory "Good morning," and headed immediately to the break room for a cup of coffee before starting work.

He set his cup in its usual spot and spotted a plain white envelope almost completely tucked under his keyboard. It was addressed to him only by first name in Johnathon's handwriting. Dillon tore open the envelope and found a single white sheet with simply Johnathon's, the Pastor's, and Lena's names and telephone numbers, all hand-written. He stared at the sheet a moment, then rubbed his index finger over Lena's name, slightly smearing the ink.

Pursing his lips, he folded the page in half and ripped it four times. Balling the paper shreds together, he threw the crumpled wad into the garbage can.

He powered up his computer and, while it booted, he stirred his coffee. He briefly wondered how Lena would prepare for her mission trip but instead focused on his successful three-week abstinence.

Perhaps a celebration was now in order? He'd head to The Cavern after work for sure. Dillon set the stir stick across the rim of his cup and signed into the Procurement Request system. Might as well pick up where he left off, he thought, and looked up Deirdre's telephone number on the computerized company telephone directory since he could no longer remember it. He stared at her number on the screen but did not dial. What was the point?

Buck plopped down in a guest chair. "So, whaddja do on holidays there, pally? Thanks for not letting your buddies know what was coming down, by the way." He slurped coffee from his usual overflowing thermal mug.

Dillon ignored the last comment. "Watched movies. Cleaned the apartment. Finally told Tiffany to fuck off about her money. She hasn't called me since, surprisingly. And here I am, all ready for my brand new life."

"Geez *Dial-on*, you're a machine, but hold on a sec, I think I need to find my violin."

Dillon ignored that jibe too. "What do you want, Buck?"

"Just coming to see if you're going for drinks after work. But if you're going to be all pissy, well . . . " Buck trailed off and slurped again.

"Now look who's pissy. Of course I'm going for drinks."

Buck hesitated a moment and said, "So, have you heard the news about Deirdre?"

Dillon glanced over at telephone directory window on his computer screen and waited for Buck to continue. Buck blew on the lid of his cup and didn't say anything.

"Heard what?" Dillon finally said.

"I talked to Deeds a couple of days after your aborted date. How you passed up on that luscious opportunity, especially when she was that drunk."

"What's your point, Buck?"

Buck took another long, loud slurp before he continued. "She didn't say too much about what you did to her to piss her off but what she did next is all your fault, you know. It's a sad, sad loss to all us healthy, red-blooded men here."

Dillon thought of his suicide pact joke and what a horrible turn such a thing could take.

"Now don't make that face, pally. It's not what you think." Buck slurped again. "She hauled that gorgeous ass off to Cancun."

"What? Why go on a holiday now? It's not winter yet."

"She's not on vacation, dummy. She gave two weeks notice and got an accounting job at some swanky five-star hotel through a relative of hers. The girl's gonna have a tough life down there. They gave her a suite in the hotel — right on the beach, no less. I sure hope she doesn't suffer too much. Look what you gave up."

"You're kidding me, right? This is another joke. It has to be."

"Not a chance. Call her number on the screen there. She won't be answering that phone no more."

"I can't believe she quit and moved away."

Buck's cup hovered in front of his lips. "To Mexico, no less."

Dillon put his hand on the telephone's handset. "I suppose there could be worse places to live."

"Yeah, like Ethiopia."

Dillon felt his face flame. What was worse was the hole burning through his stomach. He couldn't remember all that he had said to Deirdre that night, and that actually scared him.

Buck moved his cup from in front of his mouth, exposing a twisted smirk, and burst with a roaring *Bwa-ha-ha-ha.* "She told me all about your Ethiopia vacation idea and then how you ditched her. When you could have done anything to her. You must've been like a baby monkey playing with his dink." Buck pointed at Dillon with his mug. "But what's really funny is you fell for the story. Deirdre can barely talk English with that '*oh, my gawd,*' crap, let alone speak Mexican. You can be such a moron."

Buck looked at his watch and jumped up. "Well, gotta go, pally. They hired a new temp-schlub to replace that Lena chick. I gotta go break in the new meat. Great body on that one. Later."

Dillon picked up the stir stick and swirled the scum floating on his coffee. So this workday started the same as all the others. If he went drinking after work it would end the same. Maybe cleaning the coffee maker would distract him.

Instead, he seized the ripped and crumpled page from the garbage and began to reassemble the pieces.

The Jigger

Byrna Barclay

OF COURSE I HADN'T BEEN to bed. How could I sleep with so much on my mind? Boxcar Bill and I went for a walk, that's all. Oh, it was lovely in the moonlight, dappled shadows of parched leaves leading us through the shelterbelt to the road allowance. A night owl asked the question and we answered with our names.

I asked him what he thought of my sisters and he said, "Betsy is as cute as a bug's ear, and maybe some doggy dresser might call her a dead hoofer because of her twisted foot, but she would be a real flame, a regular girl to the right man." As for Lou, he said, "I could eat at her table for the rest of my life, if I didn't have to make tracks."

"I've never been anywhere," I said, swaying from side to side of the lane and picking dried leaves from the caragana. I handed one to him, and he slit it open, shelling its seeds, then closed it and whistled for the night birds. Again, the owl called the hour.

"What's your story, morning glory?" he said.

"I'm the youngest of three motherless sisters. She died giving birth to me, our mother."

"I'm sorry," he said. "I send postcards when I can to my mother, but not to my father. I have a brother I haven't seen in three years. I don't know what he's doing to survive the Crash."

Bill had simply jumped off a freight train, and came to our farm looking for work in exchange for food. "What did you do before you started riding the rails?"

"I wanted to be a railway engineer, but my father wouldn't sign the papers so I took off and haven't been home since. But someday I'll be the hog head, logger and hostler, running trains at notch 8, full power. I'll stop for the men In the Hole, and pick them up at sidings where trains wait for another to pass."

When we reached the tracks, he lay down and placed an ear on a rail, listening for the rumble of iron wheels.

"I've never ridden on a train."

"Too bad the trains aren't running right now or I'd take you for a ride." He jumped to his feet like an acrobat, and I could see how this agile fellow could race with a speeding train, grab onto someone's outstretched hand, and leap into a boxcar.

"Will you take me away from all this?" I asked, tilting my head and playing with a strand of hair escaped from the ribbon that tied my braid.

He took my hand then, and touched the palm with his lips. "The road is no place for a lady," he said. "It's full of rough and tough men, starving for food and — " He smoothed my hair, then retied the ribbon.

"There must be the odd woman riding the rails," I said. "And anyway, you would protect me."

"I tell you what, Honey Lamb. When this is all over and I've got a good job again I'll take you anywhere you want to go, but in a passenger train with a dining car and private sleeping compartment."

I tilted my head back to look at the sky, so full of winking stars from light-years away, with no clouds forming and building and darkening and lowering, no promise of the end to the drought. Times had been hard for a long time now and I had no reason to believe it would end soon, not with relief camps and thousands of men like Bill out of work. I couldn't wait, and then vowed that if he left I would follow him to the end of the line. I closed my eyes, waiting for the kiss, but it didn't arrive, not then. The warmth of his hand was replaced by the cooling air, and I opened my eyes to see him racing down the track and hollering, "Come on! Come on!" I couldn't see what he was after, but I followed, feeling as if all I had to do was lift my feet and fly to him. I'd know him by his scent in the dark: Black Cat tobacco and linseed oil he used on his tramp art.

Then he stopped and waited for me, and when I caught up to him, I discovered an abandoned railroad jigger. He lifted me up by my waist and I sat well back from the pump or whatever you call it, while he scrambled up, and then began to work the lever. The jigger moved only slightly, and he cried, "Grab the other end, and pull down when I push it up, that's it, now push up and I'll pull down." The contraption began to move, the hinges creaking, but its wheels locked onto the rail, and we were off on a night ride under the promise of deceptive moonlight. We created a small breeze that felt cool on my steaming face and sweating arms.

We were not a crew off to repair a track, hunched together, while two men worked the levers. We created our own wind, while Bill whistled the tune to "Hobo Blues" that I'd heard Wilf Carter sing on the radio.

Soon we were rolling along fast enough to let our arms rest and just coast down the track. Boxcar Bill whooped and hollered.

Most nights in June are unbearable with mosquitoes, but the ditches were too dry for breeding, so the only insects were the lightning bugs that blinked like tiny firecrackers celebrating our passage. Then we saw the lights of the city, yellow and welcoming and promising, and ahead the roundhouse where the railway bulls were sure to be waiting for drifters. The risk was great and it gave me a thrill, causing butterflies in my stomach.

"What if we get caught?" I said, loud enough for him to hear but soft enough, I hoped, to prevent anyone who might be lurking in the bushes from hearing me. I wanted to stop the jigger and race for the city. I had no idea what I might find there in the middle of the night, it wasn't Chicago after all, with nightclubs and hot jazz and boozy women and men with flirty eyes and enough in their pockets to show a farm girl a good time.

"Slow down," Bill said, and when the jigger finally stopped at a railroad crossing, he said to reverse the pumping so we would travel backwards, which meant I had to start it going, with Bill bearing down on the lever while I pushed it up. I felt some disappointment but the moon was young and the stars had fallen into my eyes.

Too quickly for me, we found ourselves back at the crossing, and I jumped off it after Bill, who turned, slid down the grade, then held out his hands and arms to catch me when I skidded down the gravel to him. He might have kissed me then, but he didn't, and I decided he just wasn't interested in a farmer's daughter. For the first time I understood my sisters' preoccupation with clothes and hairdos and makeup they found in the Eaton's catalogue and in drugstore magazines. I always told them that if a man didn't like me the way I am that would just be too bad for him. Take me as I am or not at all. Yet, just for a moment I could see myself stepping out with Bill in a slinky dress and maybe a fox-fur wrap, with a jaunty hat with a veil to make me look mysterious. He'd take me to a gin joint in Chicago and I wouldn't look out of place and embarrass him.

"Won't your father be worried?" he said, tugging me along the road allowance homeward.

I swung our arms. "He'll be asleep by now. His daughters aren't in the habit of going out at night and never with a drifter." He dropped my hand then as if it were a hot coal from my sister Betsy's stove. "Oh, I'm sorry. I didn't mean — "

"Well maybe I won't ever settle down. Maybe this is the life for me. By the time I'm thirty I hope to have seen all of America and most of Canada."

"So far, what place do you like best?" I expected him to say New York or maybe Hollywood. Chicago for sure.

He stopped then, turned and stood close to me, his fingers tracing the oval line of my face, my upper lip. "Right now," he said, "I like it here just fine."

"And tomorrow?"

"I can't know, maybe I'll hear a train whistle calling me and I won't be able to ignore it." He stooped and picked a dandelion.

"I know what's going to happen to you."

"Oh you do, do you?" He bopped my nose with the flower.

"You're going to fall for one of my sisters, and break the other one's heart. Just like you do all the girls you meet. Like in the song: *Love me or leave me.*"

"Don't let me be lonely." He made sad eyes at me then, like a puppy in a shelter needing a home.

Yes, I was asking for trouble, but it didn't find me, not that night.

I could well imagine a group of grubby men sitting around a fire, smoking and passing a mickey of whisky and telling tales of lonely widows and ugly stepsisters. The jokes about travelling salesmen and farmers' daughters spread from the city streets to the farms, and my sisters and I had overheard plenty of them. Betsy, of course, didn't think they were funny, and Lou didn't get the gag lines, she was so naïve, just like the clichéd farmer's daughter. The only thing I liked about the jokes was when the farmer had three daughters, just like us.

"I'm a farmer's daughter," I said, "and it's no joke, so watch it, fella."

"Then we're a match," he said, "because I'm a travelling salesman." All he had to sell besides hard work were his bird cages, and I had the cardinals, while my sisters got a cage each.

Lou had plunked hers on top of her dresser and said, "What use is that? A cage with no birds."

"Mine is full to bursting, even if you can't see what it holds," Betsy said. She never could keep a secret or a dream to herself so she added: "Hope, peace, and prosperity." She set her birdcage on the windowsill, with its little door open to the night air. Maybe she hoped his cardinals would find it. But I had their larger cage and it was empty too since the cardinals had taken to nest-building in the underbrush of the shelterbelt.

Then Lou did the weirdest thing: she put Betsy's baby shoes inside her cage. She had saved them, saying it's what our mother would have done. I just can't figure out what it means: baby shoes trapped in a cage. Maybe only an isolated farmer's daughter would think to do something like that. Dumb dodo bird.

"Did you hear about the farmer who had three daughters?" I said now.

"I'd love to hear it from you."

"There was this farmer who had three beautiful daughters, and the word spread among the travelling salesmen. One night at eight thirty, there was a knock on the door and the farmer went to answer it with his shotgun. At the door stood a travelling salesman whose car had not broken down in a storm, and he wasn't looking for a place to spend the night. 'Hello,' he said, 'my name is Eddie, I'm here for Betty, is she ready?' The farmer let his first daughter go out for spaghetti with Eddie. At nine o'clock there was another knock at the door and the farmer answered it with his shotgun. 'Hello, my name is Joe and I'm here for Flo, is she ready to go?' The farmer let his second daughter go to a show with Joe. At ten o'clock there was still another knock at the door and the farmer answered it with his shotgun. 'Hello, my name is Chuck,' the travelling salesman said, and the farmer shot him."

"I get your message," Boxcar Bill said, then whistled like the male cardinal calling to his mate.

By now, we were in sight of the house.

THE GRAVEL CRUNCHED UNDER OUR feet, and he had to stop and sit down and unlace his boots and take them off, and when he turned them upside down to let out the dirt and tiny pebbles I saw the holes in the soles, the cardboard patches.

Just before we reached the house the crescent moon yielded to the first rising of the sun's light. The lawn had become a small field of dandelions, their yellow petals suddenly aglow and lifted towards the new day. They didn't need rain to survive. There would be lots of dandelion wine available from the bootleggers. It was childish of me, but I picked one flower and held it under his chin to see if he liked butter, but there wasn't enough daylight yet to cast a shadow on his square jaw. What I really wanted was to throw myself onto the bed of flowers and languish and roll around like a retriever we once had and called Rover. I held back, not wanting to appear forward and bold and overly eager to have this man as my first beau.

But I had to do something to lay claim to him. Having danced with him and then ridden on a jigger gave me an advantage, a head start, but it was not enough to hold him back and want me, only me. If I seem calculating, it comes from having to compete with my sisters for my father's attention; I've never really thought of that before, how Papa taught us that in order to survive if we left the farm and went out into the world controlled by men. "It's a dog-eat-dog world out there, girls," Papa would say outside the city limits. "So watch yourselves."

Whenever Lou and Betsy fought over their messy room, with Lou being neat and tidy and Betsy tossing her clothes every which way, Papa would storm into their room and take sides with Betsy. "She started it," Lou complained. And Papa would say, "Doesn't matter who started it, I'm ending it." And, when they ganged up on me and said I hadn't fed the chickens, he would let them go to town to a show and make me stay home and not only finish feeding the chickens, but churn the butter after he milked the cows.

"You favour them!" I yelled once, and he made me collect and bring in kindling from the pasture for a week.

We learned to be responsible to him first, and to ourselves too late.

Now, it all had something to do with trade and commerce, skyscrapers in New York, men in expensive suits jumping out of windows of tall buildings. If one of us wanted to become a secretary or teacher or even a nurse, we'd have to please a superior, a male boss. But this night of dandelions and fireflies and city lights there was only one man I wanted to please; I'd do anything for Bill.

When we reached the barn where he slept in a cot by the end horse stall, I realized if ever I was to receive my first kiss, it was now or, I believed, never. "All or Nothing At All", the title of a song I'd heard Sinatra sing late at night when we could tune in to Major Bowes' Amateur Hour on the short wave radio. It was astounding how much he knew about love, that Frankie, and such a skinny kid he was too, with sunken cheeks and big teeth. After he was discovered by Harry James and his mug was in all the magazines, I started pinning his photos on the mirror of my dressing table. He wasn't nearly as handsome as Boxcar Bill.

"Dollface," he said. The kiss was thrilling and disappointing at the same time. His lips were soft but he pressed them too hard on mine. Yet, I lost my breath and couldn't get it back.

I knew it was only a matter of nights until Boxcar Bill left me.

And the trekkers were coming on Dominion Day.

I felt light-headed and giddy, yet I was perfectly calm, determined, absolutely confident that I would assert my will on this man who had captured me, and that he didn't stand a chance of escaping me once he knew how I felt about him.

"Come inside where we can talk."

Once inside, he closed the door and pulled me into his arms and I had to push him away or lose my purpose and my footing. I backed up and he took my hand and led me to his cot in the first horse stall. "Sit," he said "while I light the lamp."

When the yellow halo from the glass shade cast itself before my feet he sat down on the dirt floor. "Let's have it," he said.

"Who are you and why are you here?"

"I've never lied to you."

'Maybe not, but at the powwow I saw you talking to that union man, the advance man for the trekkers, Hank Whats-his-name."

He sighed and plunked down beside me. He took my hand, but I pulled it away. "I have to go away tomorrow. I can't know if I will be back or not, but I want you to know that I've never said this to a girl before. If I had a home to offer you I wouldn't hesitate, but it is my nature to wander, always has been."

"Will I never see you again?"

"I want you to keep Fred and Ginger for me." He meant the cardinals he had brought with him when he jumped off the freight train and rolled down the embankment right into our shelterbelt where I was swinging from a cottonwood, and the freed birds settled on my arms, declaring themselves mine. I'd never seen a red bird before, oh, in school books, yes, and wondered where he found them, some place south for sure, and that was proof enough that he was an American. His vowels were flat, consonants soft, and he whistled while he worked for Papa, even when hefting heavy forkfulls of hay to feed the cattle.

"If you don't come back, it won't matter," I said, "because I belong to you."

And that's when it happened, tears were running into my ears and I was in his arms and his breath warmed my neck as he lowered me onto the cot.

"You've never done this before," he said, but I couldn't answer, because I was undone and lost and didn't care about anything except what was happening to me, to him.

It was supposed to hurt the first time, Ruby Redwing had said so, but it wouldn't be so bad if you wanted it to happen and didn't fight it or tense up, but strangely it didn't hurt at all, and I felt like I was swimming underwater and could see lights of a city above me, glittering, but soft and smoky, and then they made me shiver and tremble and lifted me high until I broke through the surface, gasping for air then chirring like a mourning dove wriggling down and settling in her new nest.

When it was over and I lay on top of him, nuzzling under his chin, I whispered, "What if I'm pregnant?"

"Not likely the first time," he said.

"I don't care if I am," I said.

Then he sat up, roughly, and leaned over me and said, "Come to the city with me. I have a week's wages. I'll show you a good time, baby."

"When?"

"Right now. Go and pack a small bag, just what you'll need overnight."

I didn't think we were eloping, although I hoped that I was running away with him. I knew he couldn't stay, but there was nothing to stop me from following him wherever the wanderlust took him. I felt a pang of guilt when I thought of my father, how angry he'd be, and how he'd come after Boxcar Bill with a baseball bat.

My sisters would never forgive me.

BILL LET OUT A LOW whistle when I ran out of the house in my red coat, swinging my pocketbook. All I had in it was a change of underwear, an extra button in case one popped while tearing off my panties so Lucky could get to me, my toothbrush and a Pond's powder compact. I felt like a hussy, and that was exciting.

He was all decked out too, in the pinstriped gangster suit he arrived in that Betsy had brushed and pressed, his jaunty Bogart hat at a rakish angle. And Papa's old spectator shoes. His burlap bundles full of his birdcage hobo art were tied together with binder twine and hung from straps that looked like a harness on his back. He must have planned to sell them in the city. He had left the cardinals behind in their nest. I believed we'd be back for them.

"Let's go, dollface," he said, taking my hand, and we hastened into the dark cover of the shelterbelt, then took our time strolling up towards the railway tracks. I suddenly couldn't think of anything to say, and he halted before we broke through the underbrush to the gravelled grade. He took my face in his hands and said, “Are you sure? It’s not too late to go back.”

For me, it was too late to go back to being just the youngest sister, the one they now called Birdy Girl because the cardinals always followed me into the shelterbelt. I had already left her behind me when I stole away from the house.

“This is for me,” I said. “I’m going with you, no matter where you go.”

Then we heard the whistle, the rumble of iron wheels on steel tracks, the slowing of the midnight train as it approached the crossing where the road met the railway tracks.

“This is what we’re going to do. You have to crouch and run as fast as you can and when you’re close to the first open door, jump up and roll into the cattle car on your side.”

With Bill, I felt fearless, capable of running wild but as free as his cardinals, who could choose to stay in their new nest in the shelterbelt or fly away now.

“Now!” he said, and crouching, dashed up the grade, to the edge of the track. The midnight train east rumbled by us. Its whistle blew, a warning to anyone on the road, but to me, it was a call to freedom, an awakening of my spirit, and a promise for tomorrow.

I crouched too, and clomped as fast as I could in my chunky-heeled shoes, almost turning an ankle, the gravel thick and hard and sharp under my feet.

One car, with closed doors. Another. The third door was open but it was impossible in the dark to see if anyone lurked there. Boxcar Bill jumped, grabbed the edge of the floor, swung his left leg up, knee bent, and then he rolled inside. I already had my left hand on the rim, running and stumbling and running, my right arm flailing and I was afraid I'd lose my perky, red-feathered hat.

"Give me your hand!"

He already had hold of my left wrist but I was afraid to let go of the edge of the floor.

"Right one!"

I swung my right arm toward him, in an arc, twisting my body, and when he had hold of both hands, my feet left the ground somehow, and I was flying in the air the way Papa used to swing me around and around, playing Airplane. He pulled back as hard as he could and I flew forward and flopped right on top of him. We lay like that, panting and gasping, until the applause burst in my ears.

We were surrounded by dark human shadows, yellow eyes hungry as predators'. Someone struck a match and its brief flare illuminated hoboes leaning against the far wall, other men sleeping with hats over their faces and heads on bundles of rags. Still others huddled and squatted in the centre. The cattle car smelled of hay, manure, the sweat of men and livestock.

"*Up*," Lucky said, and I rolled off him. We squatted there, like children.

"Runners," someone said, perhaps the man who stuck the match and now puffed on a cigarette butt he'd picked out of a rusted tin that once held an ointment sold by Watkins.

"Hey, y'all," Bill said. "We're going to town for the celebrations tomorrow, to meet and greet the trekkers."

"Amen to that," said the match man.

"Slim got nowhere with Bennett, I hear. Nothin' but a shouting match. Bennett called us radicals and said Slim was an extortionist. So Evans, he called Bennett a liar."

I said, "He got away with calling the Prime Minister a liar?

"Escorted onto the street. Due back in Regina tomorrow. There's quite a crowd waiting for them."

Someone in the shadows said, "The protesters expect over two thousand people."

"So it's come to this," Bill said.

There was silence then. Men rolled into their sleep stirred and coughed while the train picked up speed again and rolled towards the yellow lights of the city. Here and there we passed a farm with a gas lamp aglow in a window and I knew some mother was up, taking care of a midnight feeding or tending to another with the lung disease. I drew up my knees, and tucked the ends of my coat around them, feeling rich because I had clean clothes and had never gone hungry for more than a few hours.

"Any food?" the smoker said.

"I'm sorry, I didn't think to pack a lunch," I said.

The laughter that brought on was not the throaty chuckle that erupts on the punch line of a joke. It wasn't sinister either. It held an ironic twist that I felt deep in my own knotted gut as if I'd swallowed a nickel tied in a hanky I'd sucked free instead of putting it in the Sunday collection plate. I wanted to say I was sorry for never going hungry.

"This is a drag," the smoker said.

"He means the train is a slow freight," Bill said.

"Not doing more than a six notch, I'd say. The first train, the one that took the trekkers in earlier, was a doubleheader. Took two engines to pull that one, it was so long and loaded. Hundreds of us, and no one dared try to stop it."

"Why didn't you get on that train?" I asked, and Bill poked me in the side with his elbow.

"Sleepin' off the rot gut on a park bench in Stanley Park." The smoker laughed, and it sounded like a dog growling in his sleep. He took a flask from the inside pocket of his ragged tweed coat. "One for the road." And the swig he took was his last. He threw the empty mickey out the open car door. We heard its soft clink on gravel.

"What time is the meeting?" Bill said.

"The protesters are camped in the Exhibition Grounds, but a public meeting has been called in Germantown near the centre of the city for tomorrow."

I huddled closer to Bill. The train created its own wind, and steamy gusts from the open doors reached me, and with them the musky scent of rosehips and the earthier smell of dandelions. Briefly, beneath the rumble of the wheels, a hound dog bounding after a rabbit caused a rustle in the underbrush and a stir among hungry men, who drooled in their sleep, perhaps dreaming of steaming rabbit stew in one of their trackside jungle campsites.

Someone played a tune on a harmonica, soft and bluesy, and I recognized Wilf Carter's "Hobo's Song to the Mounties".

I may have dozed too, with my hat in my hand, my pocketbook hidden behind my back. If a man is hungry long enough he will do anything, just like Jean Valjean that Miss Hope read to us, chapter by chapter, and it made us race home for four o'clock tea with Ruby Redwing, our father's housekeeper and second wife. Her good bannock would be hot from the frying pan and served with freshly churned butter and wild strawberry jam.

The last thing I heard Bill say was: "So what do you think? Will the Babe stay in retirement?" Men and their baseball!

When I woke up, we were near the Exhibition Grounds, the stadium lights all startling and alarming because there was no fair on and no baseball or football game ever in the early hours of the morning. It felt like a prison, and I imagined a high fence with guard towers that I'd seen in movies about Sing Sing. I get premonitions like that but I don't always realize the truth of them until later.

I wondered where the trekkers and protesters would eat, and couldn't imagine the provincial government feeding them, though, according to all newscasts I'd heard and to newspaper accounts Papa had read to us beside the gas lamp, Premier Gardiner wanted the populace to believe he was on their side. Bennett cut off the relief payments and now two thousand men had to be fed in the Exhibition Grounds. He sent eight hundred railway and Federal police to Regina to prevent the trekkers from leaving by train. A holding camp was being built in the Lumsden valley, with a barbed-wire fence. How would they ever transport that many protesters to the camp? It's only seventeen miles to the valley from Regina so I supposed they would march them under guard.

I didn't think of any of that when I took off with Boxcar Bill. I was only thinking of a good time with him. Now, I realized how worried my father would be, and maybe I could telephone him and tell him I was safe. I wouldn't let him order me back home. I'd made my bed and I couldn't wait to lie in it again with Bill.

Bill said we'd find a hotel first, then have breakfast, get some proper sleep in a real bed, then do the town before the public meeting. I hoped I'd have enough egg money to pay for a day in the city, and I thought it might be just as much fun to find a corner store and buy some bread and cheese and have a picnic in the park where the swans and Canada geese were kept in a sanctuary. I vowed I'd repay my sisters for taking their egg money after I found a job waiting tables, maybe at a train station wherever Boxcar Bill took me.

He had promised to make tracks to Chicago where we would pitch woo all day and then shake a leg at night to hear the world's best skin ticklers, scat singers, and canaries in the finest gin mills in America. I imagined myself in a red backless gown, with a halter neckline, long white gloves up to my armpits, and I'd wave a diamond cigarette holder. I'd find out what a champagne cocktail tasted like, and after dancing cheek-to-cheek with Bill till dawn, he'd take me for a carriage ride along the shore of Lake Michigan.

He had told Betsy that he was born on Park Avenue and told me he was born in Chicago. When we questioned him about it he just laughed and said there was a Park Avenue in Chicago Heights and one in New York so he hadn't fibbed to either of us.

Now, the old-timer gave Bill and I instructions before the train stopped at its destination. "Watch out for the cinder dicks. Word has it that there's more than usual looking for vagrants and any excuse to club a hungry man. You can tell 'em from the road masters by their size. Got grabbers the size of meathooks. Sure, you can bribe some with a five spot, but who has that kind of money?"

The train pulled into the freight yards, the men left the cattle car, jumping one by one and rolling into the gravelled siding. They were the tail end of the trekkers, mostly older men who looked like they hadn't been home for a hundred years, but were experts at avoiding the railway guards Boxcar Bill had called "the bulls". They scrambled down from the top of the train, using the couplers for footing, then jumped to the ground. Then they disappeared into the shadows between two trains that the government must have had waiting to deport the protesters back to British Columbia.

The smoker hawked and spat out the door before he jumped.

Boxcar Bill went first, his bundles bobbing on his back, and I followed, landing and rolling away from the tracks into wild sun-scorched grass and prickly weeds. We scrambled to our feet, Bill grabbed my hand, and we crept away, towards the city lights. In an empty lot, we crouched between and behind some oil cans, and watched dozens of men appear seemingly from nowhere, and they were as big as bulls, with billy clubs in their meathook grabber hands. They beat the anti-climber grilles at the front and rear of the engine, the flange on the side of the wheels that kept them on the tracks, the yaw dampers that reduced the rocking motion of a car, the noise enough to scare out a rabbit in a hunt, the way beaters go ahead of the men with guns. Several of the men didn't even try to escape, and seemed to want to be caught and herded over the tracks towards the Exhibition Grounds.

"Don't worry," Bill said. "They want to be found out and labelled a protester."

"Are they being arrested?"

"I don't think so. Let's go before one of them turns our way and finds us."

"I've lost my directions."

"The sun's coming up in the east. We want to go south, this way." He led me over more tracks, then across a wide street with no traffic. We followed a boardwalk beneath an underpass and then we were on a city street. And there on the corner was a clapboard, railway hotel. Not far from that was the large, umber-brick train station. Regretting the brilliance of my red clutch coat, I folded it around me, feeling the heat of the day rising, with a warning. My feet hurt, and I stepped out of one shoe and rubbed my toes over my Achilles heel. I dumped a bit of gravel out of the shoe. I had a blister on my heel and it was ready to burst and bleed.

He couldn't know what would happen on July 1st, 1935. There never was a Dominion Day like it before, nor will there ever be again.

I saw there in the distance the huge railway hotel, the posh one that had a ballroom and chandeliers and dances. Outside, parked in front for everyone to see was the emerald green Ford convertible sedan, top down, and a crowd surrounding it, gawking, and kicking at the tires, smoothing the shiny fenders and grille as if it were a prize racehorse. I could just imagine my father snorting and saying it belonged to a limousine socialist. No sign of Hank and his son we'd seen at the powwow when the trekkers were mustering support for their cause and march to Ottawa.

I felt like a siren, but there was only one man I wanted to attract, but not fatally, if only I could learn the right song to keep him forever on land so isolated from his life of wandering I could be an island for him.

The street was jammed with motor cars and pickup trucks moving slowly east, and they had to be driven by curious city folk. A streetcar was bursting with passengers. The main street that ran north-south right through the town was blocked off at the corner of South Railway by police barriers. The trekkers and protesters and men on strike from the BC relief camps streamed down from the Exhibition Grounds, through the underpass, and down South Railway Avenue. I know the radio and newspaper reported that only three hundred of them attended the meeting at Market Square in Germantown, but I swear there were more than that joining the march for the right to work for an honest day's wage. The big banner read: WE WANT WORK.

There were crude signs, some on bristol board,. most on cardboard with charcoal printing, while others looked like the lettering had been burned into wood with a hot ember from a campfire:

ALL HELL CAN'T STOP US.

WE WANT TO BE CITIZENS, NOT TRANSIENTS.

JOIN THE FIGHT FOR NON-CONTRIBUTORY UNEMPLOYMENT INSURANCE.

That banner was made from a white sheet and was carried by four men wearing plus fours and newsboy caps.

Another sign read: OVERTHROW THE CAPITALIST SYSTEM. I was glad Papa wasn't there to see that. He might have thrown eggs at it.

A banner that bore the signia of the WUL, the Workers' Unity League, was carried by women activists Annie Buller, Julia Care, and Jeanne Corbin. I learned their names later when I read the *Leader*; yes, I had seen all three, but did not know them, not even their names then.

It was only three long blocks till we passed the train station on South Railway just off Broad Street and came to another underpass, and Bill said in a James Cagney voice, "Mmn, if this is Broad Street where are all the broads?"

My sister Lou would have kicked his butt all the way to kingdom come. I just whapped him upside the back of his beautiful head. I couldn't think of the male version of a broad, a dame. Guy or Bruiser just didn't do it.

Just across Broad, on the corner of South Railway and Cornwall Street, was Market Square, not far from the RCMP station. There, three ice cream trucks offered a variety of flavours, some I'd never tasted — cherry and lemon-lime — but no one was selling or buying in spite of the heat of this day. Across from the Kirkaldie Garage a makeshift stage had been erected, and sure enough there was red-headed Hank and three other protest leaders who were introduced by Hank as Arthur Slim Evans, Nick Shaack, and George Black. Shaack was the oldest, about Papa's age, with a fresh haircut, the skin whiter above the collar of a crisp new shirt.

It was an enormous crowd, and at first I couldn't tell protesters from ordinary citizens come out to support the trekkers or just hoping, like me, for some entertainment. It being Dominion Day, I expected balloons and a band, maybe even clowns. There was no VIP row for politicians and their wives in big hats and white gloves, which I thought odd, given the importance of the day and the political implications of the trek.

Then, suddenly, it was easy to spot the trekkers in the crowd. They were the shabby men whose shoes were down-at-the-heel, and not polished this morning by the shoeshine boy at the CPR Hotel Saskatchewan. Their faces were gaunt, eyes sunken and ringed with dark shadows. They didn't look like they were armed, but because Bill whispered in my ear that the union men carried baseball bats and concealed knives in their boots and on belts and chains on their pants, I began to regard them with suspicion.

The speeches were short, and the signs and banners and flags waved with emphasis of an important point, and sometimes a few people clapped and cheered.

Then Hank began to really work the crowd, describing the conditions of the relief camp, how twenty cents per day wouldn't feed one man much less his wife and children back home. His son paraded back and forth beneath the stage with his sign: GIVE MY DADDY A JOB.

Disapproval moved the crowd and someone wearing a red tie shouted, "Hear! Hear!" He wore a grey flannel suit, and his shoes were polished and new.

Lucky Bill whispered, "City detective if ever I saw one."

I can't explain it, but there was an echo, not from a microphone, but from further away and above, as if a sky god had heard the plight of the poor and was cheering on the protesters. It was a rumble like the roll of train wheels. It was thunderous but distant, yet also very near and threatening. It also rang like a choir of angry angels.

'You hear that, folks? Quiet. Listen." Hank placed a finger to his lips. He raised his right arm and pointed towards the west. The crowd hushed, awed by something they understood at a level beyond reason. "That's the sound of protest," Hank said. "Here we are two thousand or more strong. Me and you. All of us citizens of this great province, of a land with the best gumbo for growing wheat, yet there is no bread for our children." He paused so the crowd would hold to silence and hang on his next and every word. "You came to support those who march for a return of lost civil liberties, but what you are witnessing is mass imprisonment of the *soul!*" There was a collective gasp from the crowd. "There are police barricades at every exit to the city in all four directions. Our trekkers cannot leave, cannot go home. We are *interred.*" He pointed westward again, and all heads raised and turned with wonder, as if a multitude of holy ghosts had filled the sky. "But over there is the largest *camp* the world has ever seen, but there is no *relief.*"

The crowd responded with shouts and catcalls meant for governments, federal and provincial and civic.

"*Hear me out*! Just a few blocks away, in the Exhibition grounds are ordinary husbands and brothers and fathers who cannot join us today because they are *locked in* a prison. With no food. No latrines. And the sound you hear is their call for help. They are fighting back, folks."

If I had been a bird — a pigeon maybe or a dove or even one of Bill's cardinals — perched on top of a steeple say, and I could look down on the people that Dominion Day, I would have seen the gates of the Exhibition ground crash down under the pressure of almost two thousand men armed with sticks and rocks, and I would have watched them swarm like angry bees down the streets and join the mob at Market Square, the numbers swelling into the thousands, so many of them it was impossible to sort them out by political persuasion or citizenship, the plain-clothes-men from city police from redcoats.

I had a sudden longing to hear my sisters' chatter about whether or not our papa should bring home a roast beef or pork chops from the meat locker in town. I wondered if either of them had put out bread crumbs for the cardinals. I missed my Papa, and I felt a cooing in my throat that threatened to turn into a cat's screech when a milk cow steps on its tail.

Was it too late to telephone home, and where would I find a call box? I asked Bill what time it was and he checked his pocket watch that hung from a chain linked to his belt and hid in his vest pocket. He said, "Eight seventeen." I'm sure of that, eight seventeen was the time that I heard the police whistle, I'm certain I did, because it was shrill and broke through the shouts of men moving like a tidal wave from the streets into the square. The back doors of the ice cream trucks burst open and out poured the RCMP riot squads. They charged the crowd with their billy clubs, hollering, "Break it up! Break it up!" And then beneath the roar of the crowd I heard the clatter of hoofs on cement and the shrilling of many horses. The RCMP had also hidden their mounted policemen in the Kirkaldie Garage. The doors broke open and flung back and out leapt the magnificent thoroughbreds, their nostrils flared and eyes rolling, yet obeying the command of each rider's spur and crop. It was thrilling and terrifying. Yet, I believed it would be enough to dispel the crowd. I looked for a fast way out of the market, but there were bunches of men every which way, and I felt suddenly weak and wobbly and dizzy.

Two men in suits and raincoats leapt upon the stage, said something to the leaders — Arthur Slim Evans and George Black as it turned out — and to my surprise both men held out their arms peacefully and let the plainclothesmen handcuff them.

Nik Shaack leapt off the stage and raced towards an empty lot next to the market, a policeman in hot pursuit.

When the plainclothesmen led them away to one of the ice cream trucks, breaking through the crowd, a whoop and a holler went up from the trekkers and they started swinging at the Mounties coming at them on foot and on horseback, fighting back with fists, knives, and mostly sticks. Above the shouts and screams of women running was the explosion of gunshots while police fired revolvers above the crowd and into groups.

A policeman swung a club at Bill. And Boxcar Bill pulled a rod from under his jacket.

I screamed: "Don't!"

But the gun fired and the policeman reared back and lost his balance and then fell on his back. I don't think the bullet struck him because I saw no blood, no hole in his fancy suit anywhere; maybe Bill had never used that gun before or else he aimed high, wanting to frighten off the detective.

Then a plainclothesman tried to help the fallen policeman. It was the guy in the city slicker suit. Immediately three or four men pounced on him and started pummelling him with their fists. No, I could never identify them. They were just a few of many hundreds. And it all happened so fast.

"Run," Bill said.

"Go home," he said.

"I'll come for you," he said.

"I'm going with you." I tugged at his sleeve, and reached up, trying to touch his sweating face. There was a crazed look in his eyes, and I stared at someone I'd never before seen. The pupils were enlarged, the white of his eyes shot with red veins. Tears streamed down his cheeks and I don't think he even knew it. He shrugged me off, dove into the crowd, came up against a Mountie who bashed him upside his head with a billy club, and when Bill fell sideways the Mountie shoved him onto the ground, kneeled over him, yanked his arms backwards, and handcuffed him. He tore the bundled birdcages from his back, ripping the burlap, and snorting with disgust he dumped them on the ground. Then he hauled Bill to his feet. Blood streamed down the left side of his face, he stumbled and staggered away, and the last time I saw him he was shoved into the back of the ice cream truck that had suddenly become a paddy wagon. Leaving empty birdcages strewn among bits of shredded burlap and candy wrappers and ice cream cones.

"I'll come for you." The last thing I ever heard him say to me.

I don't know how long I remained frozen there, like a block of ice fallen from an ice wagon. No one seemed interested in hitting a girl in a red clutch coat, stricken with fear bordering on terror. I was in the middle of a grunting, groaning, heaving mass of broken people. Continuous gunshots deafened me. It felt like war.

What brought me to my senses was the unexpected grey haze that blew in like mist from a river. My eyes stung, I gasped for breath, and tears sprang to my eyes.

An old trekker in a battered hat fell to his knees, coughing up blood. He could have been my father. I leapt away from him, and bumped into a Mountie, who grabbed my arm, whirled me around, and said, "Go home where you belong. Now. Do you hear me?" And he shoved me away, then took his billy club to a young man in a newsboy cap who looked like he should be chopping wood for my teacher, Miss Hope. The boy crumbled in a bundled heap of coughing and gagging and crying. The redcoat stood over him and he vomited on the Mountie's boot.

I found my lace hankie in my pocketbook, held it over my mouth and nose, blinking back the water leaking from my stinging eyes, and stumbled away, trying to find my way back the way we came, but determined to learn where they might be taking Bill, hopefully to a hospital. What if the man he tried but failed to shoot died from the beating? I couldn't think of that yet. I had to get away from the crowd and the tear gas.

I pushed my way through to South Railway Avenue where Union Station was, and shops, stepping carefully over horse shit and broken glass. It was mayhem here too, less fighting but more breaking of office and store windows and raiding, with one woman racing out of a womenswear shop carrying a shocking pink dress over one arm and a fox fur stole over the other. She laughed like a mockingbird at mating time. Men rushed by with radios under their arms, or jackets bulging with concealed goods.

With Broad Street blocked, an ambulance pushed its way south down Hamilton Street, its siren wailing, and a fire truck with its firemen riding the running boards headed east towards Market Square. I wondered if they planned to turn their hoses on the mob and stop the riot that way.

I didn't know which way to go, how to get home. I was lost and forlorn and frightened and frantic to know if Bill had been taken to hospital. I felt like a squab that had fallen out of its nest and could hear the other chicks squawking high up in the elm, and suddenly a cat had pounced and lay on top, batting my head back and forth with a paw.

The news would be on the radio, and Papa would be frantic with worry.

I needed him to go to the police station with me to try and find out what had happened to Boxcar Bill.

I couldn't know Papa had gone in search of me.

I was stopped by the sound of marching, not rhythmical as in a parade on Exhibition week when the Royal American Shows came to Regina. It was discordant, the high clip clop of horses' hooves breaking the slide and drag and muffled scrape of shoes patched and lined with newspapers. The RCMP had rounded up the trekkers and were marching those not arrested and taken to jail back to the Exhibition Grounds. The trekkers began to sing, as if marching to war, their anthem, "Hold the Fort, For We Are Coming".

THE RCMP STATION IN TOWN was crammed with locals trying to find out if their sons and husbands had been arrested or hurt, and most of them seemed to be shunted off to the barracks or depot at the western end of Dewdney Avenue and just outside the city. When it was my turn, finally, I said to the intake officer, "I want to report a missing person."

"Your name?" he said.

"Persson. Marna Persson."

"Lady, this is not the place or the time for jokes."

"That's my name, I'm not trying to be funny."

"The name of your missing — person?"

"I don't know. He calls himself Boxcar Bill and sometimes Lucky Bill."

"When and where did you last see him?"

"He was hit on the head and dragged into one of your police vans."

"Then you should check at the depot on Dewdney Avenue."

"I have no way of getting there!" The city streetcars had stopped running and I had no money for a taxi. I felt like breaking down, but I was no sob sister. "Can't you telephone someone out there and ask?"

"How can I check for you when you don't even know the name of the person you're missing?"

"He's not a trekker," I said. "He hasn't done anything wrong."

"How do you know him?"

"He's a hired hand on my father's farm."

"But you don't know his name."

"He goes by the name of Bill."

"Just a moment." The officer left his desk and conferred with another Mountie, who had white hair and moustaches. They both looked at me, their heads bent over some papers, then looked at me again. The senior fellow nodded and the handsome young one returned to his desk.

"We have an injured fellow. I don't know if he's the man you're looking for, but he needs identifying. Would you be willing to do that?"

"Of course. How badly?"

"Blow to the head, like so many, but he seems to have lost his memory. He can't even tell us his name." He rose. "Come with me." The senior officer took his place at the desk.

He led me to the rear of the building, then downstairs to the cells in the basement, offering his arm when I teetered at the top. "Steady now. Are you all right?"

"I will be when I find Bill." Now I felt like screaming for help, shaking, a delayed reaction to the riot.

"This is where we inter people during their trials," he said. "We've just had it painted and the walls aren't dry yet, so mind you don't get paint on your pretty coat." The smell was strong, obviously an oil base.

It was dank and musty and dark. We passed two cells full of men lying on the floor, sitting against the walls, and hanging onto the bars. They were wounded, though not too seriously, with oozing bandages on their hands and heads. I could imagine the bruises under their clothing. The sight of them made me even more afraid for Bill.

Further down the hall was a two-bed infirmary, clearly not intended for serious injuries. High above at street level was a window with bars and iron mesh. When I entered with the Mountie, the man in the first bed lifted one arm and reached out, his face contorted with pain, his face bruised, and head bandaged.

"Pain. Terrible. My gut. I need a doctor. Now."

"Soon, Shaack," the Mountie said. "You'll be taken to hospital with the first available transport ambulance."

I couldn't know it then, but Nick Shaack, one of the leaders of the trekkers, would die, not from his head injury, but from a heart attack, having been transferred to Weyburn mental hospital too late. The government's press releases and newspaper articles would emphasize the injury and death of Charles Millar, the plain-clothesman, in an effort to cover up the fact that the police had started the riot, not the protesters.

And then, there was Bill, in the second bed, almost unrecognizable, his face badly bruised and swollen, and I was sure he couldn't see out of the slits in the bandages. I'd seen only one blow to the side of his head. His chest barely rose and fell with each small breath. I approached him slowly, not wanting to disturb him if he were asleep. Then I took one of his hands, and bent over him. His eyes were open but seemed to be unseeing, and I said softly, "Bill, it's me. Marna."

The Mountie said, "He may or may not be able to hear you."

"He needs a doctor too. Right now."

"Yes, miss."

"The last time I saw him he was not in this bad shape. He spoke to me. What have you done to him?"

"It's likely a concussion. Or he could be in a comatose state. Either way, he'll be sent to Weyburn. Don't worry. He'll get good care there."

"If he lives."

I bent lower and whispered in the one exposed ear: "I'm going to get you out of here and see you get proper medical attention."

"So you can identify him."

I straightened, and said yes, this man was our hired hand, not a trekker or protester or union man or anyone else the police might have an interest in. I felt it to be true.

"Will you sign a statement to that effect?"

"Of course."

The Mountie led me back up to his station where he said something to his senior officer, who nodded and returned to his own office, and then he sat at his desk, asked me more questions, and typed my answers on a paper he scrolled into his typewriter. Then he swivelled around and left his desk. When he returned he had a brown envelope, out of which he drew a passport.

"We found this and a dozen others in the jacket he was wearing." He gave it to me, and to my surprise it was a red Canadian passport, and when I opened it there was a photo of Bill, with the name Stacy Perch. I looked up and the Mountie said, "The others were fake, but not this one, it's not a forgery, and it would appear not to have been stolen either as we checked with our division in Lloydminster. There is a Perch family there, who have not seen their son for many years."

He told us he was an American. He reinvented himself, not because he was hiding from the law or a shameful past, but just to amuse himself. And we accepted it because it entertained us too. Yet, when I think on it, it seems to me that each one of us created Lucky Bill to our own individual needs and dreams.

Then, the ambulance arrived to take un-Lucky Stacy Perch to the asylum. I begged the driver to let me go with him, but they said only next of kin were allowed transport too. They did let me say goodbye to him, and I promised to go to Weyburn to see him as soon as I could, knowing I'd have to save up more egg money for gas as Papa would never drive me there.

It didn't all hit me until I found myself outside the RCMP station, with no way to get home. I collapsed on the stairs, suddenly exhausted, barely aware of the hot summer sun beating down on my head and its promise of no relief for me or anyone until snowfall.

And that is where my Papa found me.

I didn't care about anything because that wonderful man with the silly name was no longer with me.

Of course, I would never see Boxcar Bill again. But I would discover what was left of Stacy Perch.

IT WAS THE END OF an unbearable summer of wide prairie skies that burned the inner eyelids if one looked up, searching for a faint wisp of cloud that might blossom into a bearer of rain for the parched earth. Grasshoppers plagued us, arriving in clouds, their crackling breaking the sound barrier in our ears. They left a swath of devastation, even eating the sheets and underwear left on the clothesline. The rain barrels under the eaves were emptied by the end of July, the root cellar bereft of vegetables, and there were no preserves left in the pantry.

Threshing crews did not come to Saskatchewan, and the farmers in our area helped each other salvage what they could of stunted wheat and oats. The women gathering to cook for them were sullen, ashen-faced, and grim. I was often laid up with morning sickness, a dead giveaway, but my papa was not as angry with me as I had feared, though his silences and long, sad face were often worse than if he'd yelled at me for disgracing our family name. I suspect he was really afraid I'd have trouble birthing, just like my mother. To tell the truth, I had anxieties of my own on that score. I wasn't sorry for what I'd done, only sorry for the label my child would suffer while growing up. Out-of-wedlock. Bastard baby. Born on the wrong side of the blanket.

So I was beginning to show by the end of October when I finally drove to Weyburn.

IT WAS THE LAST SUNDAY in October, almost five months since the riot, and telephone calls to the Weyburn mental hospital had been few due to the high cost of long distance and often poor connections with static on the line, never mind the party line listeners, like Miss Hope with the long pointy nose poking into everyone's business.

All the way out of Regina, I tried to tell myself not to expect too much. I only wanted to see that he was alive and getting better. I didn't hope he'd marry me and settle down on the farm. By now, I was planning on getting a job in the city after the baby was born, as a waitress in Union Station or scrubbing office floors at night, and when I had some money put by I'd take to the road and travel as far as it would take me. Before '29, when I was just a school girl, I always dreamed of becoming a small-animal veterinarian. Even then, the last thing I ever wanted was to marry a farmer and spend the rest of my days hauling water from the well, chopping wood, baking a dozen loaves of bread before the rest of the family was up, tending a garden and putting up a pantry full of preserves every autumn. Then there was the back-breaking pulling of weeds and stooking at harvest.

I needed to get away from my sisters too; living with them and their disappointments and back-biting remarks or stony silences was not the atmosphere I wanted for my child.

Already I looked like a Koala bear that had fallen out of a eucalyptus tree, so fertile I got pregnant the first time, and it felt so ironic to be surrounded by a barren plain. The fields were bereft of so much topsoil they looked abandoned, the clay cracked and broken, and the air was rank with the smell of burning stubble. Soon snow would cover this land as if trying to hide its sins, just as Betsy had made me a white shift with an empire waistline to conceal, at least for a few more weeks, the swelling of my belly. She'd even embroidered red birds and yellow daisies on the yoke in an attempt to draw the eyes of the townspeople away from my thickening waistline.

It was easy to follow the highway into the small city of Weyburn, past the tracks and the POOL elevators and idle grain cars that reminded me of my first and only ride with Boxcar Bill and the hoboes on the day of the Riot. The asylum was a large brick building on Queen Street, with the usual tree-lined lane to its grand, porticoed entrance.

I found a place to park the pickup among other visitors, it being a Sunday when families from out-of-town visited most often. I checked my hair in the rear-view mirror above the dashboard, wondering if Bill would like the short bob. One night when everyone was sleeping I had shorn it with Betsy's pinking shears then shaved my scalp with Papa's razor in a fit of madness, more at myself for giving in to my own desires than at sweet-talkin' Bill for seducing me, and now it had grown enough on the crown to cover my scalp in whorls that blended well with the finger waves that fell just long enough to cover my big, cauliflower ears. I rouged my cheeks and put another layer of Pond's lipstick on my pouty lips, then decided it was too much, and wiped it all off with my handkerchief.

With mixed feelings of excitement and trepidation, I left the truck and took a path strewn with dead asters and last summer's marigolds. The lawns swept back from the street into a grove of trees that sheltered park benches waiting for the summer of 1936 when surely grounds-keeping patients would plant tulip bulbs and geraniums and ferns for other patients well enough to bask in a young sun after a spring shower.

Inside the grand entrance, two people in overalls polished the brass newels and fittings of a magnificent stairway that looked like it was stolen from the ballroom of a palace.

I quickly followed the VISITORS sign to reception. A nurse named Clara on the ambulatory men's ward said Mister Perch was up and about, had worked in the garden, and was now enjoying arts and crafts. He had bad spells when he went into himself and didn't talk to anyone, and had to be fed and dressed, and so on. But don't get discouraged, he's come such a long way since he was admitted in June in a comatose state.

I was told I'd find Stacy Perch in the basement.

"The basement!"

"That's where everyone goes when they first come here, and once they are well enough they progress to different wards, and finally to the top floor that they call the Halfway Ward because then they are halfway home — to being discharged."

I didn't know if the person leading me to the elevator was an orderly or a nurse. He wore a white jacket over white pants, and his hair was shaved shorter than a Mountie's. He had three double chins, a protruding belly, and he waddled like a duck. I had trouble keeping a straight face when he told me his name was Donald.

Except for the night before the riot, the only time I'd ever been on an elevator before was in the Medical and Dental Building when Papa took us to the dentist in

Regina. It was like riding in a cage. This one was painted a metallic blue and looked like it fell out of a space ship manned by Orson Welles. "There's a tea for families in the auditorium," Donald said. "Maybe you'd like to join them after you visit your friend."

"How is he? Will he know me?"

"Miss, I'm sorry I don't know much about Stacy. We are bursting our mortar, with over two thousand patients now, and it's impossible to know all of them."

The elevator doors opened onto a hallway not unlike the one on the main floor, with walls painted a bilious green. One closed door had an ominous sign in brass letters: TREATMENT ROOM. "Don't be alarmed," Donald said. "We're having amaaaazing results with a new treatment developed in Switzerland by a Doctor Sakel. It's shocking!" He giggled, but I didn't understand the joke. "Shock treatments? With electricity or insulin?"

The hallway opened into a space as large as a school auditorium, but felt more like a football field because it seemed to stretch endlessly before me, with white-suited attendants spaced at intervals along the walls. It was a mob of people, women in grey housedresses and slippers, with cropped or shorn hair as if they had lice. Some squatted on the floor, picking at sores on arms and hands, or just staring off into space, others pacing, while still others huddled in groups, rocking alone or with each other. And the din of their calling and moaning and crying almost made me cover my ears with my hands.

I wanted to bring them bright, coloured balls and teach them a simple game of dodge ball.

Donald said, "There is a men's ward just like this, but your fellow is in therapy right now. I think you'll be very pleased to see what he's doing."

I expected to find a room with tables strewn with art supplies and easels and woodworking tools, lathes, and saws — well maybe not a tool that could hurt someone too sick to know better. I wanted to find Bill whittling or carving or maybe drawing a design for birdcages. The therapy room turned out to be a storage area and at first all I could see were metal shelves full of boxes and suitcases and packing cases piled in the middle of the room. Donald waddled his way into it all as if through a maze to the far end of the room, and there on a makeshift scaffold stood a man wearing overalls and a plaid shirt, his hair shorn up the back, so his neck looked as plucked as a white chicken's. The hair on the crown was spiked like the curry comb for a horse. There were multi-coloured paint stains on his overalls, even at the seat of the pants. He was painting a mural.

An attendant sat on a metal chair that looked like it was thrown out of the basement of the Lutheran Church. He was smoking and leafing through a girlie magazine.

"Give me a minute," I said to Donald.

I stood back, and my breath caught in my throat, trying to swallow the lump forming there, as if I'd swallowed a plum and it was stuck in my craw. My eyes stung the way they did when I went swimming in the saltwater pool at Watrous, the summer Papa took us north for a holiday.

It wasn't Boxcar Bill. Stacy Perch was painting a scene right out of the Regina Riot.

It already covered the top half of the wall. I couldn't see the foreground that he was working on now, but above him, a magnificent dark horse reared, its red mouth open in a shrill, its eyes rolling and shot with fear, while its red-coated rider wielded a riding crop. Behind it, two other heads of horses appeared above the crowd of men fighting with sticks and throwing stones, and wielding what looked like dowels from a stairwell. A man in a green jacket, with raised fist, to the right of Stacy was none other than Hank. To his left, a woman wearing a babushka, with a snout like a retriever, seemed to be calling or shouting at the rioters.

The attendant looked up, stubbed out his fag in a sardine tin, and said, "Hey, Donald."

Donald said, "This is Miss Persson. She's come to see Stacy Perch."

"Sure thing," the attendant said. "Stacy," he called, "you have a visitor."

Stacy Perch remained on the scaffold, mixing colours on his palate.

"He doesn't always hear," the attendant said, and he tugged on the cuff of Stacy's overalls. Still the artist I recognized as neither Boxcar Bill nor Lucky the Traveller nor Stacy Perch from Lloyd did not respond to the attendant, and just kept on applying paint to what may have been a memory of a person he saw on Dominion Day. The attendant yanked harder, and yelled, "Time to stop, Stacy."

Stacy turned and the attendant took the palette and brush from him, then helped him back down the steps of the ladder leaning against the scaffold. To my astonishment, Stacy didn't turn around. He backed up with the attendant, making sure he didn't bump into any of the boxes until he reached the metal chair, and the attendant said, "Sit." Stacy sat. He folded his hands, one on each knee, head bent slightly forward, and he just stared straight ahead at nothing and yet inward at something only he could see at the same time.

Even though my morning sickness had passed I felt queasy — and frightened and yes, appalled. Then angry. I wanted to shout at someone, a policeman or a Mountie or even a trekker: *Look what you've done to him.*

Instead, I stepped cautiously toward him. I wasn't afraid of Stacy. I was afraid of the illness, at how he had given into it, an escape from the pain of what he had seen and heard that day, or perhaps from what had sent him flying on a fast freight in the first place. I knelt before him, hoping I was in the line of sight for the outward part of his staring, but nothing registered in his face. "Bill," I said. "It's me. Marna." Not even a flicker of an eyelid. They never seemed to close, yet his eyes didn't look dried and sore. I dared to touch the side of his head where he'd received the blow from the billy club. His hair was no longer silky and soft and curling of its own around my fingers. It had been washed with hard soap, and it felt scummy and stiff and dry.

"Blink if you can hear me. Twitch your nose."

A glimmer, as if he'd turned from watching a memory unfold to looking inward to a place only he could see and hear and smell. His nostrils flared as if he were going to sneeze or he smelled Betsy's bacon frying while she poured pancake batter into a sizzling hot pan.

"Birds. Cardinals. Ginger and Fred. Bill, they're still nesting in the caragana hedge. And eggs. They've hatched, Bill. Three baby cardinals. I've not named them, thinking you might want to do that, with all your book learning. Remember how you told Betsy they were named Tristram and Isolde and then told me they were Ginger and Fred?"

My legs were stiffening, and I straightened, huffing a bit under my new weight.

"Has he ever come out of it?" I asked the attendant.

"Not to my knowledge. Some stay comatose for years. Others go in and out."

"How do you explain the mural then? It's something that really happened. He was in the riot and he was clubbed on the head."

"The brain is an amazing instrument."

"Is there something I should do or say?"

"There are no shoulds in my business."

"Can I take him for a walk or something?"

"If you like. Are you sure you don't want to join the other families for tea?"

"Oh, family. Does his family ever visit?"

"Can't say for sure. Some just give up. Too hard to help. Impossible to live with."

"Would you do something for me?"

"If I can."

"Should he wake up and I'm not here, would you tell him I'm coming back, that I know he'll be well soon, and I — "

"I know you do. And I'll tell him."

"You don't know what I was going to say."

"It's written all over your face and it's in every gesture you make. He's a lucky man to have someone waiting for him like you."

"Yes, he is a Lucky — man."

I couldn't know if the child of our love would be a girl or a boy, but I vowed that one day I would bring that small person to see Bill's mural.

Redwing

Shelley Banks

A PRAIRIE VILLAGE SO SMALL THE church has been torn down and the school playground grown into a thistle-torn lot. I haven't visited for years, but that's where my mother comes from, and where I'm driving her now.

"Directions?" I ask.

"I would like to go to the cemetery first. When you come to the crossroads, it's one mile east, then one mile south." Her frail voice takes on a singsong lilt, as if reciting instructions she learned eighty years ago as a child. "It is two miles east, and the valley farm is two miles south, after the correction line."

I fumble one-handed with the CAA map, searching for our light-grey route and the village that warrants only six-point type. "What's the distance in kilometres?"

"You don't need that Trudeau metric system here. Don't you know what a section is?"

"A field?" I roughly refold the map and toss it into the back seat.

She shakes her head and shifts the direction of the air vent in front of her.

I focus on the rattle against the undercarriage and the splatter of rain on the roof and wait. My mother likes to tell stories at her own pace.

"A section is 640 acres," she finally says. "One square mile. That means there's a grid road every mile. Or a fence, if a road can't go through."

"And you can tell which you should count, because—?"

"It doesn't matter. We turn right after the correction line. You know about those, don't you? The surveyors used lines of longitude — if they didn't build jogs every few miles, the farms would get smaller and smaller as you went north. The earth curves, you know."

I laugh. She must be feeling happy if she's in lecture mode, and I'm glad we got away quickly enough after my cousin Darla's wedding to squeeze in this drive before the evening reception.

"Next stop, Redwing!" I put my foot hard on the gas of my rented black Mazda and turn off the broken pavement of the highway onto the oiled gravel road heading south, leaving the wedding party, ranch-style houses, and commercial strip of Darla's small prairie town far behind.

"It was good to see them all, wasn't it?" I finally say.

My mother leans back in her seat and sighs. "Family," she says. It's a prayer, her benediction. She's summed up her world in that word.

Along the road, blue-green tree swallows soar and swoop above barbed wire fences, their slim bodies twisting acrobatically after bugs. A few settle on top of the birdhouses that someone has nailed to fence posts every few hundred metres, and I wonder if nestlings are still inside.

"You know, I've never felt this lot was my family," I say, watching for my mother's response in the rear-view mirror.

"Anna, Darla is your cousin!"

I grin. Bingo. As predicted, she's irritated. Animated, too, a good sign that she's recovering her energy after her long flight to Regina, and our drive further east. In her late eighties, she's had several small strokes and tires quickly.

She tugs at her seatbelt, adjusting it over her thin chest.

"Do you want help with that?" I ask. "I can pull over."

"I'm fine." She pats the seatbelt buckle. "You know, you and Darla used to play so well together when you were children."

"All I remember about Darla back then is the time she hit me on the head with her shovel."

"Were you hurt?"

"Thank you for asking. You didn't seem to care at the time. You told me to stop bawling."

"It was probably plastic."

I nod. "From the sandbox. You went back to having tea with Uncle Matt and Aunt Ettie."

"You were such a complainer." My mother laughs, and then pulls down the visor and peers at herself in the passenger-side mirror. She purses her lips and rubs a streak of lipstick off her front teeth. "I'm so glad you came back for the wedding, too. All that way."

"Toronto's no further than Victoria."

"It was in my day." She applies a fresh line of rose lipstick and smacks her lips together to soften the colour. "Isn't it good to be home?"

"Saskatchewan's not my home. We never lived here. You and Dad brought me up all over hell's half acre — "

"Anna!"

"Well, it's true. You took off and left here as soon as you could — when you were, what? Eighteen? I'm surprised your father let you leave."

I reach over and turn on the air conditioning.

She leans over and turns it off. "I went away to school."

"Hmm. As I remember the story, you left to work in a war plant in Toronto, then a clinic in BC."

"I am not a simple farm girl, you know."

"No one said you were."

Our car is the only one in sight, but I fake a right shoulder check so I can glance more closely at my mother. Her eyebrows are arched in a scowl and there is another streak of lipstick over her eyetooth. She sees me looking, shakes her head, and pulls a tissue from her purse to clean it.

She stares out the window. I turn back to the horizon. It's like driving through a sepia-toned film loop that endlessly replays: brown bales of hay, golden stubble, a few dusty yellow wildflowers, abandoned grey barns, bales, barns, flowers, stubble . . .

I grip the wheel. She relaxes back into her seat and begins humming the "Wedding March". It comes out through her dentures with a whistling sound and the notes are flat.

"Mom, what were you looking for back in the church?" The ceremony over, my mother had set off with a squeak of gum-soled Naturalizers, holding the backs of the pews for balance and bending every few paces to check each hymn-book holder.

"My pew. They moved them to town, you know, when the church in Redwing was closed."

"How could you tell which was yours?"

She smiles, the way she used to when I was little and asked her why the cat liked her better than me, or where she had hidden the cookies. "I can't tell you that, Anna."

"Well, did you find it?"

She closes her eyes.

More rain clouds are moving in from the west, but the road isn't as rough or dusty as I'd feared. My allergies will be fine and the road's oiled surface is smooth enough that I'm not nervous about losing control in loose gravel. I slide down the window and raise the volume on the Golden Oldies station. The wind is whipping knots in my hair and for the first time since I flew in from the East to meet my mother at the airport, I feel a bubble of happiness rise in my chest.

"Do you like that music?" Her voice is raised against the wind and the radio and rumble of the road. "Do you need it quite so loud?"

"Sometimes you make me feel like I'm seventeen, not thirty-seven!"

"You are thirty-six. You were born the year Ettie got her wig."

"Aunt Ettie lost her hair?"

"She was as bald as you. Nobody knew why."

I ruffle my thick brown bob. "I'm not bald!" I say, glancing over at her thinning white hair in the rear-view mirror.

"You were when you were a baby. No one expected you to have hair. But Ettie — "

"And I'm thirty-seven, Mom."

"Why ever did you say you were seventeen?"

I sigh and turn down the volume. "Remember that portable record player I had, back when we lived in Penticton? Kind of boxy? And pink? Anyway, I was the new kid, trying to make friends. I'd invited some girls over to listen to music."

"Your music was always so loud!"

"That's what you said when you burst into my room."

"I imagine your father, God rest his soul, was working." She clasps her hands tightly and nods to herself. "And you were creating a racket."

"Yep. That's what you said when you slammed the lid down."

"Why do you always argue with me?"

"I don't!" My fingers are starting staccato runs around the steering wheel. I take a deep breath and flex them straight.

"Yes, you do." She sits firmly upright, clenching the armrests. "I don't remember those girls."

"Well, they all slunk off and told everyone what a loser I was."

"How mean. If I'd known, I would have told them a thing or two. You were a lovely girl!"

"Um, thanks." I slide the window and crank the air conditioning again. "I don't remember the corner—you'll have to remind me when we get close."

"To what?" She shakes her head. "Anna, I have already said I do not want to go to the farm. I do not want to see what those new tenants of Darla's are doing to it."

"She says they're great."

"That's not the same. She should have stayed. And this hurts!" She pulls out her seatbelt again and with a grumble, clicks it open. The belt snaps back against the car door.

"You can't ride without a seatbelt!" I pull the car over, get out, and walk to her side to adjust the belt lower. Then higher. Then back close to its original position.

"Thank you," she says. "That's better."

"And I know you'd like to keep the farm in the family," I say, starting up the car again, "But I can understand why Darla wants to move to town — she was on her own long enough way out here." Like my mother, my cousin had been widowed for many years.

"You don't have to tell me. I know exactly what that's like. I hope you never have to go through what I went through, losing a husband. Someone you love the way I loved your father."

"Mom!" My nails cut into the wheel.

"What?"

"Sometimes — I don't know. You're — I mean, what about Martin?" My mother always tried hard not to acknowledge Martin, the tall crane-like man I'd lived with for fifteen years. She found excuses to not to visit me if he was in town and might be cooking his specialties, Yorkshire pudding or paella, and would sometimes even sweetly claim she had the wrong number when his deep voice answered our phone.

"You weren't married, dear."

"He died, Mom. Remember? The accident?"

"That's different."

"Holy — !" We hit a patch of gravel. I grip the steering wheel and catch myself in time to stop a blue streak of swearing. There must be more dust in the car than I realized; my eyes are starting to sting.

"You and Martin were good friends, Anna. Housemates. You are not a loose woman, not like your Aunt Freddy! No one would invite her home, not even after church! None of the ladies, anyway."

"Loose!" In spite of my frustration, I smile. I glance at my mother, but she's staring off across a field, looking vacant or sad. I point out the window and try to change the subject. "Is that wheat?"

"Barley. You always had a problem with crops and directions. Remember when you got lost just two minutes from the farm?"

"I was seven! I was carsick and dizzy from that old truck." And from the sun-baked dirt, and the glare of the wide-open skies, and the unsheltered sun. Uncle Matt had stopped to let me get some fresh air, but then he drove off without me, rushing back to the farm with the medicine he'd bought for his dog's infected paw.

"You always get so excited about things," my mother says.

"I had sunstroke." I'd stumbled down that dirt road, passing field after field after identical field, looking for anything distinct and familiar in that golden haze. I'd fallen, thrown up onto dust-caked grass, orange Freezie juice trickling over the parched earth. I'd risen, brushed sharp stones from scabby knees, and tried to keep on walking.

"My, how we laughed."

"That was funny?" I adjust the side mirror for a better look back at the same gravel and dust I'd seen all along.

"You were perfectly safe the whole time. Minutes from home. Your Aunt Ettie was with you. But what a complainer! Oh, look!" My mother's voice rises as she points across the fields. "Redwing! The elevator is still standing."

"So we're getting close?"

"I think it's terrible that they're pulling down so many and putting up those concrete monstrosities along the highway." She shakes her head, soft jowls quivering.

"Hey, what's one of the top ten signs you might be Canadian?" I wait, then say: "You think it's normal to have a grain elevator in your backyard!"

"The top ten?" She stares at me.

"You know, like David Letterman."

"Have you introduced us? I don't often get to meet your young men."

"Mom, he's on TV. In New York. And I'm hardly young."

"Well. I don't know about that. Why did he leave Toronto?"

"He never was in Toronto. He's on TV."

"Yes, dear." She turns her back and stares out the window. "You mentioned your TV already, and I'll look for that photograph of your David on it the next time you invite me to visit. And there is no need to repeat yourself. I am not deaf yet."

I punch the preset buttons on the radio and pull in another oldies station with a hefty dose of static. The Beatles are singing, "She's Leaving Home", and under my breath, I mutter, "I can understand precisely why."

"Speak up," my mother says.

"Just singing along."

I drive on, pointing first to a hawk that's landed on a fence post with a gopher in its claws, next a meadowlark singing from a willow by a slough. And then she grabs my arm. "You passed it! Redwing Cemetery!"

There are no cars on this ribbon of road that rolls into tomorrow and the day after that. I slow and turn around. "Why did they call the village Redwing?"

"Because of the blackbirds. They're all over, in the sloughs and marshes. They sit on the cattails and sing — just like in that painting by the fireplace in my living room. Your grandmother did that. It's lovely, don't you think?"

"Uh, right. Yes, it is." As I recall, the only fireplace in her senior's complex is two flights down from her small apartment, in the activity centre by the lobby. "Mom, I've never seen a red-winged blackbird here — or a cattail, either."

"You don't come back very often, do you?"

"Guess not." I help her from the car and wrap my jacket over her shoulders to shelter her from the light rain. "They're pretty birds."

"But I don't hear them anymore!" She stops and clutches my arm, her face creased with concern. "Can you, Anna? Are they gone?"

"They've probably all flown south."

She nods and stands a moment, thinking. Is she trying to remember what season it is, or when the birds migrate, or whether they were ever really here? Then she turns her attention to the chain-link fence that encloses the cemetery. It's a rectangular plot about the size of the vegetable garden back on Uncle Matt and Darla's old farm, and inside the fence, a few shiny pink and black granite gravestones are scattered among low, white-washed markers, with a wide expanse of grass beyond set aside for the rest us.

Black-eyed Susans grow along the edges of the graveyard, with a scattering of purple asters and silvery sage. I take a deep breath of dry prairie air, savouring the muted fragrance of the grass and flowers, then sneeze. This windswept country was home to my great-grand-parents and their children, and their children after that, and they never doubted that we all would stay and love the land as they had, a line never-ending under the endless prairie sky.

My mother tries to open the gate but a padlock holds it fast. She yanks at it and stumbles, and when I catch her, she is shaking. "They're gone, you know." Her voice quavers. "All of them. My parents, your father, and even — " She pauses, and for a nerve-tingling second, I think she'll mention Martin, with his high-top runners and violin, his meat pies and that red hair that always stood on end. But she carries on: "Even, oh, Darla's first husband! That fellow from Melville! What was his name?"

"Dwayne." I bend down to pick a handful of wildflowers, and arrange them in a small bouquet.

Her fingers quiver as she reaches for it. She touches the petals gently and smiles, and I wonder how our settler ancestors would have felt if they'd known that so few of us would stay. Four generations, and now only Darla living in town with her farm rented to strangers. Would they have persevered, or given up their labours on this beautiful, harsh land?

"That's right," she says, finally. "Dwayne was scouted by the Montreal Canadiens, you know. But he wanted to stay here with Darla and help your Uncle Matt run the farm, so he turned them down."

"Mom, last time you told me this, it was the Chicago Blackhawks, the time before, the Maple Leafs."

"Oh, no." She reaches for the fence around the graveyard, and rests her hand along the top as if swearing on a Bible. "It was the Canadiens. From Montreal. They spell that differently in Quebec, you know. So I'd remember."

"You're sure this even happened?"

"Oh yes, and let me tell you, the Canadiens weren't too happy about it, either, when he turned them down."

As we walk the short distance back to the car, I put my arm around her and she leans against me like a rag doll, crushing the flowers between us. I help her into her seat, turn up the heater, and hold her hand. We sit and watch the trickle of rain on the windshield. "Mom, you're still shaking." She pulls her hand away and puts it in her lap. "It's just the excitement," I say. "Flying in from Victoria, and the wedding and all."

"I want to see the village." My mother is looking straight ahead, not at me. She points to the road through the window, tracing the route down the grid road.

"But no walking? Agreed?"

She nods and looks down. Her fingers twitch.

"Okay, a quick loop past the grain elevator, then we'll head back for the reception."

The radio is playing Joni Mitchell's "Big Yellow Taxi" as we turn into Redwing, a tiny village with its church dismantled and the only phone booth hauled away. We drive past the lot where the hardware store once stood, and the rows of Manitoba maples that shaded the long-demolished school and playground, now covered in thistles. The song is still on when we pull into the field beside the rail yard.

"What kind of lyrics are those? Parking lots and paradise?"

"You don't need to criticize all the music I like."

"Or snap every time I speak."

The edge in my mother's voice startles me. When I glance at her, she is crumpled against the window, staring out at the white wooden elevator. Her hands are shaking again, the flowers dropped to the floor. Her lower lip is trembling.

I touch her shoulder, suddenly reminded of the effort it takes these days for her to remain focused and in control, wondering why my need to argue with her, challenge her, remains.

I reach for my camera. "It's in great shape, isn't it? Do you want a picture?"

She rummages through her purse and pulls out a small yellow box with Kodak written across it in red. I haven't seen this kind of disposable camera for years. "I, I have an Instamatic." She starts to open her door, then turns and hands me the box. "Could you? It's — you know, your grandfather shipped the first load of wheat back east from the station here. The first in the whole community. But — the station's gone."

Nodding, I climb out to photograph the building with its red-and-gold Wheat Pool sign. The light rain has slicked the top layer of hardpan into gumbo and it cakes my shoes with each step. Deep down, the earth is still so parched that when the mud lifts, puffs of dust rise from beneath it. Grain hasn't been stored here for years, but pigeons still rise in a cloud as I approach the building.

I click a few times with her camera, then stomp around by the tracks to get a better shot with mine, and that is where I see it: A red DANGER sign, with a demolition notice nailed above it.

When I get back to the car, my mother is silent.

"I took several photos — one even has the car, so you're in it, too."

"Did you get that sign?" she asks.

"Yes — the name is very clear."

"I'm too old to be lied to." She pinches her lips. She's so shrunken, fragile.

"Mom?"

"The one at the back. When are they tearing it down?"

I stare at her. How does she know that?

"When?" she asks again.

"Monday."

My mother takes a deep breath, like a sob, then searches in her purse for another tissue.

I put the car in reverse and skid out of the elevator yard and back onto the grid road heading north. In the rear-view mirror, the elevator thrusts against the grey-blue patchwork sky for one last weekend.

We pass fields, and suddenly I see a flock of birds rise from a low spot on the right. I slow so we can watch them wheel and turn above the marsh, their red flashes and lower yellow bars bright in the sun. A few are speckled brown like the cattails I now see below, but most shimmer like black rainbows.

My mother coughs. Finally, she speaks: "Our initials were carved in the hymn-book holder, you know. That's how I knew."

"In the church! That's what you were looking for!"

I watch her nod in the mirror.

"But carved? You marked up a church pew?" My voice rises. My ultra-respectable, ultra-conservative, church-wife mother. What else didn't I know about her, and will never know?

"He did. Jake. A hired man on our farm. With his whittling knife. Oh, he made lovely figurines with that!" She gestures back out the window at the blackbirds. "Birds, mostly. And flowers."

I clear my throat. "So you found it, then? Your pew?"

She nods. "And our names. In a corner, under all that wax and grime." Then she turns away and huddles into her seat, staring down at the wilted Black-eyed Susans she's nudging with her feet. And what she says next floors me. "I — we couldn't marry, but we were like you and your Martin, I guess. When I left home, I went to look for him. But — " My mother sniffs and wipes her nose. "I'm sorry about Martin. Your — "

"My friend." And even though I know those are the only words she wants to believe, in them I hear her own frantic love and ragged loss. I reach over and touch her hand. "Mom, I do understand. And I'm so sorry, too."

She squeezes my fingers and gives a tiny smile.

As we drive back past the cemetery, I catch a last glimpse of family gravestones in the tall, open grass. A dip in the road, then they vanish. Gravel clatters against the car and wind whips my skin. We drive back to the reception in silence.

Bus Ride

Kelly-Anne Riess

TARA LOCKED EYES WITH HIM as he was boarding the bus in Lloydminster.

He was tall, well over six feet, and had blond hair pulled back in a ponytail. Tara knew her father wouldn't like him for that reason alone, and he certainly wouldn't have been amused by his T-shirt. It had a picture of a rock talking to a ruler. The ruler told the rock it rocked and the rock was telling the ruler it ruled. She couldn't help it. Tara smiled and he returned a grin.

Tara quickly looked out the window and watched the suitcases being loaded on the bus. *Please don't sit with me. Please don't sit with me.* She regretted not putting her backpack on the seat next to her to inhibit someone sitting beside her, especially since this was an overnight trip. Tara would eventually like to sprawl out into the empty seat and sleep.

"Hi." A male voice.

Tara turned. It was him. Tara watched as he shoved his small suitcase in the overhead compartment with tanned, muscular arms. He sat down. His elbow brushed against hers as he did. She pulled away. *I should have put my bag on the other seat.*

"Hi," said Tara. She looked back out the window at the bus depot, a brown building, earth tone and dated.

Why is he sitting with me? It must be because this is the last seat available. Tara turned in her seat to look back at the other people in the bus. She was wrong. There was an open seat behind her beside a perfect blonde Barbie with eyes rimmed with black eyeliner flipping through a magazine. *Why didn't he sit with her?*

"Buses are always so uncomfortable," he said.

Tara looked at him as he stretched his long legs into the aisle. His eyes smiling. He was probably one of those people who always looked happy, Tara decided. She was not one of those people.

"I know."

"My name is Zeke, by the way." He extended his hand.

"Tara."

His handshake was firm, but his hand was clammy. Is he nervous? Tara wondered about what, certainly not about talking to her?

Tara bent down and pulled out a book, careful that the book cover was pointed down at her lap so he couldn't see what she was reading.

"Where did you get on?"

"Saskatoon," Tara answered while taking out her bookmark. *Why didn't he sit beside the Barbie? She could handle this better.*

"And you're headed to . . . "

"Jasper." She looked over at him. His eyes were still smiling. He seemed amused by her discomfort.

"Me too. I'm from there, actually." He was beaming now.

"Oh really," Tara said. She didn't smile back, though she almost couldn't resist. She hoped she wasn't blushing. "I'm just moving there."

She looked down at her book. She was reading about a surveyor named Bridgeland. Over a hundred years ago, he'd spent his summers climbing the Rockies, taking pictures he would use to draw maps in the winter. He'd invite people to his home to share his tales of adventures. His life sounded perfectly charmed, if you forgot the brutality of his climbs and his meticulous attention to detail. Tara wished she had some sort of ability for — anything.

The book was no defence from Zeke. "So, what are you going to do in Jasper?"

"I'll be working at a store called The Pussy Willow." This time she was sure she was blushing. She picked up her book again, taking the bookmark out.

Shit. She did not want to get into her life story — that she'd been waitressing in Saskatoon for three years after flunking out of engineering in her sophomore year, and was now going to Jasper to work in a gift shop.

"ONE DEAD END JOB TO ANOTHER," her mother had said when Tara had told her about the move over the phone.

"It'll be a change of scenery." She gripped the receiver tighter. She hated talking to her parents, but she called them every Thursday anyway.

"Because the mountains are going to make your life so much better."

"That's right, Mom. I'm a big failure."

"You can always go back to school."

"I don't want to talk about this again." Tara slammed the phone down. She didn't answer when her mother called back.

THE BUS PULLED OUT OF the parking lot and Tara looked out the window again, watching Lloydminster — a whir of streetlights and store signs — speed by.

"The Pussy Willow. That's a neat little shop. Half of it's a bookstore, and half of it's like crafts," said Zeke.

"The guy I did the phone interview with said it was a gift shop. He didn't say we'd be selling craft supplies."

"It is a gift shop, probably one of the best in town," he said. "When I mean crafts, I mean artisan stuff, not the sort of glue gun and sparkle stuff you made in Girl Guides. It's like handcrafted sculptures and fused glass bowls, really beautiful work."

"Oh." Tara sat silently for a moment with her cheeks burning. *Craft supplies, really, Tara, really? I am so stupid.* "I never was a Girl Guide."

"You missed out," Zeke said. "All those camping trips and hiking, it was a lot of fun."

Tara raised an eyebrow. "You were a Girl Guide then, I take it?" She had to say it; she couldn't help herself.

Zeke laughed, looking down at his lap for a minute, then back up at Tara.

"You're very pretty when you smile."

Tara hadn't noticed she had been smiling. She stopped. *Is he hitting on me?*

AT TWENTY-ONE, TARA HAD NEVER been kissed. She blamed her parents. When she was younger, they'd always made her wear her hair short, which confused other children who were taught little girls have long hair and boys have short hair. Other kids would always point at her and whisper to their parents, and not quietly: "Is that a girl?" And the parent would look at Tara with an amused smile.

When she told him about it, Tara's father would say from behind his paper at the kitchen table, "How can people think you're a boy? If you were a boy, you would sure be one effeminate-looking boy."

Her mother would always agree. "You can't have long hair," she'd say, while watching a pot come to a boil on the stove. "You wouldn't take care of it."

"How do you know?"

"Tara, we know you," her father would say.

In grade four, Ryan Desmond, one of the most popular boys, rated her as the ugliest girl in the entire school. After high school, Tara grew her hair long and always wore lots of makeup to make it clear to the world she was a girl, but the only men who ever seemed interested in her were drunk rugby players who came into Bridget's Café where she used to waitress, and she couldn't trust their judgment. They often had too much to drink and would hit on any female who walked by, including Bridget, who was twice their age.

"Come on, boys," Bridget would tell them at closing time, picking up the empty glasses from the table. "It's time to go home."

"Oh, but we were just starting to have fun," one guy, Tara heard the others call Brown, frequently said.

"I bet you'd be a lot of fun," another said once. He was referred to as Rooke.

One of the players, named J-Rock, always ended the evening for them. "Okay, we're going, but we'll see you next time."

"That's right." Brown often winked at Tara as she hovered behind Bridget.

Although an older woman, Bridget was quite fit. She ran marathons and took karate, and was in much better shape than Tara. The only exercise Tara ever got was the twenty-minute walk to and from work, and she was on her feet all day, running heavy trays from the kitchen.

Brown always asked to be seated in Tara's section. She could never get them to leave without Bridget's help.

"It's time to go," Tara would say.

A couple of times Brown tried to pull her onto his lap. "Only if you go home with me," he'd say. Bridget would break his arm if he tried that with her. Tara was sure of it. Bridget gave off that kind of *don't-mess-with-me* vibe to the rugby players that Tara could never master.

"I can't. Employees aren't allowed to date the customers," Tara would say, red-faced, then she'd take off to get Bridget.

"I MEAN IT," ZEKE SAID. "You have a nice smile. And, no, I was never a Girl Guide, but my sister was. She hated it. I was in Scouts, and I loved it. We were always doing cool things, like zip lining and kayaking."

"Did you grow up in Jasper?"

"I did. It was great. It's Canada's playground. You're going to love it."

"Well, I can hike maybe, but kayak, I don't know. I can't swim. And zip lining isn't my thing."

"You'll learn."

"Maybe," Tara said, picking up her book again. Maybe she would surprise herself, but she doubted it. She went with Bridget to karate for a little while, but she could never get any of the stances right. Her posture was always off, and the instructor, who fancied himself a military drill sergeant, was always yelling at her.

"It'll get easier," Bridget told her. "You have to ignore him." But Tara couldn't.

"So you're going to be working for David. He's quite the man around town. He owns a few businesses."

"Oh."

"He's great. He kept his faith in me even when he had no reason to, even when others told him he shouldn't. He said he always knew I'd find my way. He always saw the good in me. I wasn't always a nice guy, you know."

"I find that hard to believe, that you were ever a bad guy," said Tara, putting her book down.

Zeke looked away from her. "Sorry. I probably said too much, but I went through a rough time for a while."

"I've had my share of trouble too," Tara said.

She had an urge to put her hand on his thigh, but not in a million years would she allow herself to do anything like that. She wasn't wearing makeup today. She was wearing baggy sweatpants to be comfortable on the bus, not trendy formfitting yoga pants like Barbie behind her.

Zeke sat up from his stretched-out position. "I used to take advantage of girls like you," he said quietly so no one around them could hear.

Girls like her?

Zeke dug out a copy of *Climbing* magazine. It was the "Big Trip Issue." On the cover was a muscled blonde woman crouched impossibly vertical against a rock face. Her chalk-covered hands were gripping onto a crevasse that ran from the top of the cliff to the bottom. If there were ropes, Tara couldn't see them. It appeared Zeke was done talking.

Tara returned to her book, but Bridgeland's photographs seemed to have lost their appeal. She looked out at the night. There were flashes of isolated lights in the darkness from farms and oil derricks.

She'd never left Saskatchewan before and was only familiar with its southern prairie landscape. The last three years since graduating high school had been a waste of time. Jasper was going to be her fresh start, an adventure. *How sad was that?* It seemed like everyone had been to the Rockies, many times. It was no big deal. But Tara had never seen a moose before or a bear, let alone any mountains, except, of course, on TV.

"You've been to one place, you've been to them all," her mother had said, without looking up from her knitting when Tara had asked why they'd never gone anywhere when she was growing up. "Every city has a Walmart, a Starbucks; Winnipeg might have a zoo and a fancy statue on their government building, big deal. I don't need to drive all that way to see it."

"Well, I want to go to a zoo at least once in my life, Mom," Tara had said. "I'd like to go on an airplane."

"Air travel is too expensive."

"I'm probably the only one my age who has never been on an airplane."

"I highly doubt that," her father interjected. And that was the end of that discussion.

Her mother had been right. Air travel was expensive. The bus had been significantly cheaper than flying to Edmonton and then taking a charter to Jasper from there.

When Tara decided to move to Saskatoon to go to university instead of Regina or Brandon, cities much closer to Esterhazy, her mother had been upset. "Regina has a good engineering program. Why don't you go there? A lot of kids you've grown up with are going to Regina. It will be better for you."

"But Saskatoon is the only university that has engineering physics," Tara said, even though she had no idea what engineering physics was. But how great would it be to be able to wrap her head around physics? How great would it have been if she could have done that instead of failing?

TARA JUMPED WHEN ZEKE'S CELLPHONE rang to the tune of ABBA's "Fernando".

"I really have to change that ring." Zeke dug in his pocket for his phone. "My ex-girlfriend thought it was funny. Hello?'" He paused, listening. Tara couldn't hear who was on the other end. Who would be calling him at night while he was on a bus?

"I'll be home tomorrow." He listened again, then said, "Yeah, it will be good to see everyone again. Grandma was great and all, but it'll be great to be home. It's been such a long time." Another pause. "Yeah, you too. I hope you're keeping out of trouble. See you soon, bud." Zeke put his phone away.

"Sorry, it was my brother," he said. "Where are you coming from?"

"Saskatoon." Tara wished he'd stop talking to her. Zeke was finished with his magazine. He couldn't be that interested in her. Guys that looked like him usually had girlfriends.

"I've never been there."

"What were you doing in Lloyd?"

"My grandmother lives there. I usually try to see her once or twice a year. She taught me everything I know."

About what? Tara wondered, but didn't ask.

"What made you want to move to Jasper?"

Here we go. Now I get to tell him all about my shitty life. "I needed a fresh start," she said.

"I know all about that," he said.

"What do you do in Jasper?"

"I really want to get into day trading. I'm saving my money so I'll have some capital to play with, but, in the meantime, I'm a raft guide during the summer and I give ice walk tours of Maligne Canyon in the winter for David. One of his companies is an outdoor adventure one."

"Neat."

"It can be," he said. "Most of the tourists are smitten and happy to be in the mountains. It's rare to come across someone in a bad mood."

"Rafting sounds dangerous."

"Not really. The van ride to the water is probably the most dangerous part."

"If you can swim," Tara said.

"Even if you can't."

"What is the wildlife like?"

"There are bears, moose, mountain goats. In fact, one time when I was growing up, goats ate the rust right off my dad's old car."

"What?"

"Oh yeah, goats will eat anything. This guy who had seen the whole thing happen got angry with my dad for feeding the wildlife."

"You're making that up."

"No I'm not. Cross my heart," he said, running his finger over his chest. "But I'm sorry, I can't hope to die. I'm too young."

Tara laughed. She couldn't help herself.

He laughed too. "It's true."

Tara's parents had said wild animals would be the least of her worries. Jasper would be full of transients, Tara's father had warned, dangerous ones. "They could commit a murder and be on to the next town before anyone knows."

"Fernando" rang again. "Hello?" It had to be his girlfriend this time. "Yeah, I'm on the bus back right now. No." Zeke tensed. His voice had become stern, almost angry. "No. I don't do that anymore. I've told you that before. You're going to have to find somebody else." He paused to listen. "Yeah, maybe. I'm going to be working, but I might be able to get off early. It would be good to see everyone." Zeke relaxed again. "Okay. Well, I should get going." He looked at Tara, then at the telephone before he said, "Sorry, old friend." He hung up.

"Zeke." She hesitated. *I can't ask. Could I?*

"What?" He grinned at her.

"I was wondering what you meant when — never mind."

"No. It's okay. Go ahead, ask. I try to be an open book."

Her face flushed and she suddenly felt warm. *He likes me.* "What did you mean when you said, girls like me?"

Without losing his smile, he thought for a minute. "Girls who — " He hesitated. "Don't take this the wrong way, but girls who don't realize how pretty they are, who look sad. Girls who don't look you in the eyes."

"I look sad?" She tried to meet his gaze, but stared at his nose instead.

"Yes, but, don't worry, I won't ask you to talk about it."

Tara didn't know what to say. How could he tell she was sad? Why did he think she was pretty? How had he taken advantage of girls like her?

"I should probably get some sleep," Tara said. "I have to meet my new boss tomorrow."

"You'll really like him." Zeke closed his eyes.

"I hope so." She rested her head against the bus window, shutting her eyes.

WHEN SHE WOKE UP AN hour later, she found Zeke resting against her shoulder. Her shirt was wet. Was he drooling on her?

Zeke had used girls like Tara. What had he meant by that? Tara couldn't even guess without thinking the worst. She had to stop thinking. She sighed, looking up at the night sky through the bus window. It had to be after midnight already. Clouds hid the stars. The only light came from passing cars. She sat still so as not to wake Zeke, trying to control the twitch in her shoulder. His head was heavy. Did he not know he was leaning on her? She hoped she was making the right decision, moving to the Rockies. If there was a star visible, she'd have wished on it for happiness, to find purpose.

The bus was slowing down. Where was she? The bus made a hard right turn and drove slowly towards a town. Tara was unfamiliar with the area; she could have been anywhere. The bus lurched to a stop. Zeke sat up and looked at her.

"Did I fall asleep?" Zeke rubbed his eyes. In a daze, he looked sad himself.

"You were drooling," she said, pointing to the wet mark on her shoulder.

"Sorry. That's embarrassing."

"That's okay," she said and, on impulse, she reached out and pinched his cheek. "I like your smile too."

Why did she say that? She pulled her hand away before Zeke could feel it trembling. Before he could say anything, before he could shoot her down, Tara opened her mouth again, without thinking. "But I don't believe you're happy. Not every moment needs a smile."

Zeke stopped smiling. "Why not? My grandmother said no one can resist a smile."

"What makes you think I'd resist?" She couldn't help herself. *Ugh,* a voice screamed in her head. She was so lame. What was she doing? He couldn't possibly like a girl like her. But he said she was pretty and that she just didn't know it. Could he have been lying? Why would he lie? None of the boys she went to school with had ever liked her. Nobody had expressed any interest in her at university. She hadn't gone out much, not even with her roommate, Kathy. She had been so overwhelmed by all the homework she didn't even know where to start, so she slept and couldn't get herself out of bed for class. Often, she slept all day. Kathy said Tara was probably depressed. Adapting to city life from small-town Esterhazy had been too much, that she probably missed high school and living with her parents. The adjustment on top of the workload had been beleaguering. Kathy was full of shit.

Maybe the rugby players had been interested in her. Maybe they thought she was pretty and she was just too dumb to realize it.

"Are you flirting with me?"

"Maybe," she said. Her heart was racing so fast it felt like it would bounce right out of her chest.

"I thought you were the type that I would have to work hard to win over."

"So did I." What was she doing?

Making a new life, starting an adventure, a voice inside her told her. But Tara felt panic.

Zeke leaned down towards her and whispered, "I'd kiss you if we weren't on this bus."

Tara was terrified, yet part of her wanted to see where this would go. "I don't think you're the type to be bothered by other people," she whispered back.

"I didn't used to be," Zeke suddenly pulled away and looked out over the other seats.

Tara said, "I'm going back to sleep."

She closed her eyes, but she didn't sleep.

He had used girls like her.

As the Crow Flies

Shelley Banks

IT'S MORNING, AT LEAST TO the crows outside the open motel window. Maggie pounds the pillow against her ears as raucous calls echo from tree to tree along the dusty prairie road. If only birds weren't so damn sociable. If each lived alone, you could get some sleep.

She shoves back the covers, fumbles for the edge of the bed, and stumbles across the gritty linoleum to the window. The wooden frame sticks. She puts her weight against it and shoves. The window clatters shut.

Jenna starts to cry, a rising wail from the portable playpen in the corner.

"Shush, baby — don't wake your daddy!" Maggie picks up the baby and pats her back.

On the bed, Rob has his arms wrapped around a pillow, chest rising with a rumbling snore. *He'll be a driving maniac again.*

The chair under the window is made of 1960s plastic and pine. It's sticky on her skin, but it's the only place to sit except the bed. Maggie unbuttons her nightgown and the baby nuzzles closer, seeking her nipple with grunts and smacks.

The ceiling fan rattles.

A fly buzzes against the bathroom mirror.

The bed creaks.

And Rob is awake, searching for his watch on the bedside table. "Look at that — almost nine."

"You're still on Ottawa time." Maggie strokes Jenna's fine blonde hair and blows a kiss onto her forehead.

"You mean it's only seven?" He stretches. "Great! We'll get an early start."

"We can't leave yet."

"Sure we can. Just get Jenna settled."

"She's not finished!"

IN LESS THAN AN HOUR, they are back in the van, driving past wheat fields and stubble, small towns and grain elevators, out of Manitoba, across Saskatchewan, and into the late afternoon.

Maggie drums her fingernails on the armrest. "All these fields and fences and roads keep sliding by, but it doesn't feel like we're moving forward. The view shifts, but we're staying still."

"Gotta love the Prairies."

"Can't we find a park or ice cream somewhere?"

"You see anywhere to stop?" Rob takes his hands off the wheel and waves at the open fields that surround them.

"There's a town a few miles north on the map."

"We'll never make it to Edmonton tonight if we take detours."

"Who cares? We'll get there tomorrow." Maggie leans forward and turns on the radio.

"No, tomorrow we have to be in Prince George. They're planning a family dinner, and I'm trying to fit in a few sales calls, too."

"I can't take much more of this, racing down the highway like a bat out of hell."

"Meat Loaf. 1977."

"The point is — "

"Every extra night costs more. And cuts into the visit with Ron and Amy."

"And your precious work! We're supposed to be on vacation! And what's the point of visiting if we're exhausted?"

"I'm not exhausted." Rob hunches forward, gripping the steering wheel, his normally neat blond hair drooping over his forehead.

"Well, okay, but what about Jenna? They'll never want to see her again if she's cranky." Maggie dials up the volume and turns her back to her husband. Outside the tinted passenger window: a sea of grain and haze of dirt from dried sloughs and ditches. She half-closes her eyes and squints at insects blasted flat onto the windshield: mangled wasps, shredded butterflies, a grasshopper with one wing still fluttering against the glass.

"I'm hungry."

"Have some chips." Rob points to the cellophane bag at her feet.

"I want food, not gas station snacks!"

As if cued by stress on the word food, Jenna begins to whimper in her sleep.

"Can't you get her to settle down?"

"I'm in the front seat, she's strapped in the back — so how exactly am I supposed to do that?"

"Well, you're her mother," says Rob.

"I'm an art therapist, not a magician!"

Blacktop rolls by, and they pass gravel roads and canola fields, weathered barns and distant stands of poplars, but not a single picnic site or even a widened stretch of shoulder in the shade. Then Jenna starts to wail in earnest, her voice puckering into breathless sobs.

"Shh, baby." Maggie twists around to pat the back of Jenna's car seat. "It's okay. Daddy will stop soon."

"If we find somewhere."

"Anywhere!" Maggie unfastens her seatbelt and clambers into the back seat. She strokes Jenna's hair and coos, "There, baby, it's okay." Then she snaps, "Rob, you're acting like those guys they used to warn me about back when I thumbed rides, the ones who keep you captive in their cars."

"We all know how *that* turned out. And I'm the good guy, remember?"

Maggie rolls her eyes. "I was fine!"

Beside her, Jenna thrashes against the straps of her car seat, face red with anger and tears. "Come on, baby, it's okay," Maggie says. "Look, here's your bird toy. Your purple mousie!"

In the distance, a quarter section of flax reflects the crisp blue of the sky. From the grass along the shoulder, a bird flashes up and vanishes in a streak of gold.

Rob brakes and flips on the turn signal. "Smallville, Saskatchewan. Population: Thirty families, twenty dogs and six gophers. But they've got a motel. The Wander Inn."

"That's not its name."

"Town, no. Motel, yes. See the sign?" He pulls into an empty parking lot, tires spitting gravel as he angles the van to face the office door. "Hope you like the classics — looks like more chipped bathtubs and ant traps by the sink to me."

"Fine!" Maggie unfastens Jenna's seat straps, scoops her out, while Rob drives off in search of takeout food.

MAGGIE WAKES EARLY, summoned by Jenna's morning gurgles and coos. She rolls away from Rob and his sweaty red T-shirt, pushes back the sheet, and tiptoes over to the playpen. The baby is lying on her back, grasping a yellow disk and flapping it against her gums.

"Hey there, noisy one!" Maggie whispers, reaching down to tickle Jenna.

The baby pumps her legs with a toothless grin. She stretches out her arms to be held, letting the toy slide from her mouth to the mattress. Maggie tucks her fingers around her daughter's chubby chest and picks her up to change her and feed her. Ten minutes later, Jenna is asleep, a drool of milk leaking from her mouth onto her mother's damp breast.

Maggie looks over at Rob. It's still before 6:00 AM. And he's still snoring, his sleeping face washed clean of stress from the night before. She gently puts Jenna back in the playpen. The baby grunts and fumbles her fist towards her face until her thumb slips into her mouth. Sucking loudly, Jenna drifts into deeper sleep. Maggie breathes in the soft scent of baby powder, trying to fill herself with the baby's sated peace. Instead, her chest tightens.

A life narrowed to her daughter's needs.

Her days of freedom, over.

Even after four months home on maternity leave with Jenna, she's not used to the paralyzing tug of love and shudder of total responsibility that comes with it. Overwhelmed by the challenge of decoding the baby's signals most of her waking hours, Maggie is mystified by Rob's ability to ignore them, as if the baby is a battery-operated doll to turn on or switch off at will. Maggie's doll. Maggie's, to care for. Maggie's, to feed.

She rubs Jenna's back. "Sometimes, baby, I think you're eating me alive!"

Her hand still warm from Jenna's sleepers, Maggie kneels beside her suitcase. Soon, they'll be on the road again. Not because Rob wants a longer family visit — he won't be at his brother's house more than a couple of days before buried tensions surface. It's the travelling itself he likes. The goal of the trip? To log as much distance as possible, to challenge his personal best on the highway. The destination, irrelevant. Sights on the way, mere distractions. Motion, the only thing that matters. Once, she would have understood, back in the days when she saw a new beginning at every truck stop or access lane. But now, there is Jenna.

Maggie pulls on her jeans and a purple T-shirt, then slips a dry pair of nursing pads into her bra. Rob and the baby sleep on, their breathing deep and regular, not even a murmur as she folds and packs her pajamas, collects Jenna's toys for the carry-all and puts the scraps from Rob's foray to the café into the garbage.

Restless, she walks to the window and looks out along the oiled gravel road into town. A row of Manitoba maples, leaves shimmering in the early heat and almost imperceptible breeze. Paint peeling on the white Co-op store next door. Skiffs of dirt on the sidewalk. And beside the rusting railway track, the grass crisped brown by drought.

No people or pets.

Nothing that moves except a bluebottle launching itself against the screen.

Rob begins to mutter in his sleep.

The fly drones on.

The tabletop fan blows one puff of air over her already clammy skin and then another, redistributing the stale smell of fried chicken around the room.

Maggie glances back at the bed, slips on her sandals, and grabs her daypack from the dresser. Breakfast at the café, if it's open. A small island of independence before the day begins. She shrugs the strap over her shoulder and goes out, catching the door to prevent it slamming behind her.

Already the sun has arced high in the clear sky and the air crackles with silence, the breaks between her steps sharper than the soft sound rubber sandals make on stones. The faint buzz of insects and quivering leaves, the trills of forgotten birdsong and the far-off bark of a dog, hurling its lonely questions into the crisp morning air.

In a nearby yard, a second dog barks loudly in response. Maggie stops, breathing in the stillness, the open sky and empty streets, the chill on her arms, the fields barely visible out at the edge of town, transported by the expanse and potential of the unmarked day.

A crow flies out from the maple tree behind her, wings whirring, cascading scorn. Startled, she looks up, shielding her face with her hand against the sun's glare. The crow circles, then lands on the tree ahead, cawing loudly, like a demanding child.

Maggie scuffs her sandals in the dirt, wriggling her toes. The dirt feels warm against her feet and the sun tingles on her exposed arms. It would be a good day for rambling — poking around this small town, perhaps finding a museum with settlers' lace or dinosaur bones, a park with a creek and yellow warblers singing in the willows, a rusted advertising sign for a forgotten brand of engine oil, or simply a chance to savour the heat and wind on her skin. But instead, what's ahead is another long drive cooped up in the van.

A pickup truck passes, coated with the dust of all the grid road trips yesterday, and all the days before that, its back bumper hanging loose on one side, rattling with each bump of the road. Maggie strides faster. The driver waves.

Another crow flies shrieking into the green of a taller maple where it's joined by others soaring in from nearby trees. Heads cocked and beady eyes winking, four birds stare down at Maggie. She slows to stare back, then quickens her pace. She can see the café sign now on a low orange building two blocks down the street. Several pickups have pulled into the parking lot and two large rigs have shouldered their way in beside them. Long-distance drivers. Either the food is reasonable or this is the only place around. Like Rob, these guys won't stop unless compelled to. Unlike Rob, they value food.

An old blue Thunderbird with Ontario license plates rolls slowly down the street and turns in. The driver, a young man in a denim jacket, gets out of the car and saunters inside. Back in high school, her first real boyfriend had a car like that. He moved that like, too, muscles taut and expectant. Mike, five years older, the crew boss with his dad's construction firm in the days when backseats meant steamy caresses and plans for adventure, not baby seats, diapers, and toys. His passion was rock climbing, and they'd mapped the Shield country for ridges, cliffs, and escarpments before he moved to Alaska to tackle Mount McKinley and never returned. Trapped in a glacier, a successful guide, or a prosperous builder? Maggie never learned the rest of his story.

She tugs her T-shirt straight, puts her palm against the café door below the large green BUS sign, and shoves it open. Inside, two burly men talk on cellphones at a table beside the window, while five in baseball caps drink coffee at stools along the counter.

From a room nearby, a radio blasts Springsteen's "Born to Run". As she sinks into a booth by the door, she senses the men turn. She glances at the window. The truckers aren't missing a beat in their separate calls as they size up her G-cup nursing-bra breasts, stare as she flicks back her long loose hair. She stares back for a moment, remembering her old guessing game: how much can you tell in one glance? Can you see who a stranger really is or where he's heading? A sexual spark or hint of danger? But those days are long past. She looks away.

"Coffee?" The waitress, in her late forties with red-streaked hair and green-glossed nails, holds out the pot.

"Yes, please."

"Where you headed?"

Maggie clenches her fingers around the warmth of her mug and looks down at her menu. "BC."

"My sister lives there." The waitress points to the back of the café. "That's her daughter helping out in the kitchen for the summer. We got her baby sleeping in the office."

"Quiet baby." Maggie eases her T-shirt loose from her chest and tugs it straight, hoping the dampness is sweat, and not milk.

"Why BC? All it does there is rain."

"Family." Maggie takes a sip.

"I'm on my way to Vancouver," one of the men calls over. "That's my rig outside. Big Red. That's what they call me, too. Big Red."

The other man lets out a high cackle. "Red, maybe. I don't know about big."

The waitress shakes her head. "Don't ask me — I'm married!" She tops up Maggie's cup. "All those wheels. Guess you're on the move, but me, I'm stuck right here. One day, though, I'm going south. Somewhere hot and dry all year."

"Hey, I had a load to Sedona last April. If I'd known you wanted a ride, I'd have stopped by."

"Red, next time you get a trip like that, you come and see me. I'll just leave a note on the counter, *Help Yourself.* She waves the coffee pot towards the farmers. "One of you tell my husband, in case he doesn't notice I'm gone!"

The men guffaw. Maggie turns to the window. In the parking lot, there are eight vehicles, eight possibilities her teenaged self would have quickly evaluated, back when decisions came with no visible price tags, when she carried only an oversized shoulder bag and a hand-painted sign. BANFF. MONTREAL. TO THE SEA.

The pickup trucks probably belong to the ball-caps at the counter. Farmers who live nearby, not even beyond the next town. No point talking to them. Drivers their age were never worth the trouble. They would spend their time lecturing about the risks she was taking, or trying to convert her to their Bible-thumping ways. The truckers? A better bet, glad of the company, no judgments levied. At least one might give her a lift, east or west or whichever direction he was headed. She could catch the bus here at the café, too, and get off in Winnipeg or Saskatoon or somewhere beyond both cities.

Or she could thumb down a ride on the highway, play the guessing game again, the roadside roulette that led once to a yacht near Halifax, once to a steaming hot tub high above Vancouver's English Bay.

And once, to a knife.

And to Rob, who'd screeched to a stop when he'd seen her at the side of the road, clutching her bleeding forearm. But it had only been a surface scratch. As she kept telling him, then and in the six years thereafter, she had been fine. Shaken, yes, and more than a little excited by the attention from the tall, blond salesman intent on rescuing her. He'd remembered first aid from his teens as a lifeguard, and had bandaged her wrist when she'd refused to go to a clinic or report the assault. Love at first sight, she and Rob had said. But as time passed and the baby came, she'd begun to wonder if what she'd thought was a sexual rush might have been just adrenaline. The effects of that long steel blade were greater than one slashed windbreaker.

Maggie takes a sip of coffee. It isn't too late. She can still walk away. Step out of her life. Hit the parking lot and keep going. Do not pass the motel. Do not stop for Rob or Jenna. Head for the road and freedom. Rob will take care of Jenna. He wants to be a manager, says he likes responsibility. Let him try that with his daughter. Let him feel what it's like to be buried so deep under a barrage of demands that you forget who you are or what you wanted from life, your focus narrowed to feeding, diapering, feeding, diapering, being wrenched from your sleep by shrieks, feeding, diapering. Repeat.

She smacks the cup down. She's never seriously toyed with leaving before, although back when she was finishing her art therapy classes, there was that morning after Rob came home drunk after a week out of town, when she'd had her coat on and was almost in the car. Until Rob ran bleary-eyed to the front porch, calling her.

Maggie stares out the window past the trucks and the dusty buildings of the town to the imagined highway and wide-open land beyond. This time, she could do it. She has credentials — she could find a new job. And Rob's sober. He'd learn to be a good dad. She could ride into a new life. Choose a mountain village or a farm, drink orange juice or red wine, dance all night or crash early in a hot bath before a long, deep sleep. Be far across the prairie before Rob wakes up, before he even realizes she's gone.

A shriek. A hungry, waking newborn. A girl about seventeen runs from the kitchen, pushing a limp strand of hair out of her face. Maggie feels a jolt of recognition at her wan skin and the dark circles of fatigue below her eyes. Lips tight, the girl lopes into the office and slams the door.

Maggie listens, wondering if the baby will settle or cry again, then realizes her own breasts have begun to prickle in response to its cries. She crosses her arms tightly against her chest, hoping the pressure will stop the milk from flowing, hoping the nursing pads in her bra will soak up enough to spare her the embarrassment of two sodden circles on the front of her T-shirt, the milk dripping from her stinging nipples down to her stomach. She grits her teeth and closes her eyes. Tears of exhaustion and frustration roll down her cheeks.

Babies. That all-consuming force that keeps their mothers hostage. If only she could seize the good parts of Jenna, the babbling baby whose smiles open like rosebuds, she could take her and flee. But no, Jenna is already a complex person, happy gurgles matched by colicky rage. The one couldn't come without the other.

And it isn't from Rob or Jenna she wants to escape: it's motherhood. She remembers the nursing mother she'd seen years ago in Banff, the one who'd screeched at her partner to help diaper the kid. Maggie had been shocked then by the transformation from Madonna to fishwife; now she understands.

"Hey, I don't mean to intrude." The man in denim from the T-Bird is standing by her table. "You all right?"

Maggie lets her arms drop, elbows resting on the table. "Fine. Just fine."

"It's, well — I heard you and the waitress. You looking for a ride somewhere?" He glances down at the logo on her purple T-shirt. "Back to Hawaii, maybe?"

Maggie tries to smile. He'd take her to the nearest city. She'd be independent. Free.

Then the baby in the office sobs again, and Maggie hears Jenna's morning coos and sees her pudgy fingers drop the yellow soother to reach up for a hug. She feels a burst of joy like singing and a throb of fear so bitter that her stomach lurches.

She swallows bile. "I have a ride."

"Hey, no worries, then. Okay?"

The crackle of Dire Straits' "Love Over Gold" surges from the radio, drowning the sounds of the baby from the office. The T-Bird backs out. A van pulls into his spot, and Rob gets out, with Jenna.

He strides across the cafe, sits down across from Maggie, starts to pass Jenna over, then sees the look on her face, and stops. "What's up?"

"I was hungry."

Jenna stretches out her arms, wriggling her fingers.

Maggie ignores her and takes a sip of cold coffee.

For a few seconds, Rob holds the baby in mid-air, then he swoops her up in a circle and back onto his lap. "I woke up and you'd gone."

Maggie picks up her serviette and wipes her hands.

"I was worried," he says.

"You looked asleep to me."

Rob stares at a cowlick on the baby's head. "Weird," he says, trying to twirl it flat. "I suddenly thought you'd left me. Us, I mean."

"I'm still here, aren't I?" Maggie looks up, then out the window at Red's rig. "It's all new to me, you know."

"Me, too," says Rob. He bounces Jenna on his lap, then pulls out his keys and jiggles them to distract her. He sets the keys slowly on the table, and finally meets Maggie's eyes, his face serious and sad. "But we're figuring it out, right?"

"Are we?" Maggie leans over to touch Jenna's hair, then takes the baby. She gives Rob a half-smile and cuddles Jenna's baby-powder warmth against her chest and shoulders. Closing her eyes for a moment, she imagines swaying alone across the suspension bridge high above that canyon on the coast, cold cables in her hands, the wind rough in her hair, facing risks only of her own choosing, responsible only for her own choices.

But Jenna was a choice. And the baby has her own plans. She starts rooting in her mother's T-shirt, tiny fingers gripping her breasts. Maggie glances around the café, then sighs. Who cares what these men think, or think they are seeing? Her skin will be masked by the cloth and Jenna. She unsnaps the top of her nursing bra and lowers Jenna to her breast. With snuffles of pleasure, the baby latches on.

"Rob, this is the scariest thing I've ever done, you know? Seriously, sometimes I can't even remember who I am."

"It *is* scary," says Rob. "But I thought you liked adventure. And you're not afraid of much."

Maggie glares at him. "Don't tell me how I feel! My world has shrunk to the baby!"

"And me?" asks Rob, moving to her side of the booth.

Maggie strokes Jenna's fine hair. "You, too. But you have your own life. Your office. I never thought I'd say this so soon, but I want to go back to work." Then she winces.

"Okay?" he asks.

"Yeah, she just bit me. Gummed me, I guess. It hurt, but — " Another quick intake of breath. Maggie's lips open as the baby's greedy tugs light circles of heat from her nipple and breast down across her belly, reminding her of the fire one glance from Rob used to start. She glances up, almost shyly. "Can we just stay here today?"

Rob raises an eyebrow and slowly smiles. "Jenna will be napping soon. We don't have to check out till 11:00 AM. Want to see how it goes?" He traces an imaginary line up the scar on her arm to her shoulder, and then draws his fingers lightly across the nape of her neck.

Maggie arches her neck against his soft caress and murmurs, "Yes." Outside the window, dust devils eddy along the maples and a pair of crows hop across the sidewalk, pecking through the remains of a takeout carton in the dirt.

Beating the Devil

Annette Bower

ADRIANNA FLIPPED OVER THE ONE-EYED black jack. "Where are you when that smug red queen needs you?" The neighbours' dog barked at the reflected light that flashed across the front lawn through her smudge-free picture window. "Ralph, you'd think that little yapper would recognize the six o'clock news." In the background a TV news anchor solemnly read, "The death toll has risen in tornado alley." Her discarded cards mocked her from the top of her solitaire tableau. A red king hung at the end of the longest row with little hope of finding his place in the front of the line where he belonged because there wasn't a red five in sight for the four of spades to cover.

Adrianna counted out three cards. Before turning them over with hopes of a progressive move, she slid her wedding band back over her knuckle. She really should cook something to eat. Picturing the chicken breast on the refrigerator shelf, slick under the plastic wrap, and the cookbook cover on the island that shouted *delicious meals for one* in bold black letters. "Who are they kidding?" she said. The idea of dragging out the rolling pin, crushing Ritz crackers, cracking an egg, lifting the cast iron pan onto the stove, was too much for just her. If she won this game, she'd eat the crackers, and warm up her cup of tea in the microwave.

Before Ralph departed to the hereafter, they might have discussed the environmental cost of electricity while he butterflied the chicken breast. She would have said, "The birds are dying because they're flying into blades on wind farms."

He could have said, "Adrianna, what's a few birds when they're generating power for many?"

"But the birds will become extinct." She would have poked her finger in the air.

He would have shrugged and said, "Birds or people, take your pick."

She turned over the cards. Nothing there to change this game. "Ralph, that weather woman is wearing that short skirt, you always commented on. She says it's going to be hotter than normal tomorrow." He might have flicked a dishtowel at her. But he wouldn't be smirking and saying that he really enjoyed climate change, ever again.

There wasn't anyone for her to discuss the senseless killings she'd heard about on the news, or the way families don't seem to speak to one another.

The theme song for Ellen, "Today's the Day", snuck into the room after the Mr. Clean commercial. Adrianna scattered the game formations. Kicking the legs of the card table out of her way, it was time for her to search out the answers she wanted about euthanasia, war, overspending, and that fashion accessory, the thongs, which had taken over the name of the rubber sandals she now had to remember to call flip-flops. These questions had been shoved in the background for far too long by her flipping red and black cards and occasionally "beating the devil."

SENIORS' DAY AT SAFEWAY WAS packed with coupon cutters. Her full personal rolling cart came after her like a faithful dog and nipped at the edge of her ankle boots. Stepping aside, she allowed the occupants of the Pine Tree Assisted Living complex to trudge past her toward their bus, clutching their few sacks containing the cookies and tea placed conveniently at eye level on the shelves, and toilet paper. Another question she'd find the answer to one day: Why do seniors' purchase tissue in the quantity that would keep a Girl Guide troop serviced for their summer adventures?

She waited for the old gent to activate the electronic eye allowing his escape with his cases of Diet Coke. She hoped it would accompany a good rye whiskey like Ralph used to enjoy, even though it was contraindicated for his medications. A notice on the bulletin board shimmered from the incoming whoosh of air. A large book, like an encyclopedia, surrounded in light and with bold cursive script, announced that the Seeing Soul Congregation was recruiting septuagenarians to discuss life issues.

This could be for her, she thought: as well as the web address someone had taken the time to cut into small vertical strips with the address and phone number, reminding her of the way her generation communicated, in person, and she certainly qualified because she had a few years beyond seventy.

She tucked the information into her bra. In the old days, Ralph used to be surprised by the treasures he'd found when they were frisky. Today the cashier had leaned toward her when her rusty voice croaked small, uneven, and unused.

BOARDING THE NUMBER NINE BUS, she flashed her senior's pass, collected her transfer to the number two and rode to the stop outside the beige brick, flat-roofed building with SEEING SOUL flashing in blue and yellow neon.

Adrianna recognized the repurposed elementary school. Back in the day there had been many children in this area, but that had obviously changed.

She pressed the bell as she had been instructed when she had phoned. Then she spoke her name into the intercom. The locking system clicked and the door slid open. The receptionist, with a face absent of wrinkles, glossy lips against twinkling white dentures, extended a smooth but age-spotted hand. "Welcome, Adrianna." On her other palm lay a deep purple binder she offered like a platter of treats. "As I informed you on the phone, this book contains the course study and a schedule for group meetings."

"When can I start?" Adrianna asked, "Ms?" glancing around the reception area for a name plate. Ms. No-name's lids dropped and displayed crepey eyelids before they lifted wide and she glanced at the clock. "You're just in time. Reverend Seeker's introductory seminar just started. Follow me."

Instead of the school motto painted on the wall or children's art work, there were inspirational sayings. Adrianna knew all about these words. They were similar to the sympathy cards telling her that Ralph was in a better place and her pain would pass. Murmurs came from an opening door where a figure emerged, covered from head to hem in a winter white robe. The apparition bowed slightly to Ms. No-name before carrying on down the hall and turned the corner. Notes on a piano followed by harmonized voices abruptly began and stopped as if a door had been opened and closed. They passed several rooms with the lights glowing from the small windows in the doors. Ms. No-name put her finger to her lips as she opened a door to a small room with five tub chairs. Three men and one woman occupied four and Ms. No-name pointed to a fifth. Adrianna's soles squeaked against the tiled floor while she crossed the room and took her seat. None of the other occupants looked up from their binders, while a man with flowing chestnut hair sat with his hands on his knees, swivelling his chair side to side. His voice, smooth and persuasive, brought to mind the salesman who convinced Ralph that every working man needed a car to match his personality. He drove the red Mustang until the end. Adrianna hugged her purse and binder to her chest, trying to focus on the topic of "a well-lived life".

Adrianna assumed this man, who stood and called upon the highest powers with a deep resonant voice that bounced off her chest like the too-loud drum beats at a dance, was the Seeing Soul's Reverend Seeker. Someone's hearing aid squealed, while another someone clicked his teeth. There wasn't any discussion but rather a one-way doctrine teaching. Adrianna was not going to jump to conclusions; she was sure once she read the material she'd be up to speed and ready when the discussion groups took place. The binders whispered closed, the leader stood, approached each chair, and laid his hands against the occupant's forehead. In turn, one bald, two thin-haired, and one tight-curled head dropped back with eyes closed. When the white-robed man approached Adrianna she looked straight into his hazel eyes. He merely bowed his head to her and floated out of the room on his Jesus sandals.

Slowly, one by one, the other occupants gathered their belongings and left the room without a word. This is the strangest bunch she'd witnessed in a long time. She too gathered her coat around herself, tucked her binder under her arm, and walked out of the building without seeing another soul.

AFTER THE SIX O'CLOCK NEWS, Adrianna spread a white-linen cloth over the card table and sharpened a pencil with Ralph's Legion crest. She checked the ink in the yellow highlighter. The purple binder in the centre looked as if it was floating in the cloud of white. She rummaged in the bottom drawer for a notebook. It had been years since she studied much of anything. Paging through the scribbled notes of Ralph's last doctor's appointments and which side effects of the drugs were worthy of an ambulance wasn't considered study, but necessary knowledge for survival. That hadn't worked anyway. This was a new time for her, discovering and discussing ideas with people in the same boat as her. *That's a lot of biblical references,* Ralph would have said, but he wasn't the one trying to find his way in a couples' world.

Coffee, black coffee is what she'd need to stay awake past nine; she wanted to be prepared. *You sound like a Boy Scout.*

"Go away, Ralph." With a sip and a deep sigh she opened the table of contents, and unscrewing the cap of the highlighter, she underlined "Pain Elimination."

At the mere mention of pain, her knee throbbed. She could do without pain.

Her eyes watered at the charts of the rising cost of drugs in direct relation to the pharmaceutical companies' rise in profits and then the declining donations to seniors' programs. Adrianna closed the book and poured herself a generous shot of brandy.

THE NEXT MORNING, BEFORE SHE began her double bus ride, she remembered Ralph's old briefcase, the perfect bag to cart the supplies.

In their room, Adrianna was pleased Seeker did all the talking because she hadn't gotten around to reading the whole book. But she wondered why their chairs didn't swivel.

Today the others nodded recognition when they left the building.

After the news and then procrastinating with *The Price is Right*, she finally sat at her table with her highlighter in hand. Adrianna thought about the blackened chicken Ralph used to make, giggling, at her crazy association because the assigned reading was "Cremation versus Casket" and huge hole in the earth.

With coffee and brandy by her side, she highlighted, "Dearly Departed." She hadn't exactly been "dearly" about anything in Ralph's departure. She was bloody angry. They were supposed to go on that Alaskan cruise and see the icebergs before they disappeared, but Ralph sailed instead. She had purchased gold thongs, to wear to the cruise ship's pool. Ralph had mimicked *flip flop, flip flop* when she modelled them for him.

Tipping the last drop of brandy over her tongue, she closed the book. Even during her secretarial courses, it had taken her a few days to find her study rhythm.

For the rest of the week, while Seeker's voice rose in earnest or dipped to a confidential whisper, Adrianna noticed Never-been-married's fingernails were bitten to the quick and washed-out black socks hung over Man-about-town's shoes. She knew there wasn't a woman in this man's life. After the class on Friday, he held the door and winked at her. Ha! She wasn't shopping for socks anytime soon.

On the weekend, it was easier to study with the brandy burning her throat raw when she read about living wills, trusts, appointing executors, and powers of attorney.

The following week, Adrianna noticed there were more men in the long winter white habits floating through the halls with black patent shoes sliding in and out of the fabric. They seemed to be the team leaders who handed out assignments when groups were ready for open discussions.

In the evenings, she studied her binder, and during the day she took her place of silence in the tub chair that seemed to be reserved for her.

At the end of the week, Reverend Seeker placed his hand on her forehead, and goosebumps pimpled her arms. This had been the first time a man had touched her in months. He proclaimed that next week the group could now have open discussions.

Adrianna was ready but Philip, the widower, was first. He pushed his palm across his sweaty scalp and asked the others if their pain had disappeared as his had done. They murmured in agreement. Philip praised the teaching that said there was no longer a need for their body's cells to fight each other and the money they'd spend on medications could be used for more meaningful endeavours.

Adrianna hoped her painful arthritis in her knees would disappear. She could use a little extra each month rather than spending it on pills and salves.

When it was Divorced Hugo's turn, he pointed to a section in their teachings that stated the evil in their lives was over. This meant that Adrianna would no longer have to hurry through the crosswalks because drivers would stop just for her, and if they didn't, well she wouldn't be here to worry about the consequences. *Wait a minute, if I'm not killed outright, I'll have one heck of a lot of pain.*

Never-been-married Marcia's assignment included holding hands and committing to doing no harm to anyone for the remainder of his or her life.

Adrianna winced. "That's a tall order for me, I have a short fuse for fools."

Marcia said she'd keep Adrianna in her thoughts.

Then, Reverend Seeker said, "Seeing Soul brothers and sisters, it is better to die on schedule, because it takes away the uncertainty for you and your loved ones." There was a small sigh of resignation and a few hopeful murmurs. That pronouncement sounded reasonable even though Adrianna didn't have anyone concerned with her demise. It had always been just her and Ralph.

While Marcia and Adrianna waited for the bus together, Marcia confided that she had looked after her parents who only recently passed away after depleting what they had always promised her for her future. But Marcia couldn't, or wouldn't, have them living in separate homes after sixty-five years of marriage.

At the next meeting, No-kids-for-me-John, the retired attorney, gave a lecture. "There are legal ramifications if you request someone to spread your ashes. It is against the law."

"Gives a new meaning to 'scattered to the four corners of the world'," Adrianna said.

Man-about-town Maurice, the retired financial adviser, turned on his computer, opened his laser pointer, and showed charts. "Unless you have prepaid arrangements, a casket with pallbearers is very expensive, whereas an urn with a drawstring bag needing only a small hole in the ground is much more economical."

"Wait a minute," Adrianna said, "I'm not sure about the ride into the furnace that would render me a pile of ash that would fit into a jar."

A white-robed man appeared by her side, to provide comfort she assumed. She'd noticed this silent support during other discussions from other groups.

"You'll be dead," Philip said.

Maurice, who had been downsized and never again found a position in his career field, continued with enthusiasm, "If you are considering leaving your worldly possessions to an animal shelter or hospital," he said, then paused.

The Reverend Seeker bent his head and said, "Please consider the needs of the Seeing Soul congregation."

"Yes, of course I was getting to the necessity of creating living wills to include our new home, the Seeing Soul community."

"Thank you, Maurice," the Seeker said.

BY THE END OF THE THIRD WEEK Adrianna had participated in the discussions, considered the arguments, and received her gold guild Right to Decide certificate in a fake oak frame.

Reverend Seeker said, "Congratulations Adrianna, you are ready to discover some answers from within by entering the vault of self-discovery."

Adrianna looked around and said, "Many of you have been in?"

Everyone near her shook their heads, but Reverend Seeker lowered his eyes.

"Adrianna, because of your age, we have put you on a top-priority list," said the white-robed man in attendance that day, slipping the shiny black toe of his shoe in and out of his habit. "It sometimes happens that members can't keep their appointments due to illness or an unscheduled death, so you may receive a call any time."

Though her heart seemed to stop for a moment, this was what she wanted: answers. "I'll be ready."

On the number nine bus, she recalled bits of financial history being written in notebooks. Adrianna wasn't wealthy, but after she sold her house she wouldn't have to worry about money. The hotel company wanted her property bad enough to keep her in clover, Ralph had said, but she wasn't quite ready. She wanted to learn things. She just kept hoping this was the right venue. Besides, she was considering having her fellow students over for dinner.

The bus driver commented on her scarf. "Weather's getting warmer, you've left your toque at home."

HER PHONE DIDN'T RING OFTEN, and her hand shook when she received the call. She agreed to be there within two hours and splurged on a taxi.

One of the white-robed elders met her at reception and led her down hallways she hadn't been before to a room where what looked like the door of an old-fashioned bank safe faced her. Adrianna raised her eyebrow at Maurice, Marcia, and John, who watched quietly from a corner. "Vault of Discovery."

"I need to blindfold you, Adrianna." The sleeves on the white robe billowed while he held up a purple bandana.

Her heart bumped against her ribs. "Okay."

"Take my hand." His fingers were cool and bony. "Now place both your hands on the door frame." He helped her lift one foot over the threshold, and then she pulled the other over the ledge. She steadied herself with one hand on the cold, dimpled wall. Neither spoke. Her bladder tightened when she heard the door being closed. Adrianna breathed deeply, her back against a cold wall. The physical dimensions of the space were a secret. The air circulated with a definite chill.

She reached up, untied her blindfold, and placed it beside the door. The room was in total darkness. Her words filled the space in long, drawn out syllables. "Euthanasia." *Deep breath.* "War." *Deep breath.* "Overspending." A giggle bubbled from her lips. "Thong."

With the back of her head touching the cold concrete wall she sunk to her bottom and when her feet stretched out in front of her, her polyester slacks snagged on the cement floor. Her silver-coloured, silk thong underwear slid tight between her cold butt cheeks and pulled against parts of her that hadn't been stimulated since Ralph died. Aha! Her usual full brief was a layer of protection against sensual memories. How could she argue with that answer?

She snapped her fingers and extended her arms as far out as she could reach. She felt as if she had lost her eyes. Her heart banged and her stomach acids babbled. Her new blood-red gel fingernails were out there somewhere. She felt formless.

Adrianna crossed her arms over her soft breasts. Her fingers found the cross-your-heart presence and underwire support. She was real.

The steady *tick, tick* of her watch calmed her. Her mind stilled for a second, then longer. She shifted her legs. Her hip brushed up against a corner. With her head turned, her nose pressed into a smooth surface. The aroma of Evening in Paris perfume filled the space. Could it be? She walked her fingers from one cement join to another until she stood. Her nose followed the scent. Her head filled with the memory of her grandma's voice singing, *Good night Adrianna, good night. I'll meet you in your dreams.* Then Grandma whispered, *Adrianna, be five again. Play Cowboys and Indians. Here's your gun.*

Adrianna's tongue clicked against the roof of her mouth and the edges of her dentures.

She swallowed the saliva that pooled between her gums and cheeks. She pulled air in through her nostrils and pushed it slowly out of her mouth. She scrunched down but she kept one toe against the wall.

A sound shattered in her room.

"Get out of my space," she commanded. "Bang." She pulled her trigger finger. Invasion of space equals war. Adrianna struck another question from her list.

The Reverend Seeker's voice surrounded her and echoed: "Seeing Soul Adrianna, your hour is up."

"I'm not ready. Charge the extra time to my Visa." Suddenly it made sense, credit cards were for overspending.

The sound system buzzed, then silence. She breathed deeply. Her curious mind contemplated her answers.

Flattening her hand against her thigh, she knelt on both knees then crawled away from the wall. She lay on the floor with her arms outstretched, her hair snagged against the cement, her pelvis tilted and her back arched. Then her feet automatically crossed at her ankles. She felt a familiarity in the pose. She had seen it on the crucifix that hung in many churches. Since she believed in a human's right-to-life, didn't it follow then that she also believed that she had a right to end her life when she saw fit?

The reverend promised a gentle and easy death when the time came.

Adrianna stretched. A tingling began in her perhaps-again region and joy akin to beating the solitaire devil in record time pulsed through her body. She could control her overspending, she wouldn't fight for space, she didn't have to submit to euthanasia yet, but she could purchase a different style of underwear and be a sensual woman again. She rolled over and crawled to the wall. She felt along it until her fingernails poked the door hinges.

"I'm ready. Open up."

The door swung open and the Reverend Seeker was surrounded by light.

"Seeing Soul Adrianna, did you find your answers from within?"

"Yes, and strangely from without, too." She felt her lips twitch toward a smile. She stepped over the ledge.

His green eyes with brown spearing out from the pupils focused on her while he extended his arm toward her. "Would you like me to arrange a meeting with our lawyer?"

Adrianna reached up and tapped the reverend on the side of his head, her concession to not causing harm.

"I won't be returning."

She walked away without looking back.

Hello in There

Annette Bower

MY NAME IS MURIEL SEYMOUR. I live at 433 Jackson Avenue, in Destiny, Saskatchewan.

Memory in place. Check. Today, I don't have to make the call to move to the next level of restricted living. My armpits sweat just thinking about a four-bed ward with the smell of old breath, skin, the sight of empty teeth containers on the bedside table, and care aides swearing at me while they search the sheets for my dentures. I should be able to microchip my teeth like they do for a dog or cat's ear. I'll ask my denturist at my next appointment. He'll probably tell me that anything is possible with enough money.

About twenty years ago, a bunch of us attended a walking fitness class at the community hall. To maximize inner thigh muscle strength, the instructor, in her Lycra exercise outfit, suggested we practice walking as if we were wearing a diaper. We laughed. Now, I need leakage protection when I go out. Those muscles are used. I only wish I could dance like the woman who wears her protection in the TV advertisement.

Enough, you can walk with your walker. The stroke didn't steal everything. The sun still rises in the morning and sets at night and I have my wheels, both push power and gasoline driven.

Nora, Inga, and I are friends but oddities in Destiny. We don't host bridge or bake for the church sales. None of us have children living near so we depend on each other to check if we are alive each morning. More so for Inga and me because we're on our own. Nora has Joe when he's not in hospital.

But today is our freedom day when I drive us out of the valley onto straight blacktop to the city where no one knows our history. *Relax rectum! You clench every time I lock the front door and stand at the top of this ramp, wishing my old student, Raymond, now local handyman, would have scored higher in his geometry test.* "We manifest what we see." I see going down this ramp at a controlled speed.

It's good times, when my baby purrs to life with just the turn of a key, a full gas tank, and because my mechanic friend Inga knew all about hand controls for a car and how to get them, I have freedom.

"Here I come, Angel of Mercy, Nora."

There are segments in our lives that determine the paths we take. Nora almost became a Sister of Mercy, until Joe found his way past her habit. Now he calls her his Angel of Mercy. She deserves this title from him, half the town, and me, too. She appeared at my door when I came out of hospital, and still needed help having a shower. "You don't have anything I've never seen before," and "I'll keep you safe," she said. Then on Tuesdays and

Thursdays, for months, she brought soup and fresh baked bread. I asked permission to address her as my angel, but she laughed and said, no, that was something special between her and Joe.

I steer around the ruts in Nora's driveway. After three short bursts on the horn, I watch the front room curtain, until it twitches and Nora waves. The trees are bare and the air smells of burning poplar. Fall is definitely here and winter not far behind.

Finally, Nora grips the handrail while moving slowly down the steps of her mobile home, and shuffles toward the car. Propping her rear onto the seat, she pushes with her thick legs until she is inside, and then closes the door. Kissing her fingertips, she turns them toward the window of her home.

"Everything okay, Nora? You're looking a little pale."

"Fine." Nora huffs. "I have a lot to do before the anniversary party on Sunday."

"I thought the kids were doing everything."

"You know how it is. It's just easier to do it myself." Nora wiggles for comfort.

"You're supposed to have learned how to delegate by your age." Times like this, I'm glad I don't have kids of my own.

"Forget it, Muriel." Nora says. "Joe's not getting better. I want everything perfect. This could be our last anniversary together."

Nora wipes the perspiration from her forehead with a wad of tissue. "Do you have our lottery numbers?"

"Not this week. It's Inga's turn." And I'm worried about *my* memory.

"When we get into the city, can we go to a kiosk in a mall? I need to pick up a few more things.

"There's a strip mall on the east side, it has a Safeway."

Nora nods. "That'll do."

"You haven't cracked one joke or passed on the tiniest bit of gossip since we left your house," I say. "You're definitely not yourself."

Nora doesn't answer. She pulls at the seat belt and extends it farther from her chest, and sucks air noisily through her teeth.

"Is the belt not working properly?"

"It must be caught on something. It's tight."

"Maybe it's your coat. It was okay the last time we went out."

"There's Inga!" Nora wags her hand in the general vicinity of a small, clapboard cottage behind a white picket fence. I slow the car and it drifts to a stop.

While we watch Inga stride to the passenger back door Nora whispers, "Where does she find her hats? At Value Village?"

"Hi der, ho der, ladies."

"What in the world are you doing with that car?" I wave at a rusted green Lada in the driveway.

"We're putting on the winter tires. Soon it will snow and it will be ready."

"You know, Inga, just because a car has four wheels doesn't mean it should be driven." Nora winks at me without her usual enthusiasm.

"You make do with what you have," Inga chants. Then she talks about tire treads, jacks, and lug nuts as if they were old friends, while I drive over speed bumps, around potholes, and stop for a mom pushing a stroller across the street.

My friends help me enjoy what I have, and if anything happens to me before them, they'll benefit from my estate. I check my mirrors before I merge onto the highway and the town of Destiny disappears from view behind us.

"But I have to admit," Inga leans forward, her hands pressing against the front seat, "this week I put on my lottery list a brand new red, half-ton truck."

"What . . . the hell are you going to do with a truck?" Nora asks. "You'll be seventy soon."

"What does that have to do with a truck? A truck hauls things. I just drive."

"What's next? A garage?" Nora asks, her breathlessness hiding some of the consonants.

"Sure, if there is enough lottery money." Inga sits back. "I'm helping Shirley's boy figure out four- and two-stroke engines. If you know engines, then you can understand life." A residual garlic scent rides out on a big breath. "I just wish I could help him with the new engines."

"I taught Pete in high school," I say. "He had a slower way about him even then."

Inga presses her hand to her forehead. "Engines brought food to my table and something to puzzle about when life wasn't so good."

The winter tires growl along the pavement. "Maybe after I teach him, he'll be able to make a living in this fast world. Someone needs to keep the old ways alive."

"Sort of like us," Nora says.

"Muriel, did you think of something new to add to your wish list?" Inga asks. Her familiar *eau d'oil* wafts toward us.

"No, it's the same as always," I say, glancing quickly over my shoulder. "I'd buy blue-chip to firm up my portfolio."

"That bear market really bit you," Inga says as if she's been watching a market pundit on CNN.

"True, and every day it seems harder for me to manage alone. But when we win, I'll hire anyone I need so I can stay at home."

"Yah, then no one has to worry about where to put you. It's good to be positive, Muriel." Inga reaches to the front seat and pats my shoulder.

"Guess what I added this week?" Nora wheezes.

"Something silly again, I suppose," Inga calls from the back seat.

"You might say that!" Nora breathes deeply, "now that Joe's on oxygen twenty-four hours a day."

"You're sounding like you could use some of that oxygen, Nora." Her skin is tinged blue around her mouth.

"Let me finish. The TV's always on. So, I got this idea. Joe likes to look at pretty girls. I'll have one of those hot-tub beer parties in our backyard, for Joe. I saw a hot tub rental ad." Nora coughs into her sleeve. "They send the girls in the bathing suits, too."

"That'd keep his ticker going for a while longer," Inga says.

"Nora, that's sexist!" I frown and purse my lips.

"But fun," Nora says.

"You don't take this very serious." Inga folds down each thick finger as she lists. "You have a trip to the fat farm, a face lift, and a home security system so you can lock yourself in and out."

"That's me," Nora sputters, "always kidding around."

"Nora, stop pulling on the seat belt, it's annoying!" I'm agitated when things don't function properly.

"You sick, Nora?" Inga asks.

"Just indigestion." Nora's head arches back as she rubs her chest. "It's hot. Open a window."

"Inga! Nora's in trouble. I'm pulling onto the shoulder. Come 'round the front and help her."

"Sure. Hurry, Muriel." Inga touches Nora's shoulder.

The Skylark grinds to a halt. The back door flies open. The front door pulls free. The highway traffic continues humming past us at one hundred kilometres an hour.

I turn on the four way flashers, crane my neck and scan the passenger floorboards. "Her purse is next to her feet. Find her nitroglycerin! I'll call 9-1-1."

"We have a friend with heart trouble . . . Yes, she's still conscious . . . "Nitroglycerin . . . Highway 11, ten kilometres from the city . . . Hurry. Yes, I'll stay on the line."

"Nora? Nora, how're you feeling?" Inga releases the seat belt.

"Pretty good, and you?"

"Nora, stop fooling! How's the pain?" Inga reaches for Nora's wrist.

"Big."

"Here, let me put these pills under your tongue." Inga glances my way worriedly. "What did the ambulance say?"

"Stay where we are. They'll be here as soon as possible. Nora, don't you do anything stupid. You've got that anniversary on Sunday."

"Shh, Muriel," Inga says.

"I feel so bloody useless. My walker is in the trunk." I jab my thumb against the seat belt release button.

"What you going to do? Walk for help? No. We stay. Should we call Nora's kids?"

"Those no-good-for-nothings. If they'd help her out once in a while this wouldn't happen." I'm scared.

"Hey, gals, I'm still here."

"Shh, Nora." Inga pats our friend's puffy hand.

"Do you know how they make holy water?" Nora asks.

"Nora, enough already, keep your strength!" Inga says.

"They boil the hell out of it," Nora whispers.

"One of your nun jokes, I assume." I scan the clear blue bowl of a prairie sky and the horizon for a dot with flashing lights to crest the hill. "Yes, look, the ambulance is coming."

"I can't hear a thing." Nora gulps for air, "They say hearing is the last to go."

"Maybe they got some cute paramedics to keep your ticker going, Nora," Inga says.

"I like a good bum," Nora's eyes glisten with unshed tears. "Joe has a nice bum."

"Your humour might save you, but it will be the death of me." My muttering is swallowed by the windshield while the ambulance parks in front of the car.

Inga searches Nora's purse, and passes on the practical information, and health insurance card.

Nora waves Inga over to the gurney.

The attendant closes the back door and climbs into the passenger seat. The ambulance speeds away and soon becomes a soundless flash of lights in the distance.

"She told me, 'Don't tell yet.' She doesn't want Joe worrying." Inga scrambles into the front seat. "Come, Muriel, let's get going!"

"I need a minute. Something like this makes me think about life."

"Sure, but can you think and drive?" Inga reaches over and turns off the flashers.

The Skylark flies down the highway past the last combines moving across the field, harvesting a crop before the snow comes.

"What should we do now?" I ask Inga, the practical one.

"I'll petition the Holy Mother to save Nora." Inga's hand drags worn rosary beads from her pocket. She kisses the crucifix.

"Do you really think Nora's and your God might take her before the anniversary?"

"Muriel, you do your positive thoughts to the universe and I'll petition my way." Inga's beads clatter.

"Survival isn't always the answer, you know."

"Yah, I know. But she's not ready. She and Joe need this party." Inga is silent. The heater fan roars. The tires thud across the repaired cracks in the asphalt.

"My way is working. Look at all the green lights to help us get there faster." Inga holds up her beads.

"Or it's my steady speed that is getting us through the city." I switch on the left turning signal. For a change, a handicap spot is empty at the emergency entrance of the Pasqua Hospital. I pop the trunk latch and Inga hops out of the car, then lifts the wheeled walker. "We're a good team." Inga snaps the trunk closed.

My legs feel heavier than usual and my head aches. Inga strides confidently through the doors.

When I'm beyond the swing of the automatic door, I see that she is talking to the information clerk. The antiseptic odour worms its way up my nose; it demands recognition of arbitrary and unexplained illnesses and deaths, which take place in beds behind the doors.

"We've got to wait in here." Inga turns toward the dimly-lit, climate-controlled waiting area with its grey high-back chairs and buzzing TV.

We sit side by side. Inga wearing her plaid driver's cap and me with fly-away, blue-tinged hair, staring at the emergency room door.

Inga fumbles the pages of a dog-eared *Readers' Digest* on her lap.

I pick lint from my black polyester pants, trying to calm the pain behind my right ear.

"Muriel, what's the matter?"

"I have to find the restroom."

"The nurse is coming."

"You go to Nora."

Inga helps me stand. "I'll catch up."

"You don't look so good."

"Go."

I bump the walker through the wide door with the universal sign for toilet, bolt it, and then the pain rips through my skull.

The tiles feel cool against my cheek. My name is Muriel.

Flying

Linda Biasotto

DEE LIFTS FROM HER CHAIR on the Reeds' front porch.

Gino Andrelli is too engrossed in a long anecdote to notice her rise. He keeps his Sicilian-blue eyes on Elizabeth Reed's crossed legs while she admires how the dimple on his cheek deepens with each puff on his pipe. It's only her husband Gregory Reed, face mottled by the shadows of the young oak, who salutes Dee with his glass.

With a half-rotation, she passes through the Reed's front door, a diver gliding through glass. She floats into the living room where scrims shiver with each breath of the young man, the tip of his tongue exposed as he lies on the velvet couch. One hand follows the rise and fall of his breast; the other rests on his blue-jeaned thigh.

Like a weather vane pirouetted by a changing wind, Dee swings and flies to the foot of the stairs. Mr. Andrelli's laugh scoops her to the second floor while Pryor sleeps below on the velvet couch, exposing the tip of his tongue.

Tanya's cat swaggers along the upstairs hallway, yellow fur trailing sulfurous smoke. He angles his head against Tanya's door, pushes it wide enough for Dee to follow. And she does follow, swimming in the grey room where Tanya lies on her side like a tipped statuary. Carved curls frame her smooth face. A hand beneath her chin curves in a question mark.

The cat leaps to the bed, settles against Tanya's bare leg. It bares its fangs and hisses when Dee reaches to touch the scar on Tanya's chin.

Dee whirls toward the window. Porcelain dolls on the dressing table hike their ruffled skirts in a frenzied cancan, the mirror reflecting the bed but not Dee, who hovers before it.

She flies out between the grey curtains until she stops suspended over the pointed leaves of the lilac hedges and the dried husks of their dead flowers. The heat dances about her, snapping yellow and white streamers against her bare arms. The sun bleaches the air into white translucence and dazzles the windows below.

Dee closes her eyes, gives in to the light and the red-spangled stars. Slowly at first, then faster, she falls.

WHEN SHE AWAKES MRS. REED looks ready to jab her with a pink fingernail. Instead, she gives Dee a dirty look and turns back to Mr. Andrelli. "I apologize for the girl's bad manners, Gino. Do go on with your story."

He waves a hand. "Is funny, no, how hot weather makes the young ones sleep like *bambini* and here we old ones sit, wide awake?"

Dee is grateful her hair hides her face as she reaches down for her lemonade. How will she make it through the rest of today and Sunday morning? Why did she agree to a sleepover at Tanya's when girls at school told her she was crazy? Couldn't she see how stuck-up Tanya was and how she thought she was better than Dee? But come Monday morning, they'll want to know everything, and Dee already has enough information to keep them interested for days.

THIS MORNING, SHE RODE TO the Reed's black and white two-story on the bike she bought with babysitting money. Everything about the new house sparkled, from the windows to the brass doorknob. The veranda was a white barge ready to detach and float across the new lawn. She pushed her bike round the side to where she leaned it against the garage, and then carried her paper bag to the door. Through the screen she smelled bleach and onions. She pressed the bell.

Tanya bounced into the porch and opened the door. "Take off your shoes." She grabbed the paper bag. "Did you bring me something?"

Dee unbuckled her sandals, and then Tanya thrust the bag back at her. "Most people use suitcases."

"A suitcase won't fit in my bike basket."

"Why didn't your mother drive you?"

"She doesn't drive."

Tanya swivelled away. "What do you think of our kitchen?" The appliances were the same brown as the cupboards and countertops. Brown and white curtains framed the window.

"I like it. Nicer than ours, for sure."

Mrs. Reed stood at the chrome-edged counter about to smack a hard-boiled egg with a spoon.

"This is my mother."

Mrs. Reed turned. She wore a black, sleeveless top and a pink apron longer than her white shorts. "So you're Tanya's little friend." Her green eyes seemed to pick up Dee and set her down. "What's in the bag?"

"Mo-ther. Egg salad *again*?"

Mrs. Reed lifted the spoon and hardboiled egg next to her ear as though expecting a transmission. "I'm sure your friend doesn't mind egg salad."

Dee hugged the bag to her chest. "I'll eat anything. Mom says I have a cast-iron stomach."

"Tanya told me your mother has a job, but I forget doing what."

"Mother, you know I told you this morning she's a cleaning lady."

"Good at sewing, too." Mrs. Reed's eyes scrambled over Dee's homemade green paisley top and matching shorts before she turned back to her eggs.

"Come on."

Dee followed Tanya through a red-carpeted dining room with an oval table and eight chairs. On the table stood a large dish of toffees. The red carpet continued into the living room with its velvet sofa and two matching chairs. On one wall hung a starburst clock and beneath it a golden cat curled on a chair. It watched through slit eyes.

Tanya waited with one foot on the bottom stair facing the front door. "I wouldn't pet Wilbur if I were you. He bites."

Dee withdrew her hand and followed Tanya. Halfway upstairs, she stopped to look at a framed photograph of a girl holding a baby.

"That's me and my sister, Beth. She's twelve, now, but still chubby. Boys make fun of her at school and Mother keeps putting her on diets. Father says she'll slim out but Mother and I don't believe him."

Upstairs, Tanya pointed down the hall. "Bathroom's the one with the toilet. This is my room."

A pattern of three-dimensional diamonds covered the wallpaper and the bedspread; the drapes sheets and pillowcases were the same lime green. How could Dee ever invite Tanya into her room with the bumpy walls and broken blind?

Tanya dropped onto the bed and tucked her sleeveless white blouse into her shorts. "I expected you sooner. Close the door."

Dee shut the door and set down her bag. Besides the bed, the only place to sit was the stool in front of the dressing table. She studied the china dolls lined up there, each with a painted face and bright ruffled skirt. After sitting, she checked the mirror to make sure the narrow straps of her top covered her white bra. "I couldn't leave until I finished vacuuming and dusting my room. Mom makes me do it every Saturday."

"Really? My mother does everything for me and Beth. My sister plays the cello in her school band and wants to be in an orchestra when she grows up. I can see her, this woman with two chins going at it on stage. The orchestra dresses in black, you know." Tanya used both hands to smooth her brown curls. "I suppose she'll become famous and make loads of money. I don't know what it is about this family; we can't seem to do anything without making heaps of money. My grandfather's rich and owns a humongous house and a cottage and a boat."

Sunlight snagged on Tanya's scar and turned it into a luminous glow-worm.

She stretched her arms overhead and fluttered her hands to her chest. "Pryor thinks I could be a ballet dancer. He says I have the figure for it." She flopped onto her side and looked at Dee. "Oh, I haven't told you about him. He's my boyfriend and lives next door with his father. They're Italian, but Pryor was born in Canada. He has the dreamiest eyes. My summer romance. He'll do anything for me. It's kind of pathetic, but I like it. Some men will do anything for love. You don't have a boyfriend, do you?"

"Sure I do." Dee couldn't admit her mom wouldn't allow her to date, yet. Not that anyone had asked.

"Funny you never mention him. What's his name?"

"Mark. And he's finished school. He works pumping gas and stuff. At a gas station. We broke up two weeks ago and that's why I don't talk about him."

"I've had four boyfriends, not counting my secret romances. I think Pryor looks just like James Dean before he went and got himself killed in a car accident. Wasn't that *tragic*?"

"I suppose."

"Golly, you're such a yacker in class, always putting up your hand, Miss Know-it-all. What are we going to do with you until tomorrow? Oh. Mother says you have to come with us to mass. I said you wouldn't mind and she said she didn't care *what* you minded."

"I've been to church before. I got baptized at St. Theresa's."

"Do tell."

"Hail, Mary." Dee pretended to look out the window. "Nope. Sun, Mary."

"Pryor didn't want me to ask you over for the weekend, but Mother made me. She thinks I'm spending too much time with him." Tanya pulled a green cushion to her stomach. "She's scared I'm going to get p.g. like she did."

"What's p.g?"

"Gosh, you're dumb. *Pregnant.* Mother was pregnant with me before my parents got married. They think I don't know. Okay. So if you could date any Beatle, who would it be?"

P.g. was information Dee's mom had neglected to pass on to her. She wanted a drink of water but was afraid Tanya would make her face Mrs. Reed alone. "Ringo's funny."

"A guy shouldn't waste his time being funny. He should tell you you've got beautiful eyes. And buy you stuff. Did your boyfriend give you things?"

"Sure."

Tanya lowered her voice. "Do you want to know a secret?" She patted the bed next to her. "Sit here because we have to whisper."

Dee, perched at the edge of the bed, squeezed her knees together and smelled Tanya's skin, a mixture of talcum powder and sweat. "Why do we have to whisper?"

"Mother listens. Once when I had a friend over, I tiptoed to the door and opened it fast. Mother fell right in. Do you wonder why Pryor's name is Pryor?"

"No."

"I told you his father's Italian," Tanya said in an impatient voice.

"So?"

"Pryor's mother is from *England,* not Italy like Mr. Andrelli tells everyone. He says she got sick and died, but she didn't. She ran away with another man. Whatever you do, you can't breathe a word of this to anyone. Pryor made me swear never to tell. He told me because he said lovers tell each other everything so of course I had to tell him about my romance at church camp."

There was a click.

"Lunch," said Mrs. Reed before withdrawing her head. She left the door open.

Tanya raised her brows. "Not a word."

In the bathroom was a dish of guest soaps. Afraid to ruin any, Dee merely rinsed her hands before using a green towel. The tub and sink and toilet were gold. Green covers stretched across the toilet's seat and tank; a small rug fit at the base. Everything in the room matched. It was only Dee who was out of place.

She felt out of place at the dining room table, too, where Mr. Reed waited and tapped the tablecloth with his fingers. He stood to take her hand, shook it gently as though afraid her bones were fragile. "I'm pleased to meet you." He waved to the chair placed between his and Tanya's.

The table was set with white plates trimmed in gold. The egg salad sandwiches were cut diagonally, the triangles layered on a platter matching the plates. A small plate held two kinds of pickles. Lemon slices and ice cubes floated in a glass jug. On the sideboard waited a homemade, frosted carrot cake.

Mr. Reed lifted the white platter and offered Dee a sandwich. He asked what her favourite subject was, if she'd read any exciting books, did she think bell-bottom pants would stay in style, and then listened as though her answers mattered. He made her nervous, the way a good-looking boy made her feel if he nodded hello.

Beth dropped onto her chair and reached for a sandwich. She didn't say a word during the meal. Mrs. Reed told her to stop slouching and slapped her hand when she reached for a third sandwich.

Tanya told Dee about the trip to Banff her family took last summer and described the fancy hotel with a pool they stayed in. "How much did it cost to stay there, Mother? Each night."

Mr. Reed shook his head. "Sweetheart, that subject's a bit rude."

"Since when? You and Mother talk about money all the time. You told Mr. and Mrs. Ahl how much you paid for Beth's cello and I could tell they weren't interested."

No one answered. Mrs. Reed stood, collected plates and passed out clean ones for the dessert. Dee forced herself to eat a slice of cake, said no to a second helping, and told Mrs. Reed how good it tasted. It was the first time Dee ate cake that had no taste.

AFTER LUNCH, MR. REED DROVE Beth and two friends to the swimming pool at Kildonan Park. Mrs. Reed poured glasses of lemonade over ice and insisted they all relax on the front porch and work on their tans. She took care to face her chair to one side and told Dee to take the chair next to hers, while Tanya moved her chair closer to the house.

The front door of the neighbour's opened and two men emerged. Mrs. Reed stood and waved. Both men had slicked hair and bright blue eyes, but the younger was taller and although they declined Mrs. Reed's offer of lemonade, the older man did accept the offer of an ashtray. Mrs. Reed sent Tanya inside to fetch one and after she returned, Pryor stood against the wall by her chair. Mr. Reed was the only one in the shade, his chair angled halfway between the street and the house.

Mrs. Reed crossed her legs. "What do you think, Gino, will there be a storm tonight? It's been incredibly hot."

"Ah, Sicily is *mucho* hotter."

"Aren't you glad there are refrigerators now and not those awful iceboxes that dripped all over the floor?"

"In my hometown, no one has this. When I visited my mamma and say 'I have a stove, is electric,' she can no believe."

Dee expected Tanya to stand and say they were going up to her room. Instead, she announced she was sleepy and left without a word to Dee who expected Mrs. Reed to call Tanya back and tell her it was rude to leave a guest. But Mrs. Reed said no such thing. Was this how it was with families who had both parents and lived in two-storied houses with crystal bowls heaped with caramels? (Help yourself, Mrs. Reed had told Dee after lunch, and then frowned after Dee scooped a handful.)

The older man pulled a pipe from his breast pocket and struck a match. Not until he made a point of staring over the flame at Dee did Mrs. Reed make introductions. "Gino, this is Tanya's friend from school. Dee, this is Mr. Andrelli."

He rose, took Dee's hand in a strong grip, which he held for several seconds. "Am pleased to meet you. And this is my son, Pryor." Mr. Andrelli clapped his hand on Pryor's shoulder.

As soon as his father sat, again, Pryor headed for the veranda stairs. "I had a late night and I'm going home for a nap. See you later, *Babbo*."

Dee watched him disappear around the corner of the Reeds' house. If he was headed home, he was going the wrong way. The ensuing conversation centred on people she didn't know and she wondered what excuse she could give for going inside. When Mr. Andrelli began a story about himself and another passenger on a train,

Dee set her glass on the boards beneath her chair and leaned back. She closed her eyes then opened them. How embarrassing it would be if she fell asleep in front of these people.

And then she felt herself rise.

Contributor Notes

SHELLEY BANKS

THE WOMAN AT THE REST stop hums a Beatles' song and stares across the fields. There's someone in her blue SUV, but instead of joining them, she saunters to a strip of weeds beside the road. Is she a naturalist looking for wildflowers or dragonflies? Deep in thought, perplexed by a family crisis? Or simply stretching her legs before heading back on the road?

On the highway, a black van eases alongside me. Its cruise control must be set only slightly faster than mine, and we drive in tandem for a while. First glance: The woman in the passenger seat is scowling. Next: She's waving her arms. Last: She's scrambling into the back seat. I slow down to let them pull away, wishing I could see through their darkened rear windows. Was she getting a drink from a back-seat cooler? Finding the map? Or comforting a child?

There are no answers on the road, only stories. "Redwing" and "As the Crow Flies" came from moments like these.

My fiction, non-fiction, and poetry appear in literary magazines, and I have one poetry collection, *Exile on a Grid Road* (Thistledown Press, 2015).

BYRNA BARCLAY

THE STORY OF THE THREE sisters in love with the same man is the most completely fictive novel I've ever written, especially since I was an only child with no notion of what it's like to have a sibling. I stumbled upon the story at the Saturday Art under the Umbrellas in La Quinta, California when I found three clay and ceramic sculptures by Joanne Collins. "They're three sisters," I cried, "and they're in love with the same man." The first had branches for arms on which perched two red cardinals. The second held a birdcage which contained a pair of baby shoes that I decided belonged to the third sister, who, the artist told me, had a dowel in one leg. The third sister's birdcage held only words: Peace, Hope, Love. The cages looked like hobo art, which led me to invent the character of Boxcar Bill alias Lucky, a mysterious trekker who jumps off a freight train in June of 1935 just before the Regina Riot — and into the arms of the sisters. When published the novel will be my eleventh publication, the most recent being *Forest Horses*, from Coteau Books, and *House of the White Elephant*, Burton House Books, which won Best Fiction in the inaugural Whistler/Tidewater Awards, 2016.

Many years ago, while president of the Saskatchewan Division of the Canadian Mental Health Association, I toured the Weyburn hospital and was awed by the mural of the Regina Riot painted in the basement by former patient Jim Eadie, who was nine years old during the Riot. Because I know nothing more about the man, the character of Lucky Boxcar Bill, like the women he loved and left, is completely fictitious.

LINDA BIASOTTO

I WRITE TO ILLUMINATE THE plights of the disadvantaged, those experiencing common, yet seldom articulated problems. Besides greed and hate, my stories dabble with different types of mental illnesses, including madness, depression, and PTSD. My writing explores the psychological challenges experienced by real people dealing with anarchic events.

"The Virgin in the Grotto" was first published in *Sweet Life,* a collection of short stories published by Coteau Books.

ANNETTE BOWER

MY STORIES REFLECT MY DAY-TO-DAY experiences as a nurse, administrator, town councillor, teacher's assistant, and student. They are about the place where I live and my neighbours. My short stories and novels are read around the world. They are set in Saskatchewan because I believe my home is as exotic as anywhere else in the wide world I have visited.

An earlier version of "Hello in There" was published as "The Friends' Way", *Green's Magazine,* Spring 2003. The title was inspired by the song, written and performed by John Prine. With the publication of "Beating the Devil" and "Hello in There", I will have published thirty-four short stories and three novels, the most recent being *Fearless Destiny.*

BRENDA NISKALA

I GREW UP IN, AND will always return to, the hills near a small Finnish settlement in west-central Saskatchewan called Rock Point. It's not on any map. When I visit my Finnish relatives, I am always struck by how their world view was shaped by compromise, and protected by isolation. I wanted to look at this a bit closer, at the time before city-states, before Christianity. How did this small group of people, the ancestors of my parents, maintain not only their language and their culture, but their distinct world view when up against the power of the Viking? As a Canadian the issue of cultural retention is of deep significance to me. I believe we are enriched by diversity, and I am saddened by the prospect of a homogenous world.

The Khanty giant, Bogatyr, was the subject of a recent archeological dig. His injuries are documented, but the manner of his death is not known. He was greatly honoured in burial. He is the only actual historical character in this excerpt from a yet-to-be-published novel.

My books include several chapbooks of poetry and two books of poetry: *Ambergris Moon* (Thistledown Press) and *How to Be River* (Wild Sage Press). I have also published *Of All the Ways to Die* (Quattro), a novella, and *For the Love of Strangers* (Coteau Books), a collection of linked stories.

KELLY-ANNE RIESS

I AM INTERESTED IN THE unhappy character — the person who doesn't have it all, who doesn't fit in and has to struggle to find her or his place in the world. These are characters on the cusp of change. "Bus Ride" is a chapter in a novel in which not much external happens. It is a story of rumination.

JAMES TRETTWER

I ONCE ATTENDED A DIALOGUE workshop lead by the wonderful Stephen Heatley. As an introductory exercise, Stephen asked the participants from where they got their inspiration. When it was my turn to answer. I said, "I hear voices." I listened in on a conversation in my mind between an alcoholic father and his daughter. He was trying to explain why he forgot her birthday, but would not admit the real reason. The gist of what I imagined I heard strongly suggested that this was not the first time he had lied to her. "Godsend" and "Leaving with Lena" are two stories from a collection entitled *Thornfields* that takes place in a fictitious potash company called Liverwood Mines. It was a winner in the 2016 John V. Hick's Long Manuscript Award for Fiction sponsored by the Saskatchewan Writers' Guild.